R

~~VAN~~ THAL von

The bedside book of sea stories

FICTION

other books by Herbert van Thal

The Bedside Book of Horror
Great Ghost Stories
The Bedside Book of Strange Stories
The Bedside Book of Great Detective Stories
Tales of History
The Second Bedside Book of Strange Stories
The Second Bedside Book of Great Detective Stories
The Third Bedside Book of Great Detective Stories
The Fourth Bedside Books of Great Detective Stories

The Bedside Book of SEA STORIES

edited by Herbert van Thal

Arthur Barker Limited London
A subsidiary of Weidenfeld (Publishers) Limited

Published in Great Britain by
Arthur Barker Limited
91 Clapham High Street, London SW4 7TA

ISBN 0 213 16705 0

Printed in Great Britain by
Willmer Brothers Limited,
Rock Ferry, Merseyside

Contents

Acknowledgements

The editor is grateful to the following for permission to reprint material in this volume:

Michael Joseph Ltd and Penguin Books Ltd for *A Dip in the Pool* from *Someone Like You* by Roald Dahl.

The Estate of the late Gordon Meyer and William Blackwood and Sons Ltd for *The Strait* by Gordon Meyer.

Ernest Benn for *The Ghost Ship* by Richard Middleton, originally published by T. Fisher Unwin in 1912.

The author for *The Sea Tryst* by Harry E. Turner.

The Estate of the late H. G. Wells and A. P. Watt Ltd for *In the Abyss* by H. G. Wells.

While every attempt has been made to ascertain the owners of rights and to secure the necessary permission to include the stories in the present collection, the editor and publisher wish to offer their apologies in any case of accidental infringement.

Foreword

I have no business with assembling a book of stories about the sea. I am a complete landlubber, although I live by the sea and am able to watch all her moods.

In prospect wide,
The boundless tide!
Waves cease to foam, and winds to roar,
Without a breeze,
The curling seas
Dance on, in measure, to the shore.*

The sea is a playmate that can be very fickle, and angry and rough with us poor mortals. It is better for those of us who are unused to her ways to use her with equanimity, to read of her vagaries.

Within this book is a collection of what I hope are varied stories about the sea by English and American authors. Our literature is much 'pebbled', if we can coin a sea-word, with wonderful accounts of sea voyages, for we are by nature a sea-loving nation, a country girt by the sea, and we have a legacy of many masterpieces of exploration by sea. Hakluyt, Drake, Shackleton are names that come immediately to mind, and are reminders of the foundation of our sea-power. The stories here should entertain both those who love and those who hate the sea.

H. v. T.

*From 'The Ocean' by Edward Young

Joseph Conrad

A SMILE OF FORTUNE

EVER SINCE THE SUN ROSE I had been looking ahead. The ship glided gently in smooth water. After a sixty days' passage I was anxious to make my landfall, a fertile and beautiful island of the tropics. The more enthusiastic of its inhabitants delight in describing it as the 'Pearl of the Ocean'. Well, let us call it the 'Pearl'. It's a good name. A pearl distilling much sweetness upon the world.

This is only a way of telling you that first-rate sugar-cane is grown there. All the population of the Pearl lives for it and by it. Sugar is their daily bread, as it were. And I was coming to them for a cargo of sugar in the hope of the crop having been good and of the freights being high.

Mr Burns, my chief mate, made out the land first; and very soon I became entranced by this blue, pinnacled apparition, almost transparent against the light of the sky, a mere emanation, the astral body of an island risen to greet me from afar. It is a rare phenomenon, such a sight of the Pearl at sixty miles off. And I wondered half seriously whether it was a good omen, whether what would meet me in that island would be as luckily exceptional as this beautiful, dreamlike vision so very few seamen have been privileged to behold.

But horrid thoughts of business interfered with my enjoyment of an accomplished passage. I was anxious for success and I wished, too, to do justice to the flattering latitude of my owners' instructions contained in one noble phrase: 'We leave it to you to do the best you can with the ship.' . . . All the world being thus given me for a stage, my abilities appeared to me no bigger than a pinhead.

Meantime the wind dropped, and Mr Burns began to make disagreeable remarks about my usual bad luck. I believe it was his devotion for me which made him critically outspoken on every occasion. All the same, I would not have put up with his humours if it had not been my lot at one time to nurse him through a desperate illness at sea.

After snatching him out of the jaws of death, so to speak, it would have been absurd to throw away such an efficient officer. But sometimes I wished he would dismiss himself.

We were late in closing with the land, and had to anchor outside the harbour till next day. An unpleasant and unrestful night followed. In this roadstead, strange to us both, Burns and I remained on deck almost all the time. Clouds swirled down the porphyry crags under which we lay. The rising wind made a great bullying noise amongst the naked spars, with interludes of sad moaning. I remarked that we had been in luck to fetch the anchorage before dark. It would have been a nasty, anxious night to hang off a harbour under canvas. But my chief mate was uncompromising in his attitude.

'Luck, you call it, sir! Aye – our usual luck. The sort of luck to thank God it's no worse!'

And so he fretted through the dark hours, while I drew on my fund of philosophy. Ah, but it was an exasperating, weary, endless night, to be lying at anchor close under that black coast! The agitated water made snarling sounds all round the ship. At times a wild gust of wind out of a gully high up on the cliffs struck on our rigging a harsh and plaintive note like the wail of a forsaken soul.

I

By half-past seven in the morning, the ship being then inside the harbour at last and moored within a long stone's-throw from the quay, my stock of philosophy was nearly exhausted. I was dressing hurriedly in my cabin when the steward came tripping in with a morning suit over his arm.

Hungry, tired, and depressed, with my head engaged inside a white shirt irritatingly stuck together by too much starch, I desired him peevishly to 'heave round with that breakfast'. I wanted to get ashore as soon as possible.

'Yes, sir. Ready at eight, sir. There's a gentleman from the shore waiting to speak to you, sir.'

This statement was curiously slurred over. I dragged the shirt violently over my head and emerged staring.

'So early!' I cried. 'Who's he? What does he want?'

On coming in from sea one has to pick up the conditions of an utterly unrelated existence. Every little event at first has the peculiar emphasis of novelty. I was greatly surprised by that early caller but there was no reason for my steward to look so particularly foolish.

'Didn't you ask for the name?' I enquired in a stern tone.

'His name's Jacobus, I believe,' he mumbled shamefacedly.

'Mr Jacobus!' I exclaimed loudly, more surprised than ever, but with a total change of feeling. 'Why couldn't you say so at once?'

But the fellow had scuttled out of my room. Through the momentarily opened door I had a glimpse of a tall, stout man standing in the cuddy by the table on which the cloth was already laid; a 'harbour' table-cloth, stainless and dazzlingly white. So far good.

I shouted courteously through the closed door, that I was dressing and would be with him in a moment. In return the assurance that there was no hurry reached me in the visitor's deep, quiet undertone. His time was my own. He dared say I would give him a cup of coffee presently.

'I am afraid you will have a poor breakfast,' I cried apologetically. 'We have been sixty-one days at sea, you know.'

A quiet little laugh, with a 'That'll be all right, Captain,' was his answer. All this, words, intonation, the glimpsed attitude of the man in the cuddy, had an unexpected character, a something friendly in it – propitiatory. And my surprise was not diminished thereby. What did this call mean? Was it the sign of some dark design against my commercial innocence?

Ah! These commercial interests – spoiling the finest life under the sun. Why must the sea be used for trade – and for war as well? Why kill and traffic on it, pursuing selfish aims of no great importance after all? It would have been so much nicer just to sail about with here and there a port and a bit of land to stretch one's legs on, buy a few books and get a change of cooking for awhile. But, living in a world more or less homicidal and desperately mercantile, it was plainly my duty to make the best of its opportunities.

My owners' letter had left it to me, as I have said before, to do my best for the ship, according to my own judgment. But it contained also a postscript worded somewhat as follows:

'Without meaning to interfere with your liberty of action we are writing by the outgoing mail to some of our business friends there who may be of assistance to you. We desire you particularly to call on Mr Jacobus, a prominent merchant and charterer. Should you hit it off with him he may be able to put you in the way of profitable employment for the ship.'

Hit it off! Here was the prominent creature absolutely on board asking for the favour of a cup of coffee! And life not being a fairy-tale the improbability of the event almost shocked me. Had I discovered an enchanted nook of the earth where wealthy merchants rush fasting on board ships before they are fairly moored? Was this white magic or merely some black trick of trade? I came in the end (while making the bow of my tie) to suspect that perhaps I did not get the name right. I had been thinking of the prominent Mr Jacobus pretty frequently during the passage and my hearing might have been deceived by some remote similarity of sound. . . . The steward might have said Antrobus – or maybe Jackson.

But coming out of my state-room with an interrogative 'Mr Jacobus?' I was met by a quiet 'Yes,' uttered with a gentle smile. The 'yes' was rather perfunctory. He did not seem to make much of the fact that he was Mr Jacobus. I took stock of a big, pale face, hair thin on the top, whiskers also thin, of a faded nondescript colour, heavy eyelids. The thick, smooth lips in repose looked as if glued together. The smile was faint. A heavy, tranquil man. I named my two officers, who just then came down to breakfast; but why Mr Burns's silent demeanour should suggest suppressed indignation I could not understand.

While we were taking our seats round the table some disconnected words of an altercation going on in the companion-way reached my ear. A stranger apparently wanted to come down to interview me, and the steward was opposing him.

'You can't see him.'

'Why can't I?'

'The Captain is at breakfast, I tell you. He'll be going on shore presently, and you can speak to him on deck.'

'That's not fair. You let – '

'I've had nothing to do with that.'

'Oh, yes you have. Everybody ought to have the same chance. You let that fellow – '

The rest I lost. The person having been repulsed successfully, the steward came down. I can't say he looked flushed – he was a mulatto – but he looked flustered. After putting the dishes on the table he remained by the sideboard with that lackadaisical air of indifference he used to assume when he had done something too clever by half and was afraid of getting into a scrape over it. The contemptuous expression of Mr Burns's face as he looked from him to me was really extraordinary. I couldn't imagine what new bee had stung the mate now.

The Captain being silent, nobody else cared to speak, as is the way in ships. And I was saying nothing simply because I had been made dumb by the splendour of the entertainment. I had expected the usual sea-breakfast, whereas I beheld spread before us a veritable feast of shore provisions: eggs, sausages, butter which plainly did not come from a Danish tin, cutlets, and even a dish of potatoes. It was three weeks since I had seen a real, live potato. I contemplated them with interest, and Mr Jacobus disclosed himself as a man of human, homely sympathies, and something of a thought-reader.

'Try them, Captain,' he encouraged me in a friendly undertone. 'They are excellent.'

'They look that,' I admitted. 'Grown on the island, I suppose.'

'Oh, no, imported. Those grown here would be more expensive.'

I was grieved at the ineptitude of the conversation. Were these the topics for a prominent and wealthy merchant to discuss? I thought the simplicity with which he made himself at home rather attractive; but what is one to talk about to a man who comes on one suddenly, after sixty-one days at sea, out of a totally unknown little town in an island one has never seen before? What were (besides sugar) the interest of that crumb of the earth, its gossip, its topic of conversation? To draw him on business at once would have been almost indecent – or even worse: impolitic. All I could do at the moment was to keep on in the old groove.

'Are the provisions generally dear here?' I asked, fretting inwardly at my inanity.

'I wouldn't say that,' he answered placidly, with that appearance of saving his breath his restrained manner of speaking suggested.

He would not be more explicit, yet he did not evade the subject. Eyeing the table in a spirit of complete abstemiousness (he wouldn't let me help him to any eatables) he went into details of supply. The beef was for the most part imported from Madagascar; mutton of course was rare and somewhat expensive, but good goat's flesh –

'Are these goat's cutlets?' I exclaimed hastily, pointing at one of the dishes.

Posed sentimentally by the sideboard, the steward gave a start.

'Lor', no, sir! It's real mutton!'

Mr Burns got through his breakfast impatiently, as if exasperated by being made a party to some monstrous foolishness, muttered a curt excuse, and went on deck. Shortly afterwards the second mate took his smooth red countenance out of the cabin. With the appetite of a schoolboy, and after two months of sea-fare, he appreciated the generous spread. But I did not. It smacked of extravagance. All the same, it was a remarkable feat to have produced it so quickly, and I congratulated the steward on his smartness in a somewhat ominous tone. He gave me a deprecatory smile and, in a way I didn't know what to make of, blinked his fine dark eyes in the direction of the guest.

The latter asked under his breath for another cup of coffee, and nibbled ascetically at a piece of very hard ship's biscuit. I don't think he consumed a square inch in the end; but meantime he gave me, casually as it were, a complete account of the sugar crop, of the local business houses, of the state of the freight market. All that talk was interspersed with hints as to personalities, amounting to veiled warnings, but his pale, fleshy face remained equable, without a gleam, as if ignorant of his voice. As you may imagine I opened my ears very wide. Every word was precious. My ideas as to the value of business friendship were being favourably modified. He gave me the names of all the disposable ships together with their tonnage and the names of their commanders. From that, which was still commercial information, he condescended to mere harbour gossip. The *Hilda* had unaccountably lost her figurehead in the Bay of Bengal, and her captain was greatly affected by this. He and the ship had been getting on in years together and the old gentleman imagined this strange event to be the forerunner of his own early dissolution. The *Stella* had experienced awful weather off the Cape – had her decks swept, and the chief officer washed overboard. And only a few hours before reaching port the baby died. Poor Captain H—— and his wife were terribly cut up. If they had only been able to bring it into port alive it could have been probably saved; but the wind failed them for the last week or so, light breezes, and . . . the baby was going to be buried this afternoon. He supposed I would attend –

'Do you think I ought to?' I asked, shrinkingly.

He thought so, decidedly. It would be greatly appreciated. All the captains in the harbour were going to attend. Poor Mrs—— was quite prostrated. Pretty hard on H—— altogether.

'And you, Captain – you are not married, I suppose?'

'No, I am not married,' I said. 'Neither married nor even engaged.'

Mentally I thanked my stars; and while he smiled in a musing, dreamy fashion, I expressed my acknowledgements for his visit and for the interesting business information he had been good enough to impart to me. But I said nothing of my wonder thereat.

'Of course, I would have made a point of calling on you in a day or two,' I concluded.

He raised his eyelids distinctly at me, and somehow managed to look rather more sleepy than before.

'In accordance with my owners' instructions,' I explained. 'You have had their letter, of course?'

By that time he had raised his eyebrows too but without any particular emotion. On the contrary he struck me then as absolutely imperturbable.

'Oh! You must be thinking of my brother.'

It was for me, then to say 'Oh!' But I hope that no more than civil surprise appeared in my voice when I asked him to what, then, I owed the pleasure. ... He was reaching for an inside pocket leisurely.

'My brother's a very different person. But I am well known in this part of the world. You've probably heard – '

I took a card he extended to me. A thick business card, as I lived. Alfred Jacobus – the other was Ernest – dealer in every description of ship's stores! Provisions salt and fresh, oils, paints, rope, canvas, etc., etc. Ships in harbour victualled by contract on moderate terms –

'I've never heard of you,' I said brusquely.

His low-pitched assurance did not abandon him.

'You will be very well satisfied,' he breathed out quietly.

I was not placated. I had the sense of having been circumvented somehow. Yet I had deceived myself – if there was any deception. But the confounded cheek of inviting himself to breakfast was enough to deceive anyone. And the thought struck me: Why! The fellow had provided all these eatables himself in the way of business. I said:

'You must have got up mighty early this morning.'

He admitted with simplicity that he was on the quay before six o'clock waiting for my ship to come in. He gave me the impression that it would be impossible to get rid of him now.

'If you think we are going to live on that scale,' I said, looking at the table with an irritated eye, 'you are jolly well mistaken.'

'You'll find it all right, Captain. I quite understand.'

Nothing could disturb his equanamity. I felt dissatisfied, but I could not very well fly out at him. He had told me many useful things – and besides he was the brother of that wealthy merchant. That seemed queer enough.

I rose and told him curtly that I must now go ashore. At once he offered the use of his boat for all the time of my stay in port.

'I only make a nominal charge,' he continued equably. 'My man remains all day at the landing-steps. You have only to blow a whistle when you want the boat.'

And, standing aside at every doorway to let me go through first, he carried me off in his custody after all. As we crossed the quarter-deck two shabby individuals stepped forward and in mournful silence offered me business cards which I took from them without a word under his heavy eye. It was a useless and gloomy ceremony. They were the touts of the other ship-chandlers, and he, placid at my back, ignored their existence.

We parted on the quay, after he had expressed quietly the hope of seeing me often 'at the store'. He had a smoking-room for captains there, with newspapers and a box of 'rather decent cigars'. I left him very unceremoniously.

My consignees received me with the usual business heartiness, but their account of the state of the freight-market was by no means so favourable as the talk of the wrong Jacobus had led me to expect. Naturally I became inclined now to put my trust in his version, rather. As I closed the door of the private offices behind me I thought to myself: 'H'm. A lot of lies. Commercial diplomacy. That's the sort of thing a man coming from sea has got to expect. They would try to charter the ship under the market rate.'

In the big, outer room, full of desks, the chief clerk, a tall, lean, shaved person in immaculate white clothes and with a shiny, closely-cropped head on which silvery gleams came and went, rose from his place and detained me affably. Anything they could do for me, they would be most happy. Was I likely to call again in the afternoon? What? Going to a funeral? Oh, yes, poor Captain H——.

He pulled a long, sympathetic face for a moment, then, dismissing from this workaday world the baby, which had got ill in a tempest and had died from too much calm at sea, he asked me with a dental, shark-like smile – if sharks had false teeth – whether I had yet made my little arrangements for the ship's stay in port.

'Yes, with Jacobus,' I answered carelessly. 'I understand he's the brother of Mr Ernest Jacobus to whom I have an introduction from my owners.'

I was not sorry to let him know I was not altogether helpless in the hands of his firm. He screwed his thin lips dubiously.

'Why,' I cried, 'isn't he the brother?'

'Oh, yes. . . . They haven't spoken to each other for eighteen years,' he added impressively after a pause.

'Indeed! What's the quarrel about?'

'Oh, nothing! Nothing that one would care to mention,' he protested primly. 'He's got quite a large business. The best ship-chandler here, without a doubt. Business is all very well, but there is such a things as character, too, isn't there? Good morning, Captain.'

He went away mincingly to his desk. He amused me. He resembled an old maid, a commercial old maid, shocked by some impropriety. Was it a commercial impropriety? Commercial impropriety is a serious matter, for it aims at one's pocket. Or was he only a purist in conduct who disapproved of Jacobus doing his own touting? It was certainly undignified. I wondered how the merchant brother liked it. But then different countries, different customs. In a community so isolated and so exclusively 'trading' social standards have their own scale.

II

I would have gladly dispensed with the mournful opportunity of becoming acquainted by sight with all my fellow-captains at once. However I found my way to the cemetery. We made a considerable group of bareheaded men in sombre garments. I noticed that those of our company most approaching to the now obsolete sea-dog type were the most moved – perhaps because they had less 'manner' than the new generation. The old sea-dog, away from his natural element, was a simple and sentimental animal. I noticed one – he was facing me across the grave – who was dropping tears. They trickled down his weather-beaten face like drops of rain on an old rugged wall. I learned afterwards that he was looked upon as the terror of sailors, a hard man; that he had never had a wife or chick of his own, and that, engaged from his tenderest years in deep-sea voyages, he knew women and children merely by sight.

Perhaps he was dropping those tears over his lost opportunities, from sheer envy of paternity and in strange jealousy of a sorrow which he could never know. Man, and even the sea-man, is a capricious animal, the creature and the victim of lost opportunities. But he made me feel ashamed of my callousness. I had no tears.

I listened with horribly critical detachment to that service I had had to read myself, once or twice, over childlike men who had died at sea. The words of hope and defiance, the winged words so inspiring in the free immensity of water and sky, seemed to fall wearily into the little grave. What was the use of asking Death where her sting was, before that small, dark hole in the ground? And then my thoughts escaped me altogether – away into matters of life – and no very high matters at that – ships, freights, business. In the instability of his emotions man resembles deplorably a monkey. I was disgusted with my thoughts – and I thought: Shall I be able to get a charter soon? Time's money. . . . Will that Jacobus really put good business in my way? . . . I must go and see him in a day or two.

Don't imagine that I pursued these thoughts with any precision. They pursued me rather: vague, shadowy, restless, shamefaced. Theirs was a callous, abominable, almost revolting, pertinacity. And it was the presence of that pertinacious ship-chandler which had started them. He stood mournfully amongst our little band of men from the sea, and I was angry at his presence, which, suggesting his brother the merchant, had caused me to become outrageous to myself. For indeed I had preserved some decency of feeling. It was only the mind which –

It was over at last. The poor father – a man of forty with black, bushy side-whiskers and a pathetic gash on his freshly-shaven chin – thanked us all, swallowing his tears. But for some reason, either because I lingered at the gate of the cemetery being somewhat hazy as to my way back, or because I was the youngest, or ascribing my moodiness caused by remorse to some more worthy and appropriate sentiment, or simply because I was even more of a stranger to him than the others – he singled me out. Keeping at my side, he renewed his thanks, which I listened to in a gloomy, conscience-stricken silence. Suddenly he slipped one hand under my arm and waved the other after a tall, stout figure walking away by itself down a street in a flutter of thin, grey garments:

'That's a good fellow – a real good fellow' – he swallowed down a belated sob – 'this Jacobus.'

And he told me in a low voice that Jacobus was the first man to board his ship on arrival, and, learning of their misfortune, had taken charge of everything, volunteered to attend to all routine business, carried off the ship's papers on shore, arranged for the funeral –

'A good fellow. I was knocked over. I had been looking at my wife for ten days. And helpless. Just you think of that! The dear little chap died the very day we made the land. How I managed to take the ship in God alone knows! I couldn't see anything; I couldn't speak; I couldn't. . . . You've heard, perhaps, that we lost our mate overboard on the passage? There was no one to do it for me. And the poor woman nearly crazy down there all alone with the. ... By the Lord! It isn't fair.'

We walked in silence together. I did not know how to part from him. On the quay he let go my arm and struck fiercely his fist into the palm of his other hand.

'By God, it isn't fair!' he cried again. 'Don't you ever marry unless you can chuck the sea first. ... It isn't fair.'

I had no intention to 'chuck the sea', and when he let me go aboard his ship I felt convinced that I would never marry. While I was waiting at the steps for Jacobus's boatman, who had gone off somewhere, the captain of the *Hilda* joined me, a slender silk umbrella in his hand and the sharp points of his archaic, Gladstonian shirt-collar framing a small, clean-shaved, ruddy face. It was wonderfully fresh for his age, beautifully modelled and lit up by remarkably clear blue eyes. A lot of white hair, glossy like spun glass, curled upwards slightly under the brim of his valuable, ancient, panama hat with a broad black ribbon. In the aspect of that vivacious, neat, little old man there was something quaintly angelic and also boyish.

He accosted me, as though he had been in the habit of seeing me every day of his life from my earliest childhood, with a whimsical remark on the appearance of a stout negro woman who was sitting upon a stool near the edge of the quay. Presently he observed amiably that I had a very pretty little barque.

I returned this civil speech by saying readily:

'Not so pretty as the *Hilda*.'

At once the corners of his clear-cut, sensitive mouth dropped dismally.

'Oh, dear! I can hardly bear to look at her now.'

Did I know, he asked anxiously, that he had lost the figurehead of his ship; a woman in a blue tunic edged with gold, the face perhaps not so very, very pretty, but her bare white arms beautifully shaped and extended as if she were swimming? Did I? Who would have expected such a thing! ... After twenty years too!

Nobody could have guessed from his tone that the woman was made of wood; his trembling voice, his agitated manner gave to his lamentations a ludicrously scandalous flavour.... Disappeared at night – a clear fine night with just a slight swell – in the gulf of Bengal. Went off without a plash; no one in the ship could tell why, how, at what hour – after twenty years last October.... Did I ever hear! ...

I assured him sympathetically that I had never heard – and he became very doleful. This meant no good he was sure. There was something in it which looked like a warning. But when I remarked that surely another figure of a woman could be produced I found myself being soundly rated for my levity. The old boy flushed pink under his clear tan as if I had proposed something improper. One could replace masts, I was told, or a lost rudder – any working part of a ship; but where was the use of sticking up a new figurehead? What satisfaction? How could one care for it? It was easy to see that I had never been shipmates with a figurehead for over twenty years.

'A new figurehead!' he scolded in unquenchable indignation. 'Why! I've been a widower now for eight-and-twenty years come next May and I would just as soon think of getting a new wife. You're as bad as that fellow Jacobus.'

I was highly amused.

'What has Jaobus done? Did he want you to marry again, Captain?' I enquired in a deferential tone. But he was launched now and only grinned fiercely.

'Procure – indeed! He's the sort of chap to procure you anything you like for a price. I hadn't been moored here for an hour when he got on board and at once offered to sell me a figurehead he happens to have in his yard somewhere. He got Smith, my mate, to talk to me about it. "Mr Smith," says I, "don't you know me better than that? Am I the sort that would pick up another man's cast-off figurehead?" And after all these years too! The way some of you young fellows talk – '

I affected great compunction, and as I stepped into the boat I said soberly:

'Then I see nothing for it but to fit in a neat fiddlehead – perhaps. You know, carved scrollwork, nicely gilt.'

He became very dejected after his outburst.

'Yes. Scrollwork. Maybe. Jacobus hinted at that too. He's never at a loss when there's any money to be extracted from a sailorman. He would make me pay through the nose for that carving. A gilt fiddlehead did you say – eh? I daresay it would do for you. You young fellows don't seem to have any feeling for what's proper.'

He made a convulsive gesture with his right arm.

'Never mind. Nothing can make much difference. I would just as soon let the old thing go about the world with a bare cutwater,' he cried sadly. Then as the boat got away from the steps he raised his voice on the edge of the quay with comical animosity:

'I would! If only to spite that figurehead-procuring bloodsucker. I am an old bird here and don't you forget it. Come and see me on board some day?'

I spent my first evening in port quietly in my ship's cuddy; and glad enough was I to think that the shore life which strikes one as so pettily complex, discordant; and so full of new faces on first coming from sea, could be kept off for a few hours longer. I was however fated to hear the Jacobus note once more before I slept.

Mr Burns had gone ashore after the evening meal to have, as he said, 'a look round'. As it was quite dark when he announced his intention I didn't ask what it was he expected to see. Some time about midnight, while sitting with a book in the saloon, I heard cautious movements in the lobby and hailed him by name.

Burns came in, stick and hat in hand, incredibly vulgarized by his smart shore togs, with a jaunty air and an odious twinkle in his eye. Being asked to sit down he laid his hat and stick on the table and after we had talked of ship affairs for a little while:

'I've been hearing pretty tales on shore about that ship-chandler fellow who snatched the job from you so neatly, sir.'

I remonstrated with my late patient for his manner of expressing himself. But he only tossed his head disdainfully. A pretty dodge indeed: boarding a strange ship with breakfast in two baskets for all hands and calmly inviting himself to the captain's table! Never heard of anything so crafty and so impudent in his life.

I found myself defending Jacobus's unusual methods.

'He's the brother of one of the wealthiest merchants in the port.' The mate's eyes fairly snapped green sparks.

'His grand brother hasn't spoken to him for eighteen or twenty years,' he declared triumphantly. 'So there!'

'I know all about that,' I interrupted loftily.

'Do you, sir? H'm!' His mind was still running on the ethics of commercial competition. 'I don't like to see your good nature taken advantage of. He's bribed that steward of ours with a five-rupee note to let him come down – or ten for that matter. He don't care. He will shove that and more into the bill presently.'

'Is that one of the tales you have heard ashore?' I asked.

He assured me that his own sense could tell him that much. No; what he had heard on shore was that no respectable person in the whole town would come near Jacobus. He lived in a large old-fashioned house in one of the quiet streets with a big garden. After telling me this Burns put on a mysterious air. 'He keeps a girl shut up there who, they say – '

'I suppose you've heard all this gossip in some eminently respectable place?' I snapped at him in a most sarcastic tone.

The shaft told, because Mr Burns, like many other disagreeable people, was very sensitive himself. He remained as if thunderstruck, with his mouth open for some further communication, but I did not give him the chance. 'And, anyhow, what the deuce do I care?' I added, retiring into my room.

And this was a natural thing to say. Yet somehow I was not indifferent. I admit it is absurd to be concerned with the morals of one's ship-chandler, if ever so well connected; but his personality had stamped itself upon my first day in harbour, in the way you know.

After this initial exploit Jacobus showed himself anything but intrusive. He was out in a boat early every morning going round the ships he served, and occasionally remaining on board one of them for breakfast with the captain.

As I discovered that this practice was generally accepted, I just nodded to him familiarly when one morning, on coming out of my room, I found him in the cabin. Glancing over the table I saw that his place was already laid. He stood awaiting my appearance, very bulky and placid, holding a beautiful bunch of flowers in his thick hand. He offered them to my notice with a faint, sleepy smile. From his own garden; had a very fine old garden; picked them himself that morning before going out to business; thought I would like. . . . He turned away 'Steward, can you oblige me with some water in a large jar, please.'

I assured him jocularly, as I took my place at the table, that he made me feel as if I were a pretty girl, and that he mustn't be surprised if I blushed. But he was busy arranging his floral tribute at the sideboard. 'Stand it before the Captain's plate, steward, please.' He made this request in his usual undertone.

The offering was so pointed that I could do no less than to raise it to my nose, and as he sat down noiselessly he breathed out the opinion that a few flowers improved notably the appearance of a ship's saloon. He wondered why I did not have a shelf fitted all round the skylight for flowers in pots to take with me to sea. He had a skilled workman able to fit up shelves in a day, and he could procure me two or three dozen good plants –

The tips of his thick, round fingers rested composedly on the edge of the table on each side of his cup of coffee. His face remained immovable. Mr Burns was smiling maliciously to himself. I declared that I hadn't the slightest intention of turning my skylight into a conservatory only to keep the cabin-table in a perpetual mess of mould and dead vegetable matter.

'Rear most beautiful flowers,' he insisted with an upward glance. 'It's no trouble really.'

'Oh, yes, it is. Lots of trouble,' I contradicted. 'And in the end some fool leaves the skylight open in a fresh breeze, a flick of salt water gets at them and the whole lot is dead in a week.'

Mr Burns snorted a contemptuous approval. Jacobus gave up the subject passively. After a time he unglued his thick lips to ask me if I had seen his brother yet. I was very curt in my answer.

'No, not yet.'

'A very different person,' he remarked dreamily and got up. His movements were particularly noiseless. 'Well – thank you, Captain. If anything is not to your liking please mention it to your steward. I suppose you will be giving a dinner to the office-clerks presently.'

'What for?' I cried with some warmth. 'If I were a steady trader to the port I could understand it. But a complete stranger! . . . I may not turn up again here for years. I don't see why I . . . Do you mean to say it is customary?'

'It will be expected from a man like you,' he breathed out placidly. 'Eight of the principal clerks, the manager, that's nine, you three gentlemen, that's twelve. It needn't be very expensive. If you tell your steward to give me a day's notice – '

'It will be expected of me! Why should it be expected of me? Is it because I look particularly soft – or what?'

His immobility struck me as dignified suddenly, his imperturbable quality as dangerous. 'There's plenty of time to think about that,' I concluded weakly with a gesture that tried to wave him away. But before he departed he took time to mention regretfully that he had not yet had the pleasure of seeing me at his 'store' to sample those cigars. He had a parcel of six thousand to dispose of, very cheap.

'I think it would be worth your while to secure some,' he added with a fat, melancholy smile and left the cabin.

Mr Burns struck his fist on the table excitedly.

'Did you ever see such impudence! He's made up his mind to get something out of you one way or another, sir.'

At once feeling inclined to defend Jacobus, I observed philosophically that all this was business, I supposed. But my absurd mate, muttering broken disjointed sentences, such as: 'I cannot bear! . . . Mark my words! . . .' and so on, flung out of the cabin. If I hadn't nursed him through that deadly fever I wouldn't have suffered such manners for a single day.

III

Jacobus having put me in mind of his wealthy brother I concluded I would pay that business call at once. I had by that time heard a little more of him. He was a member of the Council, where he made himself objectionable to the authorities. He exercised a considerable influence on public opinion. Lots of people owed him money. He was an importer on a great scale of all sorts of goods. For instance, the whole supply of bags for sugar was practically in his hands. This last fact I did not learn till afterwards. The general impression conveyed to me was that of a local personage. He was a bachelor and gave weekly card-parties in his house out of town, which were attended by the best people in the colony.

The greater, then, was my surprise to discover his office in shabby surroundings, quite away from the business quarter, amongst a lot of hovels. Guided by a black board with white lettering, I climbed a narrow wooden staircase and entered a room with a bare floor of planks littered with bits of brown paper and wisps of packing straw. A great number of what looked like wine-cases were piled up against one of the walls. A lanky, inky, light-yellow, mulatto youth, miserably long-necked and generally recalling a sick chicken, got off a three-legged stool behind a cheap deal desk and faced me as if gone dumb with fright. I had some difficulty in persuading him to take in my name, though I could not get from him the nature of his objection. He did it at last with an almost agonized reluctance which ceased to be mysterious to me when I heard him being sworn at menacingly with savage, suppressed growls, then audibly cuffed and finally kicked out without any concealment whatever; because he came back flying head foremost through the door with a stifled shriek.

To say I was startled would not express it. I remained still, like a man lost in a dream. Clapping both his hands to that frail part of his anatomy which had received the shock, the poor wretch said to me simply:

'Will you go in, please.'

His lamentable self-possession was wonderful; but it did not do away with the incredibility of the experience. A preposterous notion that I had seen this boy somewhere before, a thing obviously impossible, was like a delicate finishing touch of weirdness added to a scene fit to raise doubts as to one's sanity. I stared anxiously about me like an awakened somnambulist.

'I say,' I cried loudly, 'there isn't a mistake, is there? This is Mr Jacobus's office.'

The boy gazed at me with a pained expression – and somehow so familiar! A voice within growled offensively:

'Come in, come in, since you are there. . . . I didn't know.'

I crossed the outer room as one approaches the den of some unknown wild beast; with intrepidity but in some excitement. Only no wild beast that ever lived would rouse one's indignation; the power to do that belongs to the odiousness of the human brute. And I was very indignant, which did not prevent me from being at once struck by the extraordinary resemblance of the two brothers.

This one was dark instead of being fair like the other; but he was as big. He was without his coat and waistcoat; he had been doubtless snoozing in the rocking-chair which stood in a corner farthest from the window. Above the great bulk of his crumpled white shirt, buttoned with three diamond studs, his round face looked swarthy. It was moist; his brown moustache hung limp and ragged. He pushed a common, cane-bottomed chair towards me with his foot.

'Sit down.'

I glanced at it casually, turning my indignant eyes full up on him, I declared in precise and incisive tones that I had called in obedience to my owners' instructions.

'Oh! Yes. H'm! I didn't understand what that fool was saying. . . . But never mind! It will teach the scoundrel to disturb me at this time of the day,' he added, grinning at me with savage cynicism.

I looked at my watch. It was past three o'clock – quite the full swing of afternoon office work in the port. He snarled imperiously: 'Sit down, Captain.'

I acknowledged the gracious invitation by saying deliberately:

'I can listen to all you may have to say without sitting down.'

Emitting a loud and vehement 'Pshaw!' he glared for a moment, very round-eyed and fierce. It was like a gigantic tomcat spitting at one suddenly. 'Look at him! . . . What do you fancy yourself to be? What did you come here for? If you won't sit down and talk business you had better go to the devil.'

'I don't know him personally,' I said. 'But after this I wouldn't mind calling on him. It would be refreshing to meet a gentleman.'

He followed me, growling behind my back:

'The impudence! I've a good mind to write to your owners what I think of you.'

I turned on him for a moment:

'As it happens I don't care. For my part I assure you I won't even take the trouble to mention you to them.'

He stopped at the door of his office while I traversed the littered anteroom. I think he was somewhat taken aback.

'I will break every bone in your body,' he roared suddenly at the miserable mulatto lad, 'if you ever dare to disturb me before half-past three for anybody. D'ye hear? For anybody! ... Let alone any damned skipper,' he added, in a lower growl.

The frail youngster, swaying like a reed, made a low moaning sound. I stopped short and addressed this sufferer with advice. It was prompted by the sight of a hammer (used for opening the wine-cases, I suppose) which was lying on the floor.

'If I were you, my boy, I would have that thing up my sleeve when I went in next and at the first occasion I would – '

What was there so familiar in that lad's yellow face? Entrenched and quaking behind the flimsy desk, he never looked up. His heavy, lowered eyelids gave me suddenly the clue of the puzzle. He resembled – yes, those thick glued lips – he resembled the brothers Jacobus. He resembled both, the wealthy merchant and the pushing shopkeeper (who resembled each other); he resembled them as much as a thin, light-yellow mulatto lad may resemble a big, stout, middle-aged white man. It was the exotic complexion and the slightness of his build which had put me off so completely. Now I saw in him unmistakably the Jacobus strain, weakened, attenuated, diluted as it were in a bucket of water – and I refrained from finishing my speech. I had intended to say: 'Crack this brute's head for him.' I still felt the conclusion to be sound. But it is no trifling responsibility to counsel parricide to anyone, however deeply injured.

'Beggarly – cheeky – skippers.'

I despised the emphatic growl at my back; only, being much vexed and upset, I regret to say that I slammed the door behind me in a most undignified manner.

It may not appear altogether absurd if I say that I brought out from that interview a kindlier view of the other Jacobus. It was with a feeling resembling partisanship that, a few days later, I called at his 'store'. That long, cavern-like place of business, very dim at the back and stuffed full of all sorts of goods, was entered from the street by a lofty archway. At the far end I saw my Jacobus exerting himself in his shirt-sleeves among his assistants. The captains' room was a small, vaulted apartment with a stone floor and heavy iron bars in its windows like a dungeon converted to hospitable purposes. A couple of cheerful bottles and several gleaming glasses made a brilliant cluster round a tall, cool red earthenware pitcher on the centre table which was littered with newspapers from all parts of the world. A well-groomed stranger in a smart grey check suit, sitting with one leg flung over his knee, put down one of these sheets briskly and nodded to me.

I guessed him to be a steamer-captain. It was impossible to get to know these men. They came and went too quickly and their ships lay moored out, at the very entrance of the harbour. Theirs was another life altogether. He yawned slightly.

'Dull hole, isn't it?'

I understood this to allude to the town.

'Do you find it so?' I murmured.

'Don't you? But I'm off tomorrow, thank goodness.'

He was a very gentlemanly person, good-natured and superior. I watched him draw the open box of cigars to his side of the table, take a big cigar-case out of his pocket and begin to fill it very methodically. Presently, on our eyes meeting, he winked like a common mortal and invited me to follow his example. 'They are really decent smokes.' I shook my head.

'I am not off tomorrow.'

'What of that? Think I am abusing old Jacobus's hospitality? Heavens! It goes into the bill, of course. He spreads such little matters all over his account. He can take care of himself! Why, it's business – '

I noted a shadow fall over his well-satisfied expression, a momentary hesitation in closing his cigar-case. But he ended by putting it in his pocket jauntily. A placid voice uttered in the doorway: 'That's quite correct, Captain.'

The large noiseless Jacobus advanced into the room. His quietness, in the circumstances, amounted to cordiality. He had put on his jacket before joining us, and he sat down in the chair vacated by the steamer-man, who nodded to me again and went out with a short, jarring laugh. A profound silence reigned. With his drowsy stare Jacobus seemed to be slumbering open-eyed. Yet, somehow, I was aware of being profoundly scrutinized by those heavy eyes. In the enormous cavern of the store somebody began to nail down a case, expertly: tap-tap . . . tap-tap. Two other experts, one slow and nasal, the other shrill and snappy, started checking an invoice.

'A half-coil of three-inch manilla rope.'

'Right!'

'Six assorted shackles.'

'Right!'

'Six tins assorted soups, three of paté, two asparagus, fourteen pounds tobacco, cabin.'

'Right!'

'It's for the captain who was here just now,' breathed out the immovable Jacobus. 'These steamer orders are very small. They pick up what they want as they go along. That man will be in Samarang in less than a fortnight. Very small orders indeed.'

The calling over of the items went on in the shop; an extraordinary jumble of varied articles, paint-brushes, Yorkshire Relish, etc, etc. . . . 'Three sacks of best potatoes,' read out the nasal voice.

At this Jacobus blinked like a sleeping man roused by a shake, and displayed some animation. At his order, shouted into the shop, a smirking half-caste clerk with his ringlets much oiled and with a pen stuck behind his ear, brought in a sample of six potatoes which he paraded in a row on the table.

Being urged to look at their beauty I gave them a cold and hostile glance. Calmly, Jacobus proposed that I should order ten or fifteen tons – tons! I couldn't believe my ears. My crew could not have eaten such a lot in a year and potatoes (excuse these practical remarks) are a highly perishable commodity. I thought he was joking – or else trying to find out whether I was an unutterable idiot. But his purpose was not so simple. I discovered that he meant me to buy them on my own account.

'I am proposing you a bit of business, Captain. I wouldn't charge you a great price.'

I told him that I did not go in for trade. I even added grimly that I knew only too well how that sort of spec. generally ended.

He sighed and clasped his hand on his stomach with exemplary resignation. I admired the placidity of his impudence. Then waking up somewhat:

'Won't you try a cigar, Captain?'

'No, thanks. I don't smoke cigars.'

'For once!' he exclaimed, in a patient whisper. A melancholy silence ensued. You know how sometimes a person discloses a certain unsuspected depth and acuteness of thought; that is, in other words, utters something unexpected. It was unexpected enough to hear Jacobus say:

'The man who just went out was right enough. You might take one, Captain. Here everything is bound to be in the way of business.'

I felt a little ashamed of myself. The remembrance of his horrid brother made him appear quite a decent sort of fellow. It was with some compunction that I said a few words to the effect that I could have no possible objection to his hospitality.

Before I was a minute older I saw where this admission was leading me. As if changing the subject, Jacobus mentioned that his private house was about ten minutes' walk away. It had a beautiful old walled garden. Something really remarkable. I ought to come round some day and have a look at it.

He seemed to be a lover of gardens. I too take extreme delight in them; but I did not mean my compunction to carry me as far as Jacobus's flower-beds, however beautiful and old. He added, with a certain homeliness of tone:

'There's only my girl there.'

It is difficult to set everything down in due order; so I must revert here to what happened a week or two before. The medical officer of the port had come on board my ship to have a look at one of my crew who was ailing, and naturally enough he was asked to step into the cabin. A fellow-shipmaster of mine was there too; and in the conversation, somehow or other, the name of Jacobus came to be mentioned. It was pronounced with no particular reverence by the other man, I believe. I don't remember now what I was going to say. The doctor – a pleasant, cultivated fellow, with an assured manner – prevented me by striking in, in a sour tone:

'Ah! You're talking about my respected papa-in-law.'

Of course, that sally silenced us at the time. But I remembered the episode, and at this juncture, pushed for something non-committal to say, I enquired with polite surprise:

'You have your married daughter living with you, Mr Jacobus?'

He moved his big hand from right to left quietly. No! That was another of his girls, he stated, ponderously and under his breath as usual. She... He seemed in a pause to be ransacking his mind for some kind of descriptive phrase. But my hopes were disappointed. He merely produced his stereotyped definition.

'She's a very different sort of person.'

'Indeed. . . . And bye-the-bye, Jacobus, I called on your brother the other day. It's no great compliment if I say that I found him a very different sort of person from you.'

He had an air of profound reflection, then remarked quaintly:

'He's a man of regular habits.'

He might have been alluding to the habit of late siesta; but I mumbled something about 'beastly habits anyhow' – and left the store abruptly.

IV

My little passage with Jacobus the merchant became known generally. One or two of my acquaintances made distant allusions to it. Perhaps the mulatto boy had talked. I must confess that people appeared rather scandalized, but not with Jacobus's brutality. A man I knew remonstrated with me for my hastiness.

I gave him the whole story of my visit, not forgetting the tell-tale resemblance of the wretched mulatto boy to his tormentor. He was not surprised. No doubt, no doubt. What of that? In a jovial tone he assured me that there must be many of that sort. The elder Jacobus had been a bachelor all his life. A highly respectable bachelor. But there had never been open scandal in that connection. His life had been quite regular. It could cause no offence to anyone.

I said that I had been offended considerably. My interlocutor opened very wide eyes. Why? Because a mulatto lad got a few knocks? That was not a great affair, surely. I had no idea how insolent and untruthful these half-castes were. In fact he seemed to think Mr Jacobus rather kind than otherwise to employ that youth at all; a sort of amiable weakness which could be forgiven.

This acquaintance of mine belonged to one of the old French families, descendants of the old colonists; all noble, all impoverished, and living a narrow domestic life in dull, dignified decay. The men, as a rule, occupy inferior posts in Government offices or in business houses. The girls are almost always pretty, ignorant of the world, kind and agreeable and generally bilingual; they prattle innocently both in French and English. The emptiness of their existence passes belief.

I obtained my entry into a couple of such households because some years before, in Bombay, I had occasion to be of use to a pleasant, ineffectual young man who was rather stranded there, not knowing what to do with himself or even how to get home to his island again. It was a matter of two hundred rupees or so, but, when I turned up, the family made a point of showing their gratitude by admitting me to their intimacy. My knowledge of the French language made me specially acceptable. They had meantime managed to marry the fellow to a woman nearly twice his age, comparatively well off: the only profession he was really fit for. But it was not all cakes and ale. The first time I called on the couple she spied a little spot of grease on the poor devil's pantaloons and made him a screaming scene of reproaches so full of sincere passion that I sat terrified as at a tragedy of Racine.

Of course there was never question of the money I had advanced him; but his sisters, Miss Angele and Miss Mary, and the aunts of both families, who spoke quaint archaic French of pre-Revolution period, and a host of distant relations adopted me for a friend outright in a manner which was almost embarrassing.

It was with the eldest brother (he was employed at a desk in my consignee's office) that I was having this talk about the merchant Jacobus. He regretted my attitude and nodded his head sagely. An influential man. One never knew when one would need him. I expressed my immense preference for the shopkeeper of the two. At that my friend looked grave.

'What on earth are you pulling that long face about?' I cried impatiently. 'He asked me to see his garden and I have a good mind to go some day.'

'Don't do that,' he said, so earnestly that I burst into a fit of laughter; but he looked at me without a smile.

This was another matter altogether. At one time the public conscience of the island had been mightily troubled by my Jacobus. The two brothers had been partners for years in great harmony, when a wandering circus came to the island and my Jacobus became suddenly infatuated with one of the lady-riders. What made it worse was that he was married. He had not even the grace to conceal his passion. It must have been strong indeed to carry away such a large placid creature. His behaviour was perfectly scandalous. He followed that woman to the Cape, and apparently travelled at the tail of that beastly circus to other parts of the world, in a most degrading position. The woman soon ceased to care for him, and treated him worse than a dog. Most extraordinary stories of moral degredation were reaching the island at that time. He had not the strength of mind to shake himself free. . . .

The grotesque image of a fat, pushing ship-chandler, enslaved by an unholy love-spell, fascinated me; and I listened rather open-mouthed to the tale as old as the world, a tale which had been the subject of legend, of moral fables, of poems, but which so ludicrously failed to fit the personality. What a strange victim for the gods!

Meantime his deserted wife had died. His daughter was taken care of by his brother, who married her as advantageously as was possible in the circumstances.

'Oh! The Mrs Doctor!' I exclaimed.

'You know that? Yes. A very able man. He wanted a lift in the world, and there was a good bit of money from her mother, besides the expectations. . . . Of course, they don't know him,' he added. 'The doctor nods in the street, I believe, but he avoids speaking to him when they meet on board a ship, as must happen sometimes.'

I remarked that this surely was an old story by now.

My friend assented. But it was Jacobus's own fault that it was neither forgiven nor forgotten. He came back ultimately. But how? Not in a spirit of contrition, in a way to propitiate his scandalized fellow-citizens. He must needs drag along with him a child – a girl. . . .

'He spoke to me of a daughter who lives with him,' I observed, very much interested.

'She's certainly the daughter of the circus-woman,' said my friend. 'She may be his daughter too; I am willing to admit that she is. In fact I have no doubt – '

But he did not see why she should have been brought into a respectable community to perpetuate the memory of the scandal. And that was not the worst. Presently something much more distressing happened. That abandoned woman turned up. Landed from a mail-boat. . . .

'What! Here? To claim the child perhaps,' I suggested.

'Not she!' My friendly informant was very scornful. 'Imagine a painted, haggard, agitated, desperate hag. Been cast off in Mozambique by somebody who paid her passage here. She had been injured internally by a kick from a horse; she hadn't a cent on her when she got ashore; I don't think she even asked to see the child. At any rate, not till the last day of her life. Jacobus hired for her a bungalow to die in. He got a couple of Sisters from the hospital to nurse her through these few months. If he didn't marry her *in extremis* as the good Sisters tried to bring about, it's because she wouldn't even hear of it. As the nuns

B

said: "The woman died impenitent." It was reported that she ordered Jacobus out of the room with her last breath. This may be the real reason why he didn't go into mourning himself; he only put the child into black. While she was little she was seen sometimes about the streets attended by a negro woman, but since she became of age to put her hair up I don't think she has set foot outside that garden once. She must be over eighteen now.'

Thus my friend, with some added details; such as, that he didn't think the girl had spoken to three people of any position in the island; that an elderly female relative of the brothers Jacobus had been induced by extreme poverty to accept the position of gouvernante to the girl. As to Jacobus's business (which certainly annoyed his brother) it was a wise choice on his part. It brought him in contact only with strangers of passage; whereas any other would have given rise to all sorts of awkardness with his social equals. The man was not wanting in a certain tact – only he was naturally shameless. For why did he want to keep that girl with him? It was most painful for everybody.

I thought suddenly (and with profound disgust) of the other Jacobus, and I could not refrain from saying slyly:

'I suppose if he employed her, say, as a scullion in his household and occasionally pulled her hair or boxed her ears, the position would have been more regular – less shocking to the respectable class to which he belongs.'

He was not so stupid as to miss my intention, and shrugged his shoulders impatiently.

'You don't understand. To begin with, she's not a mulatto. And a scandal is a scandal. People should be given a chance to forget. I dare-say it would have been better for her if she had been turned into a scullion or something of that kind. Of course he's trying to make money in every sort of petty way, but in such a business there'll never be enough for anybody to come forward.'

When my friend left me I had a conception of Jacobus and his daughter existing, a lonely pair of castaways, on a desert island; the girl sheltering in the house as if it were a cavern in a cliff, and Jacobus going out to pick up a living for both on the beach – exactly like two shipwrecked people who always hope for some rescuer to bring them back at last into touch with the rest of mankind.

But Jacobus's bodily reality did not fit in with this romantic view. When he turned up on board in the usual course, he sipped the cup of coffee placidly, asked me if I was satisfied – and I hardly listened to the harbour gossip he dropped slowly in his low, voice-saving enunciation. I had then troubles of my own. My ship chartered, my thoughts dwelling on the success of a quick round voyage, I had been suddenly confronted by a shortage of bags. A catastrophe! The stock of one especial kind, called pockets, seemed to be totally exhausted. A consignment was shortly expected – it was afloat, on its way, but, meantime, the loading of my ship dead stopped, I had enough to worry about. My consignees, who had received me with such heartiness on my arrival, now, in the character of my charterers, listened to my complaints with polite helplessness. Their manager, the old-maidish, thin man, who so prudishly didn't even like to speak about the impure Jacobus, gave me the correct commercial view of the position.

'My dear Captain' – he was retracting his leathery cheeks into a condescending, shark-like smile – 'we were not morally obliged to tell you of a possible shortage before you signed the charter-party. It was for you to guard against the contingency of a delay – strictly speaking. But of course we shouldn't have taken any advantage. This is no one's fault really. We ourselves have been taken unawares,' he concluded primly, with an obvious lie.

This lecture I confess had made me thirsty. Suppressed rage generally produces that effect; and as I strolled on aimlessly I bethought myself of the tall earthenware pitcher in the captains' room of the Jacobus 'store'.

With no more than a nod to the men I found assembled there, I poured down a deep, cool draught on my indignation, then another, and then, becoming dejected, I sat plunged in cheerless reflections. The others read, talked, smoked, bandied over my head some unsubtle chaff. But my abstraction was respected. And it was without a word to anyone that I rose and went out, only to be quite unexpectedly accosted in the bustle of the store by Jacobus the outcast.

'Glad to see you, Captain. What? Going away? You haven't been looking so well these last few days, I notice. Run down, eh?'

He was in his shirt-sleeves, and his words were in the usual course of business, but they had a human note. It was commercial amenity, but I had been a stranger to amenity in that connection. I do verily believe (from the direction of his heavy glance towards a certain shelf) that he was going to suggest the purchase of Clarkson's Nerve Tonic, which he kept in stock, when I said impulsively:

'I am rather in trouble with my loading.'

Wide awake under his sleepy, broad mask with glued lips, he understood at once, had a movement of the head so appreciative that I relieved my exasperation by exclaiming:

'Surely there must be eleven hundred quarter-bags to be found in the colony. It's only a matter of looking for them.'

Again that slight movement of the big head, and in the noise and activity of the store that tranquil murmur:

'To be sure. But then people likely to have a reserve of quarter-bags wouldn't want to sell. They'd need that size themselves.'

'That's exactly what my consignees are telling me. Impossible to buy. Bosh! They don't want to. It suits them to have the ship hung up. But if I were to discover the lot they would have to – Look here, Jacobus! *You* are the man to have such a thing up your sleeve.'

He protested with a ponderous swing of his big head. I stood before him helplessly, being looked at by those heavy eyes with a veiled expression as of a man after some soul-shaking crisis. Then suddenly:

'It's impossible to talk quietly here,' he whispered. 'I am very busy. But if you could go and wait for me in my house. It's less than ten minutes walk. Oh, yes, you don't know the way.'

He called for his coat and offered to take me there himself. He would have to return to the store at once for an hour or so to finish his business, and then he would be at liberty to talk over with me the matter of quarter-bags. This programme was breathed out at me through slightly parted, still lips; his heavy, motionless glance rested upon me placid as ever, the glance of a tired man – but I felt that it was searching, too. I could not imagine what he was looking for in me and kept silent, wondering.

'I am asking you to wait for me in my house till I am at liberty to talk this matter over. You will?'

'Why, of course!' I cried.

'But I cannot promise –'

'I daresay not,' I said. 'I don't expect a promise.'

'I mean I can't even promise to try the move I've in my mind. One must see first . . . h'm!'

'All right. I'll take the chance. I'll wait for you as long as you like. What else have I to do in this infernal hole of a port!'

Before I had uttered my last words we had set off at a swinging pace. We turned a couple of corners and entered a street completely empty of traffic, of semi-rural aspect, paved with cobblestones nestling in grass tufts. The house came to the line of the roadway; a single storey on an elevated basement of rough stones, so that our heads were below the level of the windows as we went along. All the jalousies were tightly shut, like eyes, and the house seemed fast asleep in the afternoon sunshine. The entrance was at the side, in an alley even more grass-grown than the street: a small door, simply on the latch.

With a word of apology as to showing me the way, Jacobus preceded me up a dark passage and led me across the naked parquet floor of what I supposed to be the dining-room. It was lighted by three glass doors which stood wide open onto a verandah or rather loggia running its brick arches along the garden side of the house. It was really a magnificent garden: smooth green lawns and a gorgeous maze of flowerbeds in the foreground, displayed around a basin of dark water framed in a marble rim, and in the distance the massed foliage of varied trees concealing the roofs of other houses. The town might have been miles away. It was a brilliantly coloured solitude, drowsing in a warm, voluptuous silence. Where the long, still shadows fell across the beds, and in shady nooks, the massed colours of the flowers had an extraordinary magnificence of effect. I stood entranced. Jacobus grasped me delicately above the elbow, impelling me to a half-turn to the left.

I had not noticed the girl before. She occupied a low, deep, wicker-work armchair, and I saw her in exact profile like a figure in a tapestry, and as motionless. Jacobus released my arm.

'This is Alice,' he announced tranquilly; and his subdued manner of speaking made it sound so much like a confidential communication that I fancied myself nodding understandingly and whispering: 'I see, I see.' ... Of course, I did nothing of the kind. Neither of us did anything; we stood side by side looking down at the girl. For quite a time she did not stir, staring straight before her as if watching the vision of some pageant passing through the garden in the deep, rich glow of light and the splendour of flowers.

Then, coming to the end of her reverie, she looked round and up. If I had not at first noticed her, I am certain that she too had been unaware of my presence till she actually perceived me by her father's side. The quickened upward movement of the heavy eyelids, the widening of the languid glance, passing into a fixed stare, put that beyond doubt.

Under her amazement there was a hint of fear, and then came a flash of anger. Jacobus, after uttering my name fairly loud, said: 'Make yourself at home, Captain – I won't be gone long,' and went away rapidly. Before I had time to make a bow I was left alone with the girl – who, I remembered suddenly, had not been seen by any man or woman of that town since she had found it necessary to put up her hair. It looked as though it had not been touched again since that distant time of first putting up; it was a mass of black, lustrous locks, twisted anyhow high on her head, with long, untidy wisps hanging down on each side of the clear sallow face; a mass so thick and strong and abundant that, nothing but to look at, it gave you a sensation of heavy pressure on the top of your head and an impression of magnificently cynical untidiness. She leaned forward, hugging herself with crossed legs; a dingy, amber-coloured, flounced wrapper of some thin stuff revealed the young supple body drawn together tensely in the deep low seat as if crouching for a spring. I detected a slight, quivering start or two, which looked uncommonly like bounding away. They were followed by the most absolute immobility.

The absurd impulse to run after Jacobus (for I had been startled, too) once repressed, I took a chair, placed it not very far from her, sat down deliberately, and began to talk about the garden, caring not what I said, but using a gentle caressing intonation as one talks to soothe a startled wild animal. I could not even be certain that she understood me. She never raised her face nor attempted to look my way. I kept on talking only to prevent her from taking flight. She had another of those quivering repressed starts which made me catch my breath with apprehension.

Ultimately I formed the notion that what prevented her perhaps from going off in one great, nervous leap, was the scantiness of her attire. The wicker armchair was the most substantial thing about her person. What she had on under that dingy, loose, amber wrapper must have been of the most flimsy and airy character. One could not help being aware of it. It was obvious. I felt it actually embarrassing at first; but that sort of embarrassment is got over easily by a mind not enslaved by narrow prejudices. I did not avert my gaze from Alice. I went on talking with ingratiating softness, the recollection that, most likely, she had never before been spoken to by a strange man adding to my assurance. I don't know why an emotional tenseness should have crept into the situation. But it did. And just as I was becoming aware of it a slight scream cut short my flow of urbane speech.

The scream did not proceed from the girl. It was emitted behind me, and caused me to turn my head sharply. I understood at once that the apparition in the doorway was the elderly relation of Jacobus, the companion, the gouvernante. While she remained thunderstruck, I got up and made her a low bow.

The ladies of Jacobus's household evidently spent their days in light attire. This stumpy old woman with a face like a large wrinkled lemon, beady eyes, and a shock of iron-grey hair, was dressed in a garment of some ash-coloured, silky, light stuff. It fell from her thick neck down to her toes with the simplicity of an unadorned nightgown. It made her appear truly cylindrical. She exclaimed 'How did you get here?'

Before I could say a word she vanished and presently I heard a confusion of shrill protestations in a distant part of the house. Obviously no one could tell her how I got there. In a moment, with great outcries from two negro women following her, she waddled back to the doorway, infuriated.

'What do you want here?'

I turned to the girl. She was sitting straight up now, her hands posed on the arms of the chair. I appealed to her.

'Surely, Miss Alice, you will not let them drive me out into the street?'

Her magnificent black eyes, narrowed, long in shape, swept over me with an indefinable expression, then in a harsh, contemptuous voice she let fall in French a sort of explanation:

'*C'est papa.*'

I made another low bow to the old woman.

She turned her back on me in order to drive away her black henchwomen, then surveying my person in a peculiar manner with one small eye nearly closed and her face all drawn up on that side as if with a twinge of toothache, she stepped out on the verandah, sat down in a rocking-chair some distance away, and took up her knitting from a little table. Before she started at it she plunged one of the needles into the mop of her grey hair and stirred it vigorously.

Her elementary nightgown-sort of frock clung to her ancient, stumpy, and floating form. She wore white cotton stockings and flat brown velvet slippers. Her feet and ankles were obtrusively visible on the footrest. She began to rock herself slightly, while she knitted. I had resumed my seat and kept quiet, for I mistrusted that old woman. What if she ordered me to depart? She seemed capable of any outrage. She had snorted once or twice; she was knitting violently. Suddenly she piped at the young girl in French a question which I translate colloquially:

'What's your father up to, now?'

The young creature shrugged her shoulders so comprehensively that her whole body swayed within the loose wrapper; and in that unexpectedly harsh voice which yet had a seductive quality to the sense, like certain kinds of natural rough wines one drinks with pleasure:

'It's some captain. Leave me alone – will you!'

The chair rocked quicker, the old, thin voice was like a whistle.

'You and your father make a pair. He would stick at nothing – that's well known. But I didn't expect this.'

I thought it high time to air some of my own French. I remarked modestly, but firmly, that this was business. I had some matters to talk over with Mr Jacobus.

At once she piped out a derisive 'Poor innocent!' Then, with a change of tone: 'The shop's for business. Why don't you go to the shop to talk with him?'

The furious speed of her fingers and knitting-needles made one dizzy; and with squeaky indignation:

'Sitting here staring at that girl – is that what you call business?'

'No,' I said suavely. 'I call this pleasure – an unexpected pleasure. And unless Miss Alice objects – '

I half turned to her. She flung me an angry and contemptuous 'Don't care!' and leaning her elbow on her knees took her chin in her hand – a Jacobus chin undoubtedly. And those heavy eyelids, this black irritated stare reminded me of Jacobus, too – the wealthy merchant, the respected one. The design of her eyebrows also was the same, rigid and ill-omened. Yes! I traced in her a resemblance to both of them. It came to me as a sort of surprising remote inference that both these Jacobuses were rather handsome men after all. I said:

'Oh! Then I shall stare at you till you smile.'

She favoured me again with an even more viciously scornful 'Don't care!'

The old woman broke in blunt and shrill:

'Hear his impudence! And you too! Don't care! Go at least and put some more clothes on. Sitting there like this before this sailor riff-raff.'

The sun was about to leave the Pearl of the Ocean for other seas, for other lands. The walled garden full of shadows blazed with colour as if the flowers were giving up the light absorbed during the day. The amazing old woman became very explicit. She suggested to the girl a corset and petticoat with a cynical unreserve which humiliated me. Was I of no more account than a wooden dummy? The girl snapped out: 'Sha'n't!'

It was not the naughty retort of a vulgar child; it had a note of desperation. Clearly an intrusion had somehow upset the balance of their established relations. The old woman knitted with furious accuracy, her eyes fastened down on her work.

'Oh, you are the true child of your father! And *that* talks of entering a convent! Letting herself be stared at by a fellow.'

'Leave off.'

'Shameless thing!'

'Old sorceress,' the girl uttered distinctly, preserving her meditative pose, chin in hand, and a far-away stare over the garden.

It was like the quarrel of the kettle and the pot. The old woman flew out of the chair, banged down her work, and with a great play of thick limb perfectly visible in that weird, clinging garment of hers, strode at the girl – who never stirred. I was experiencing a sort of trepidation when, as if awed by that unconscious attitude, the aged relative of Jacobus turned short upon me.

She was, I perceived, armed with a knitting-needle; and as she raised her hand her intention seemed to be to throw it at me like a dart. But she only used it to scratch her head with, examining me the while at close range, one eye nearly shut and her face distorted by a whimsical, one-sided grimace.

'My dear man,' she asked abruptly, 'do you expect any good to come of this?'

'I do hope so indeed, Miss Jacobus.' I tried to speak in the easy tone of an afternoon caller. 'You see, I am here after some bags.'

'Bags! Look at that now! Didn't I hear you holding forth to that graceless wretch?'

'You would like to see me in my grave,' uttered the motionless girl hoarsely.

'Grave! What about me? Buried alive before I am dead for the sake of a thing blessed with such a pretty father!' she cried; and turning to me: 'You're one of these men he does business with. Well – why don't you leave us in peace, my good fellow?'

It was said in a tone – this 'leave us in peace!' There was a sort of ruffianly familiarity, a superiority, a scorn in it. I was to hear it more than once, for you would show an imperfect knowledge of human nature if you thought that this was my last visit to that house – where no respectable person had put foot for ever so many years. No, you would be very much mistaken if you imagined that this reception had scared me away. First of all I was not going to run before a grotesque and ruffianly old woman.

And then you mustn't forget these necessary bags. That first evening Jacobus made me stay to dinner; after, however, telling me loyally that he didn't know whether he could do anything at all for me. He had been thinking it over. It was too difficult, he feared. . . . But he did not give it up in so many words.

We were only three at table; the girl by means of repeated 'Won't!' 'Sha'n't!' and 'Don't care!' having conveyed and affirmed her intention not to come to the table, not to have any dinner, not to move from the verandah. The old relative hopped about in her flat slippers and piped indignantly, Jacobus towered over her and murmured placidly in his throat; I joined jocularly from a distance, throwing in a few words, for which under the cover of the night I received secretly a most vicious poke in the ribs from the old woman's elbow or perhaps her fist. I restrained a cry. And all the time the girl didn't even condescend to raise her head to look at any of us. All this may sound childish – and yet that stony, petulant sullenness had an obscurely tragic flavour.

And so we sat down to the food around the light of a good many candles while she remained crouching out there, staring in the dark as if feeding her bad temper on the heavily scented air of the admirable garden.

Before leaving I said to Jacobus that I would come next day to hear if the bag affair had made any progress. He shook his head slightly at that.

'I'll haunt your house daily till you pull it off. You'll be always finding me here.'

His faint, melancholy smile did not part his thick lips.

'That will be all right, Captain.'

Then seeing me to the door, very tranquil, he murmured earnestly the recommendation: 'Make yourself at home,' and also the hospitable hint about there being always 'a plate of soup.' It was only on my way down to the quay, down the ill-lighted streets, that I remembered I had been engaged to dine that very evening with the S—— family. Though vexed with my forgetfulness (it would be rather awkward to explain) I couldn't help thinking that it had procured me a more amusing evening. And besides – business. The sacred business –

In a barefooted negro who overtook me at a run and bolted down the landing-steps I recognized Jacobus's boatman, who must have been feeding in the kitchen. His usual 'Good night, sah!' as I went up my ship's ladder had a more cordial sound than on previous occasions.

have sounded like the murmur of a pleading lover. Whenever I paused expectantly there was only a deep silence. It was like offering food to a seated statue.

'I haven't been able to swallow a single morsel thinking of you out here starving yourself in the dark. It's positively cruel to be so obstinate. Think of my sufferings.'

'Don't care.'

I felt as if I could have done her some violence – shaken her, beaten her maybe. I said:

'Your absurd behaviour will prevent me coming here any more.'

'What's that to me?'

'You like it.'

'It's false,' she snarled.

My hand fell on her shoulder; and if she had flinched I verily believe I would have shaken her. But there was no movement and this immobility disarmed my anger.

'You do. Or you wouldn't be found on the verandah every day. Why are you here, then? There are plenty of rooms in the house. You have your own room to stay in – if you did not want to see me. But you do. You know you do.'

I felt a slight shudder under my hand and released my grip as if frightened by that sign of animation in her body. The scented air of the garden came to us in a warm wave like a voluptuous and perfumed sigh.

'Go back to them,' she whispered, almost pitifully.

As I re-entered the dining-room I saw Jacobus cast down his eyes. I banged the plate on the table. At this demonstration of ill-humour he murmured something in an apologetic tone, and I turned on him viciously as if he were accountable to me for these 'abominable eccentricities', I believe I called them.

'But I daresay Miss Jacobus here is responsible for most of this offensive manner,' I added loftily.

She piped out at once in her brazen, ruffianly manner:

'Eh? Why don't you leave us in peace, my good fellow?'

I was astonished that she should dare before Jacobus. Yet what could he have done to repress her? He needed her too much. He raised a heavy, drowsy glance for an instant, then looked down again. She insisted with shrill finality:

'Haven't you done your business, you two? Well, then – '

She had the true Jacobus impudence, that old woman. Her mop of iron-grey hair was parted on the side like a man's, raffishly, and she made as if to plunge her fork into it, as she used to do with the knitting-needle, but refrained. Her little black eyes sparkled venomously. I turned to my host at the head of the table – menacingly as it were.

'Well, and what do you say to that, Jacobus? Am I to take it that we have done with each other?'

I had to wait a little. The answer when it came was rather unexpected, and in quite another spirit than the question.

'I certainly think we might do some business yet with those potatoes of mine, Captain. You will find that – '

I cut him short.

'I've told you before that I don't trade.'

His broad chest heaved without a sound in a noiseless sigh.

'Think it over, Captain,' he murmured tenacious and tranquil; and I burst into a jarring laugh, remembering how he had stuck to the circus-rider woman – the depth of passion under that placid surface, which even cuts with a riding-whip (so the legend had it) could never ruffle into the semblance of a storm; something like the passion of a fish would be if one could imagine such a thing as a passionate fish.

That evening I experienced more distinctly than ever the sense of moral discomfort which always attended me in that house lying under the ban of all 'decent' people. I refused to stay on and smoke after dinner; and when I put my hand into the thickly-cushioned palm of Jacobus, I said to myself that it would be for the last time under his roof. I pressed his bulky paw heartily nevertheless. Hadn't he got me out of a serious difficulty? To the few words of acknowledgement I was bound, and indeed quite willing, to utter, he answered by stretching his closed lips in his melancholy, glued-together smile.

'That will be all right, I hope, Captain,' he breathed out weightily.

'What do you mean?' I asked alarmed. 'That your brother might yet – '

'Oh no,' he assured me. 'He . . . he's a man of his word, Captain.'

My self-communion as I walked away from his door, trying to believe that this was for the last time, was not satisfactory. I was aware myself that I was not sincere in my reflections as to Jacobus's motives, and, of course, the very next day I went back again.

How weak, irrational, and absurd we are! How easily carried away whenever our awakened imagination brings us the irritating hint of desire! I cared for the girl in a particular way, seduced by the moody expression of her face, by her obstinate silences, her rare, scornful words; by the perpetual pout of her closed lips, the black depths of her fixed gaze turned slowly upon me as if in contemptuous provocation, only to be averted next moment with an exasperating indifference.

Of course the news of my assiduity had spread all over the little town. I noticed a change in the manner of my acquaintances and even something different in the nods of the other captains when meeting them at the landing-steps or in the offices where business called me. The old-maidish head clerk treated me with distant punctiliousness and, as it were, gathered his skirts round him for fear of contamination. It seemed to me that the very niggers on the quays turned to look after me as I passed; and as to Jacobus's boatman his 'Good night, sah!' when he put me on board was no longer merely cordial – it had a familiar, confidential sound as though we had been partners in some villainy.

My friend S—— the elder passed me on the other side of the street with a wave of the hand and an ironic smile. The younger brother, the one they had married to an elderly shrew, he, on the strength of an older friendship and as if paying a debt of gratitude, took the liberty to utter a word of warning.

'You're doing yourself no good by your choice of friends, my dear chap,' he said with infantile gravity.

As I knew that the meeting of the brothers Jacobus was the subject of excited comment in the whole of the sugary Pearl of the Ocean I wanted to know why I was blamed.

'I have been the occasion of a move which may end in a reconciliation surely desirable from the point of view of the proprieties – don't you know?'

'Of course, if that girl were disposed of it would certainly facilitate – ' he mused sagely, then, inconsequential creature, gave me a light tap on the lower part of my waistcoat. 'You old sinner,' he cried jovially, 'much you care for proprieties. But you had better look out for yourself, you know, with a personage like Jacobus who has no sort of reputation to lose.'

He had recovered his gravity of a respectable citizen by that time and added regretfully:

'All the women of our family are perfectly scandalized.'

But by that time I had given up visiting the S—— family and the D—— family. The elder ladies pulled such faces when I showed myself, and the multitude of related young ladies received me with such a variety of looks: wondering, awed, mocking (except Miss Mary, who spoke to me and looked at me with hushed, pained compassion as though I had been ill), that I had no difficulty in giving them all up. I would have given up the society of the whole town, for the sake of sitting near that girl, snarling and superb and barely clad in that flimsy, dingy, amber wrapper, open low at the throat. She looked, with the wild wisps of hair hanging down her tense face, as though she had just jumped out of bed in the panic of a fire.

She sat leaning on her elbow, looking at nothing. Why did she stay listening to my absurd chatter? And not only that; but why did she powder her face in preparation for my arrival? It seemed to be her idea of making a toilette, and in her untidy negligence a sign of great effort towards personal adornment.

But I might have been mistaken. The powdering might have been her daily practice and her presence in the verandah a sign of an indifference so complete as to take no account of my existence. Well, it was all one to me.

I loved to watch her slow changes of pose, to look at her long immobilities composed in the graceful lines of her body, to observe the mysterious narrow stare of her splendid black eyes, somewhat long in shape, half closed, contemplating the void. She was like a spellbound creature with the forehead of a goddess crowned by the dishevelled magnificent hair of a gipsy tramp. Even her indifference was seductive. I felt myself growing attached to her by the bond of an irrealizable desire, for I kept my head – quite. And I put up with the moral discomfort of Jacobus's sleepy watchfulness, tranquil, and yet so expressive; as if there had been a tacit pact between us two. I put up with the insolence of the old woman's: 'Aren't you ever going to leave us in peace, my good fellow?' with her taunts; with her brazen and sinister scolding. She was of true Jacobus stock, and no mistake.

Directly I got away from the girl I called myself many hard names. What folly was this? I would ask myself. It was like being the slave of some depraved habit. And I returned to her with my head clear, my heart certainly free, not even moved by pity for that castaway (she was as much of a castaway as anyone ever wrecked on a desert island), but as if beguiled by some extraordinary promise. Nothing more unworthy could be imagined. The recollection of that tremulous whisper when I gripped her shoulder with one hand and held a plate of chicken with the other was enough to make me break all my good resolutions.

Her insulting taciturnity was enough sometimes to make one gnash one's teeth with rage. When she opened her mouth it was only to be abominably rude in harsh tones to the associate of her reprobate father; and the full approval of her aged relative was conveyed to her by offensive chuckles. If not that, then her remarks, always uttered in the tone of scathing contempt, were of the most appalling inanity.

How could it have been otherwise? That plump, ruffianly Jacobus old maid in the tight grey frock had never taught her any manners. Manners I suppose are not necessary for born castaways. No educational establishment could ever be induced to accept her as a pupil – on account of the proprieties, I imagine. And Jacobus had not been able to send her away anywhere. How could he have done it? Who with? Where to? He himself was not enough of an adventurer to think of settling down anywhere else. His passion had tossed him at the tail of a circus up and down strange coasts, but, the storm over, he had drifted back shamelessly where, social outcast as he was, he remained still a Jacobus – one of the oldest families on the island, older than the French even. There must have been a Jacobus in at the death of the last Dodo.... The girl had learned nothing, she had never listened to a general conversation, she knew nothing, she had heard of nothing. She could read certainly; but all the reading matter that ever came in her way were the newspapers provided for the captains' room of the 'store'. Jacobus had the habit of taking these sheets home now and then in a very stained and ragged condition.

As her mind could not grasp the meaning of any matters treated there except police-court reports and accounts of crimes, she had formed for herself a notion of the civilized world as a scene of murders, abductions, burglaries, stabbing affrays, and every sort of desperate violence. England and France, Paris and London (the only two towns of which she seemed to have heard), appeared to her sinks of abomination, reeking with blood, in contrast to her little island where petty larceny was about the standard of current misdeeds, with, now and then, some more pronounced crime – and that only amongst the imported coolie labourers on sugar estates or the negroes of the town. But in Europe these things were being done daily by a wicked population of white men amongst whom, as that ruffianly, aristocratic old Miss Jacobus pointed out, the wandering sailors, the associates of her precious papa, were the lowest of the low.

It was impossible to give her a sense of proportion. I suppose she figured England to herself as about the size of the Pearl of the Ocean; in which case it would certainly have been reeking with gore and a mere wreck of burgled houses from end to end. One could not make her understand that these horrors on which she fed her imagination were lost in the mass of orderly life like a few drops of blood in the ocean. She directed upon me for a moment the uncomprehending glance of her narrowed eyes and then would turn her scornful powdered face away without a word. She would not even take the trouble to shrug her shoulders.

All that time the batches of papers brought by the last mail reported a series of crimes in the East End of London, there was a sensational case of abduction in France and a fine display of armed robbery in Australia. One afternoon crossing the dining-room I heard Miss Jacobus piping in the verandah with venomous animosity: 'I don't know what your precious papa is plotting with that fellow. But he's just the sort of man who's capable of carrying you off far away somewhere and then cutting your throat some day for your money.'

There was a good half of the length of the verandah between the chairs. I came out and sat down fiercely midway between them.

'Yes, that's what we do with girls in Europe,' I began in a grimly matter-of-fact tone. I think Miss Jacobus was disconcerted by my sudden appearance. I turned upon her with cold ferocity:

'As to objectionable old women, they are first strangled quietly, then cut up into small pieces and thrown away, a bit here and a bit there. They vanish – '

I cannot go so far as to say I had terrified her. But she was troubled by my truculence, the more so because I had been always addressing her with a politeness she did not deserve. Her plump, knitting hands fell slowly on her knees. She said not a word while I fixed her with severe determination. Then as I turned away from her at last, she laid down her work gently and, with noiseless movements, retreated from the verandah. In fact, she vanished.

But I was not thinking of her. I was looking at the girl. It was what I was coming for daily; troubled, ashamed, eager; finding in my nearness to her a unique sensation which I indulged with dread, self-contempt, and deep pleasure, as if it were a secret vice bound to end in my undoing, like the habit of some drug or other which ruins and degrades its slave.

I looked her over, from the top of her dishevelled head, down the lovely line of the shoulder, following the curve of the hip, the draped form of the long limb, right down to her fine ankle below a torn, soiled flounce; and as far as the point of the shabby, high-heeled, blue slipper, dangling from her well-shaped foot, which she moved slightly, with quick, nervous jerks, as if impatient of my presence. And in the scent of the massed flowers I seemed to breathe her special and inexplicable charm, the heady perfume of the everlastingly irritated captive of the garden.

I looked at her rounded chin, the Jacobus chin; at the full, red lips pouting in the powdered, sallow face; at the firm modelling of the cheek, the grains of white in the hairs of the straight sombre eyebrows; at the long eyes, a narrowed gleam of liquid white and intense motionless black, with their gaze so empty of thought and so absorbed in their fixity that she seemed to be staring at her own lonely image, in some far-off mirror hidden from my sight amongst the trees.

And suddenly, without looking at me, with the appearance of a person speaking to herself, she asked, in that voice slightly harsh yet mellow and always irritated:

'Why do you keep on coming here?'

'Why do I keep on coming here?' I repeated, taken by surprise. I could not have told her. I could not even tell myself with sincerity why I was coming there. 'What's the good of you asking a question like that?'

'Nothing is any good,' she observed scornfully to the empty air, her chin propped on her hand, that hand never extended to any man, that no one had ever grasped – for I had only grasped her shoulder once – that generous, fine, somewhat masculine hand. I knew well the peculiarly efficient shape – broad at the base, tapering at the fingers—of that hand, for which there was nothing in the world to lay hold of. I pretended to be playful.

'No! But do you really care to know?'

She shrugged indolently her magnificent shoulders, from which the dingy thin wrapper was slipping a little.

'Oh – never mind – never mind!'

There was something smouldering under those airs of lassitude. She exasperated me by the provocation of her nonchalance, by something elusive and defiant in her very form which I wanted to seize. I said roughly:

'Why? Don't you think I should tell you the truth?'

Her eyes glided my way for a sidelong look, and she murmured, moving only her full, pouting lips:

'I think you would not dare.'

'Do you imagine I am afraid of you? What on earth.... Well, it's possible, after all, that I don't know exactly why I am coming here. Let us say, with Miss Jacobus, that it is for no good. You seem to believe the outrageous things she says, if you do have a row with her now and then.'

She snapped out viciously:

'Who else am I to believe?'

'I don't know,' I had to own, seeing her suddenly very helpless and condemned to moral solitude by the verdict of a respectable community. 'You might believe me, if you chose.'

She made a slight movement and asked me at once, with an effort as if making an experiment:

'What is the business between you and papa?'

'Don't you know the nature of your father's business? Come! He sells provisions to ships.'

She became rigid again in her crouching pose.

'Not that. What brings you here – to this house?'

'And suppose it's you? You would not call that business? Would you? And now let us drop the subject. It's no use. My ship will be ready for sea the day after tomorrow.'

She murmured a distinctly scared 'So soon,' and getting up quickly, went to the little table and poured herself a glass of water. She walked with rapid steps and with an indolent swaying of her whole young figure above the hips; when she passed near me I felt with tenfold force the charm of the peculiar, promising sensation I had formed the habit to seek near her. I thought with sudden dismay that this was the end of it; that after one more day I should be no longer able to come into this verandah, sit on this chair, and taste perversely the flavour of contempt in her indolent poses, drink in the provocation of her scornful looks, and listen to the curt, insolent remarks uttered in that harsh and seductive voice. As if my innermost nature had been altered by the action of some moral poison, I felt an abject dread of going to sea.

I had to exercise a sudden self-control, as one puts on a brake, to prevent myself jumping up to stride about, shout, gesticulate, make her a scene. What for? What about? I had no idea. It was just the relief of violence that I wanted; and I lolled back in my chair, trying to keep my lips formed in a smile; that half-indulgent, half-mocking smile which was my shield against the shafts of her contempt and the insulting sallies flung at me by the old woman.

She drank the water at a draught, with the avidity of raging thirst, and let herself fall on the nearest chair, as if utterly overcome. Her attitude, like certain tones of her voice, had in it something masculine: the knees apart in the ample wrapper, the clasped hands hanging between them, her body leaning forward, with drooping head. I stared at the heavy black coil of twisted hair. It was enormous, crowning the bowed head with a crushing and disdained glory. The escaped wisps hung straight down. And suddenly I perceived that the girl was trembling from head to foot, as though that glass of iced water had chilled her to the bone.

'What's the matter now?' I said, startled, but in no very sympathetic mood.

She shook her bowed, overweighted head and cried in a stifled voice but with a rising inflection:

'Go away! Go away! Go away!'

I got up then and approached her, with a strange sort of anxiety. I looked down at her round, strong neck, then stooped low enough to peep at her face. And I began to tremble a little myself.

'What on earth are you gone wild about, Miss Don't Care?'

She flung herself backwards violently, her head going over the back of the chair. And now it was her smooth, full, palpitating throat that lay exposed to my bewildered stare. Her eyes were nearly closed, with only a horrible white gleam under the lids as if she were dead.

'What has come to you?' I asked in awe. 'What are you terrifying yourself with?'

She pulled herself together, her eyes open frightfully wide now. The tropical afternoon was lengthening the shadows on the hot, weary earth, the abode of obscure desires, of extravagant hopes, of unimaginable terrors.

'Never mind! Don't care!' Then, after a gasp, she spoke with such frightful rapidity that I could hardly make out the amazing words: 'For if you were to shut me up in an empty place as smooth all round as the palm of my hand, I could always strangle myself with my hair.'

For a moment, doubting my ears, I let this inconceivable declaration sink into me. It is ever impossible to guess at the wild thoughts that pass through the heads of our fellow-creatures. What monstrous imaginings of violence could have dwelt under the low forehead of that girl who had been taught to regard her father as 'capable of anything' more in the light of a misfortune than that of a disgrace; as, evidently, something to be resented and feared rather than to be ashamed of? She seemed, indeed, as unaware of shame as of anything else in the world; but in her ignorance, her resentment and fear took a childish and violent shape.

Of course she spoke without knowing the value of words. What could she know of death – she who knew nothing of life? It was merely as the proof of her being beside herself with some odious apprehension, that this extraordinary speech had moved me, not to pity, but to a fascinated, horrified wonder. I had no idea what notion she had of her danger. Some sort of abduction. It was quite possible with the talk of that atrocious old woman. Perhaps she thought she could be carried off, bound hand and foot and even gagged. At that surmise I felt as if the door of a furnace had been opened in front of me.

'Upon my honour!' I cried. 'You will end by going crazy if you listen to that abominable old aunt of yours – '

I studied her haggard expression, her trembling lips. Her cheeks even seemed sunk a little. But how I, the associate of her disreputable father, the 'lowest of the low' from the criminal Europe, could manage to reassure her I had no conception. She was exasperating.

'Heavens and earth! What do you think I can do?'

'I don't know.'

Her chin certainly trembled. And she was looking at me with extreme attention. I made a step nearer to her chair.

'I shall do nothing. I promise you that. Will that do? Do you understand? I shall do nothing whatever, of any kind; and the day after tomorrow I shall be gone.'

What else could I have said? She seemed to drink in my words with the thirsty avidity with which she had emptied the glass of water. She whispered tremulously, in that touching tone I had heard once before on her lips, and which thrilled me again with the same emotion:

'I would believe you. But what about papa – '

'He be hanged!' My emotion betrayed itself by the brutality of my tone. 'I've had enough of your papa. Are you so stupid as to imagine that I am frightened of him? He can't make me do anything.'

All that sounded feeble to me in the face of her ignorance. But I must conclude that the 'accent of sincerity' has, as some people say, a really irresistible power. The effect was far beyond my hopes – and even beyond my conception. To watch the change in the girl was like watching a miracle – the gradual but swift relaxation of her tense glance, of her stiffened muscles, of every fibre of her body. That black, fixed stare into which I had read a tragic meaning more than once, in which I had found a sombre seduction, was perfectly empty now, void of all consciousness whatever, and not even aware any longer of my presence; it had become a little sleepy, in the Jacobus fashion.

But, man being a perverse animal, instead of rejoicing at my complete success, I beheld it with astounded and indignant eyes. There was something cynical in that unconcealed alteration, the true Jacobus shamelessness. I felt as though I had been cheated in some rather complicated deal into which I had entered against my better judgment. Yes, cheated without any regard for, at least, the forms of decency.

With an easy, indolent, and in its indolence, supple, feline movement, she rose from the chair, so provokingly ignoring me now, that for very rage I held my ground within less than a foot of her. Leisurely and tranquil, behaving right before me with the ease of a person alone in a room, she extended her beautiful arms, with her hands clenched, her body swaying, her head thrown back a little, revelling contemptuously in a sense of relief, easing her limbs in freedom after all these days of crouching, motionless poses when she had been so furious and so afraid.

All this with supreme indifference, incredible, offensive, exasperating, like ingratitude doubled with treachery.

I ought to have been flattered, perhaps, but, on the contrary, my anger grew; her movements to pass by me as if I were a wooden post or a piece of furniture, that unconcerned movement brought it to a head.

I won't say I did not know what I was doing, but, certainly, cool reflection had nothing to do with the circumstance that next moment both my arms were round her waist. It was an impulsive action, as one snatches at something falling or escaping; and it had no hypocritical gentleness about it either. She had no time to make a sound, and the first kiss I planted on her closed lips was vicious enough to have been a bite.

She did not resist, and of course I did not stop at one. She let me go on, not as if she were inanimate – I felt her there, close against me, young, full of vigour, of life, a strong desirable creature, but as if she did not care in the least, in the absolute assurance of her safety, what I did or left undone. Our faces brought close together in this storm of haphazard caresses, her big, black, wide-open eyes looked into mine without the girl appearing either angry or pleased or moved in any way. In that steady gaze which seemed impersonally to watch my madness I could detect a slight surprise, perhaps – nothing more. I showered kisses upon her face and there did not seem to be any reason why this should not go on for ever.

That thought flashed through my head, and I was on the point of desisting, when, all at once, she began to struggle with a sudden violence which all but freed her instantly, which revived my exasperation with her, indeed a fierce desire never to let her go any more. I tightened my embrace in time, gasping out: 'No – you don't!' as if she were my mortal enemy. On her part not a word was said. Putting her hands against my chest, she pushed with all her might without succeeding in breaking the circle of my arms. Except that she seemed thoroughly awake now, her eyes gave me no clue whatever. To meet her black stare was like looking into a deep well, and I was totally unprepared for her change of tactics. Instead of trying to tear my hands apart, she flung herself upon my breast and with a downward, undulating, serpentine motion, a quick sliding dive, she got away from me smoothly. It was all very swift; I saw her pick up the tail of her wrapper and run for the door at the end of the verandah not very gracefully. She appeared to be limping a little – and then she vanished; the door swung behind her so noiselessly that I could not believe it was completely closed. I had a distinct suspicion of her black eye being at the crack to watch what I should do. I could not make up my mind whether to shake my fist in that direction or blow a kiss.

VI

Either would have been perfectly consistent with my feelings. I gazed at the door, hesitating, but in the end I did neither. The monition of some sixth sense – the sense of guilt, maybe, that sense which always acts too late, alas! – warned me to look round; and at once I became aware that the conclusion of this tumultuous episode was likely to be a matter of lively anxiety. Jacobus was standing in the doorway of the dining-room. How long he had been there it was impossible to guess; and remembering my struggle with the girl I thought he must have been its mute witness from beginning to end. But this supposition seemed almost incredible. Perhaps that impenetrable girl had heard him come in and had got away in time.

He stepped onto the verandah in his usual manner, heavy-eyed, with glued lips. I marvelled at the girl's resemblance to this man. Those long, Egyptian eyes, that low forehead of a stupid goddess, she had found in the sawdust of the circus; but all the rest of the face, the design and the modelling, the rounded chin, the very lips – all that was Jacobus, fined down, more finished, more expressive.

His thick hand fell on and grasped with force the back of a light chair (there were several standing about) and I perceived the chance of a broken head at the end of all this – most likely. My mortification was extreme. The scandal would be horrible; that was unavoidable. But how to act so as to satisfy myself I did not know. I stood on my guard and at any rate faced him. There was nothing else for it. Of one thing I was certain, that, however brazen my attitude, it could never equal the characteristic Jacobus impudence.

He gave me his melancholy, glued smile and sat down. I own I was relieved. The perspective of passing from kisses to blows had nothing particularly attractive in it. Perhaps – perhaps he had seen nothing? He behaved as usual, but he had never before found me alone on the verandah. If he had alluded to it, if he had asked: 'Where's Alice?' or something of the sort, I would have been able to judge from the tone. He would give me no opportunity. The striking peculiarity was that he had never looked up at me yet. 'He knows,' I said to myself confidently. And my contempt for him relieved my disgust with myself.

'You are early home,' I remarked.

'Things are very quiet; nothing doing at the store today,' he explained with a cast-down air.

'Oh, well, you know, I am off,' I said, feeling that this, perhaps, was the best thing to do.

'Yes,' he breathed out. 'Day after tomorrow.'

This was not what I had meant; but as he gazed persistently at the floor, I followed the direction of his glance. In the absolute stillness of the house we stared at the high-heeled slipper the girl had lost in her flight. We stared. It lay overturned.

After what seemed a very long time to me, Jacobus hitched the chair forward, stooped with extended arm and picked it up. It looked a slender thing in his big, thick hands. It was not really a slipper, but a low shoe of blue, glazed kid, rubbed and shabby. It had straps to go over the instep, but the girl only thrust her feet in, after her slovenly manner. Jacobus raised his eyes from the shoe to look at me.

'Sit down, Captain,' he said at last, in his subdued tone.

As if the sight of that shoe had renewed the spell, I gave up suddenly the idea of leaving the house there and then. It had become impossible. I sat down, keeping my eyes on the fascinating object. Jacobus turned his daughter's shoe over and over in his cushioned paws as if studying the way the thing was made. He contemplated the thin sole for a time; then glancing inside with an absorbed air:

'I am glad I found you here, Captain.'

I answered this by some sort of grunt, watching him covertly. Then I added: 'You won't have much more of me now.'

He was still deep in the interior of that shoe on which my eyes too were resting.

'Have you thought any more of this deal in potatoes I spoke to you about the other day?'

'No, I haven't,' I answered curtly. He checked my movement to rise by an austere, commanding gesture of the hand holding that fatal shoe. I remained seated and glared at him. 'You know I don't trade.'

'You ought to, Captain. You ought to.'

I reflected. If I left the house now I should never see the girl again. And I felt I must see her once more, if only for an instant. It was a need, not to be reasoned with, not to be disregarded. No, I did not want to go away. I wanted to stay for one more experience of that strange provoking sensation and of indefinite desire, the habit of which had made me – me of all people! – dread the prospect of going to sea.

'Mr Jacobus,' I pronounced slowly. 'Do you really think that upon the whole and taking various matters into consideration – I mean everything, do you understand? – it would be a good thing for me to trade, let us say, with you?'

I waited for awhile. He went on looking at the shoe which he held now crushed in the middle, the worn point of the toe and the high heel protruding on each side of his heavy fist.

'That will be all right,' he said, facing me squarely at last.

'Are you sure?'

'You'll find it quite correct, Captain.' He had uttered his habitual phrases in his usual placid, breath-saving voice and stood my hard, inquisitive stare sleepily without as much as a wink.

'Then let us trade,' I said, turning my shoulder to him. 'I see you are bent on it.'

I did not want an open scandal, but I thought that outward decency may be bought too dearly at times. I included Jacobus, myself, the whole population of the island, in the same contemptuous disgust as though we had been partners in an ignoble transaction. And the remembered vision at sea, diaphanous and blue, of the Pearl of the Ocean at sixty miles off; the unsubstantial and pure magic, turned into a thing of horrors too. Was this the fortune this vaporous and rare apparition had held for me in its hard heart, hidden within the shape as of fair dreams and mist? Was this my luck?

'I think' – Jacobus became suddenly audible after what seemed the silence of vile meditation – 'that you might conveniently take some thirty tons. That would be about the lot, Captain.'

'Would it? The lot! I daresay it would be convenient, but I haven't got enough money for that.'

I had never seen him so animated.

'No!' he exclaimed with what I took for the accent of grim menace. 'That's a pity.' He paused, then, unrelenting: 'How much money have you got, Captain?' he enquired with awful directness.

It was my turn to face him squarely. I did so and mentioned the amount I could dispose of. And I perceived that he was disappointed. He thought it over, his calculating gaze lost in mine, for quite a long time before he came out in a thoughtful tone with the rapacious suggestion:

'You could draw some more from your charterers. That would be quite easy, Captain.'

'No, I couldn't,' I retorted brusquely. 'I've drawn my salary up to date, and besides, the ship's accounts are closed.'

I was growing furious. I pursued: 'And I'll tell you what: if I could do it I wouldn't.' Then throwing off all restraint, I added: 'You are a bit too much of a Jacobus, Mr Jacobus.'

The tone alone was insulting enough, but he remained tranquil, only a little puzzled, till something seemed to dawn upon him; but the unwonted light in his eyes died out instantly. As a Jacobus on his native heath, what a mere skipper chose to say could not touch him, outcast as he was. As a ship-chandler he could stand anything. All I caught of his mumble was a vague – 'quite correct', than which nothing could have been more egregiously false at bottom – to my view, at least. But I remembered – I had never forgotten – that I must see the girl. I did not mean to go. I meant to stay in the house till I had seen her once more.

'Look here!' I said finally. 'I'll tell you what I'll do. I'll take as many of your confounded potatoes as my money wil buy, on condition that you go off at once down to the wharf to see them loaded in the lighter and sent alongside the ship straight away. Take the invoice and a signed receipt with you. Here's the key of my desk. Give it to Burns. He will pay you.'

He got up from his chair before I had finished speaking, but he refused to take the key. Burns would never do it. He wouldn't like to ask him even.

'Well, then,' I said, eyeing him slightingly, 'there's nothing for it, Mr Jacobus, but you must wait on board till I come off to settle with you.'

'That will be all right, Captain. I will go at once.'

He seemed at a loss what to do with the girl's shoe he was still holding in his fist. Finally, looking dully at me, he put it down on the chair from which he had risen.

'And you, Captain? Won't you come along, too, just to see – '

'Don't bother about me. I'll take care of myself.'

He remained perplexed for a moment, as if trying to understand; and then his weighty: 'Certainly, certainly, Captain,' seemed to be the outcome of some sudden thought. His big chest heaved. Was it a sigh? As he went out to hurry off those potatoes he never looked back at me.

I waited till the noise of his footsteps had died out of the dining-room, and I waited a little longer. Then turning towards the distant door I raised my voice along the verandah:

'Alice!'

Nothing answered me, not even a stir behind the door. Jacobus's house might have been made empty for me to make myself at home in. I did not call again. I had become aware of a great discouragement. I was mentally jaded, morally dejected. I turned to the garden again, sitting down with my elbows spread on the low balustrade, and took my head in my hands.

The evening closed upon me. The shadows lengthened, deepened, mingled together into a pool of twilight in which the flower-beds glowed like coloured embers; whiffs of heavy scent came to me as if the dusk of this hemisphere were but the dimness of a temple and the garden an enormous censer swinging before the altar of the stars. The colours of the blossoms deepened, losing their glow one by one.

The girl, when I turned my head at a slight noise, appeared to me very tall and slender, advancing with a swaying limp, a floating and uneven motion which ended in the sinking of her shadowy form into the deep low chair. And I don't know why or whence I received the impression that she had come too late. She ought to have appeared at my call. She ought to have . . . It was as if a supreme opportunity had been missed.

I rose and took a seat close to her, nearly opposite her armchair. Her ever discontented voice addressed me at once, contemptuously:

'You are still here.'

I pitched mine low.

'You have come out at last.'

'I came to look for my shoe – before they bring in the lights.'

It was her harsh, enticing whisper, subdued, not very steady, but its low tremulousness gave me no thrill now. I could only make out the oval of her face, her uncovered throat, the long, white gleam of her eyes. She was mysterious enough. Her hands were resting on the arms of the chair. But where was the mysterious and provoking sensation which was like the perfume of her flower-like youth? I said quietly:

'I have got your shoe here.' She made no sound and I continued: 'You had better give me your foot and I will put it on for you.'

She made no movement. I bent low down and groped for her foot under the flounces of the wrapper. She did not withdraw it and I put on the shoe, buttoning the instep-strap. It was an inanimate foot. I lowered it gently to the floor.

'If you buttoned the strap you would not be losing your shoe, Miss Don't Care,' I said, trying to be playful without conviction. I felt more like wailing over the lost illusion of vague desire, over the sudden conviction that I would never find again near her the strange, half-evil, half-tender sensation which had given its acrid flavour to so many days, which had made her appear tragic and promising, pitiful and provoking. That was all over.

'Your father picked it up,' I said, thinking she may just as well be told of the fact.

'I am not afraid of papa – by himself,' she declared scornfully.

'Oh! It's only in conjunction with his disreputable associates, strangers, the "riff-raff of Europe" as your charming aunt or great-aunt says – men like me, for instance – that you – '

'I am not afraid of you,' she snapped out.

'That's because you don't know that I am now doing business with your father. Yes, I am in fact doing exactly what he wants me to do. I've broken my promise to you. That's the sort of man I am. And now – aren't you afraid? If you believe what that dear, kind, truthful old lady says you ought to be.'

It was with unexpected modulated softness that she affirmed:

'No. I am not afraid.' She hesitated. . . . 'Not now.'

'Quite right. You needn't be. I shall not see you again before I go to sea.' I rose and stood near her chair. 'But I shall often think of you in this old garden, passing under the trees over there, walking between these gorgeous flower-beds. You must love this garden – '

'I love nothing.'

I heard in her sullen tone the faint echo of that resentfully tragic note which I had found once so provoking. But it left me unmoved except for a sudden and weary conviction of the emptiness of all things under Heaven.

'Good-bye, Alice,' I said.

She did not answer, she did not move. To merely take her hand, shake it, and go away seemed impossible, almost improper. I stooped without haste and pressed my lips to her smooth forehead. This was the moment when I realized clearly with a sort of terror my complete detachment from that unfortunate creature. And as I lingered in that cruel self-knowledge I felt the light touch of her arms falling languidly on my neck and received a hasty, awkward, haphazard kiss which missed my lips. No! She was not afraid; but I was no longer moved. Her arms slipped off my neck, she made no sound, the deep wicker armchair creaked slightly; only a sense of my dignity prevented me fleeing headlong from that catastrophic revelation.

I traversed the dining-room slowly. I thought: She's listening to my footsteps; she can't help it; she'll hear me open and shut that door. And I closed it as gently behind me as if I had been a thief retreating with his ill-gotten booty. During that stealthy act I experienced the last touch of emotion in that house, at the thought of the girl I had left sitting there in the obscurity, with her heavy hair and empty eyes as black as the night itself, staring into the walled garden, silent, warm, odorous with the perfume of imprisoned flowers, which, like herself, were lost to sight in a world buried in darkness.

The narrow, ill-lighted, rustic streets I knew so well on my way to the harbour were extremely quiet. I felt in my heart that the further one ventures the better one understands how everything in our life is common, short, and empty; that it is in seeking the unknown in our sensations that we discover how mediocre are our attempts and how soon defeated! Jacobus's boatman was waiting at the steps with an unusual air of readiness. He put me alongside the ship, but did not give me his confidential 'Good evening, sah,' and, instead of shoving off at once, remained holding by the ladder.

I was a thousand miles from commercial affairs, when on the dark quarter-deck Mr Burns positively rushed at me, stammering with excitement. He had been pacing the deck distractedly for hours awaiting my arrival. Just before sunset a lighter loaded with potatoes had come alongside with that fat ship-chandler himself sitting on the pile of sacks. He was now stuck immovable in the cabin. What was the meaning of it all? Surely I did not –

'Yes, Mr Burns, I did,' I cut him short. He was beginning to make gestures of despair when I stopped that, too, by giving him the key of my desk and desiring him, in a tone which admitted of no argument, to go below at once, pay Mr Jacobus's bill, and send him out of the ship.

'I don't want to see him,' I confessed frankly, climbing the poop-ladder. I felt extremely tired. Dropping on the seat of the skylight, I gave myself up to idle gazing at the lights about the quay and at the black mass of the mountain on the south side of the harbour. I never heard Jacobus leave the ship with every single sovereign of my ready cash in his pocket. I never heard anything till, a long time afterwards, Mr Burns, unable to contain himself any longer, intruded upon me with his ridiculously angry lamentations at my weakness and good nature.

'Of course, there's plenty of room in the after-hatch. But they are sure to go rotten down there. Well! I never heard . . . seventeen tons! I suppose I must hoist in that lot first thing tomorrow morning.'

'I suppose you must. Unless you drop them overboard. But I'm afraid you can't do that. I wouldn't mind myself, but it's forbidden to throw rubbish into the harbour, you know.'

'That is the truest word you have said for many a day, sir – rubbish. That's just what I expect they are. Nearly eighty good gold sovereigns gone; a perfectly clean sweep of your drawer, sir. Bless me if I understand!'

As it was impossible to throw the right light on this commercial transaction I left him to his lamentations and under the impression that I was a hopeless fool. Next day I did not go ashore. For one thing, I had no money to go ashore with – no, not enough to buy a cigarette. Jacobus had made a clean sweep. But that was not the only reason. The Pearl of the Ocean had in a few short hours grown odious to me. And I did not want to meet anyone. My reputation had suffered. I knew I was the object of unkind and sarcastic comments.

The following morning at sunrise, just as our stern-fasts had been let go and the tug plucked us out from between the buoys, I saw Jacobus standing up in his boat. The nigger was pulling hard; several baskets of provisions for ships were stowed between the thwarts. The father of Alice was going his morning round. His countenance was tranquil and friendly. He raised his arm and shouted something with great heartiness. But his voice was of the sort that doesn't carry any distance; all I could catch faintly, or rather guess at, were the words 'next time' and 'quite correct'. And it was only of these last that I was certain. Raising my arm perfunctorily for all response, I turned away. I rather resented the familiarity of the thing. Hadn't I settled accounts finally with him by means of that potato bargain?

This being a harbour story it is not my purpose to speak of our passage. I was glad enough to be at sea, but not with the gladness of old days. Formerly I had no memories to take away with me. I shared in the blessed forgetfulness of sailors, that forgetfulness natural and invincible, which resembles innocence in so far that it prevents self-examination. Now however I remembered the girl. During the first few days I was for ever questioning myself as to the nature of facts and sensations connected with her person and with my conduct.

And I must say also that Mr Burns' intolerable fussing with those potatoes was not calculated to make me forget the part which I had played. He looked upon it as a purely commercial transaction of a particularly foolish kind, and his devotion – if it was devotion and not mere cussedness as I came to regard it before long – inspired him with a zeal to minimize my loss as much as possible. Oh, yes! He took care of those infamous potatoes with a vengeance, as the saying goes.

Everlastingly, there was a tackle over the after-hatch and everlastingly the watch on deck were pulling up, spreading out, picking over, re-bagging, and lowering down again, some part of that lot of potatoes. My bargain with all its remotest associations, mental and visual – the garden of flowers and scents, the girl with her provoking contempt and her tragic loneliness of a hopeless castaway – was everlastingly dangled before my eyes, for thousands of miles along the open sea. And as if by a satanic refinement of irony it was accompanied by a most awful smell. Whiffs from decaying potatoes pursued me on the poop, they mingled with my thoughts, with my food, poisoned my very dreams. They made an atmosphere of corruption for the ship.

I remonstrated with Mr Burns about this excessive care. I would have been well content to batten the hatch down and let them perish under the deck.

That perhaps would have been unsafe. The horrid emanations might have flavoured the cargo of sugar. They seemed strong enough to taint the very ironwork. In addition Mr Burns made it a personal matter.

He assured me he knew how to treat a cargo of potatoes at sea – had been in the trade as a boy, he said. He meant to make my loss as small as possible. What between his devotion – it must have been devotion – and his vanity, I positively dared not give him the order to throw my commercial venture overboard. I believe he would have refused point-blank to obey my lawful command. An unprecedented and comical situation would have been created with which I did not feel equal to deal.

I welcomed the coming of bad weather as no sailor had ever done. When at last I hove the ship to, to pick up the pilot outside Port Philip Heads, the after-hatch had not been opened for more than a week and I might have believed that no such thing as a potato had ever been on board.

It was an abominable day, raw, blustering, with great squalls of wind and rain; the pilot, a cheery person, looked after the ship and chatted to me, streaming from head to foot; and the heavier the lash of the downpour the more pleased with himself and everything around him he seemed to be. He rubbed his wet hands with a satisfaction, which to me, who had stood that kind of thing for several days and nights, seemed inconceivable in any non-aquatic creature.

'You seem to enjoy getting wet, Pilot,' I remarked.

He had a bit of land round his house in the suburbs and it was of his garden he was thinking. At the sound of the word garden, unheard, unspoken for so many days, I had a vision of gorgeous colour, of sweet scents, of a girlish figure crouching in a chair. Yes. That was a distinct emotion breaking into the peace I had found in the sleepless anxieties of my responsibility during a week of dangerous bad weather. The Colony, the pilot explained, had suffered from unparalleled drought. This was the first decent drop of water they had had for seven months. The root crops were lost. And, trying to be casual, but with visible interest, he asked me if I had perchance any potatoes to spare.

Potatoes! I had managed to forget them. In a moment I felt plunged into corruption up to my neck. Mr Burns was making eyes at me behind the pilot's back.

Finally, he obtained a ton, and paid ten pounds for it. This was twice the price of my bargain with Jacobus. The spirit of covetousness woke up in me. That night, in harbour, before I slept, the Custom House galley came alongside. While his underlings were putting seals on the store-rooms, the officer in charge took me aside confidentially. 'I say, Captain, you don't happen to have any potatoes to sell.'

Clearly there was a potato famine in the land. I let him have a ton for twelve pounds and he went away joyfully. That night I dreamt of a pile of gold in the form of a grave in which a girl was buried, and woke up callous with greed. On calling at my ship-broker's office, that man, after the usual business had been transacted, pushed his spectacles up on his forehead.

'I was thinking, Captain, that coming from the Pearl of the Ocean you may have some potatoes to sell.'

I said negligently: 'Oh, yes, I could spare you a ton. Fifteen pounds.'

He exclaimed: 'I say!' But after studying my face for awhile accepted my terms with a faint grimace. It seems that these people could not exist without potatoes. I could. I didn't want to see a potato as long as I lived; but the demon of lucre had taken possession of me. How the news got about I don't know, but, returning on board rather late. I found a small group of men of the coster type hanging about the waist, while Mr Burns walked to and fro the quarter-deck loftily, keeping a triumphant eye on them. They had come to buy potatoes.

'These chaps have been waiting here in the sun for hours,' Burns whispered to me excitedly. 'They have drunk the water-cask dry. Don't throw away your chances, sir. You are too good-natured.'

I selected a man with thick legs and a man with a cast in his eye to negotiate with; simply because they were very easily distinguishable from the rest. 'You have the money on you?' I enquired, before taking them down into the cabin.

'Yes, sir,' they answered in one voice, slapping their pockets. I liked their air of quiet determination. Long before the end of the day all the potatoes were sold at about three times the price I had paid for them. Mr Burns, feverish and exulting, congratulated himself on his skilful care of my commercial venture, but hinted plainly that I ought to have made more of it.

That night I did not sleep very well. I thought of Jacobus by fits and starts, between snatches of dreams concerned with castaways starving on a desert island covered with flowers. It was extremely unpleasant. In the morning, tired and unrefreshed, I sat down and wrote a long letter to my owners, giving them a carefully-thought-out scheme for the ship's employment in the East and about the China Seas for the next two years. I spent the day at that task and felt somewhat more at peace when it was done.

Their reply came in due course. They were greatly struck with my project; but considering that, notwithstanding the unfortunate difficulty with the bags (which they trusted I would know how to guard against in the future), the voyage showed a very fair profit, they thought it would be better to keep the ship in the sugar trade – at least for the present.

I turned over the page and read on:

'We have had a letter from our good friend Mr Jacobus. We are pleased to see how well you have hit it off with him; for, not to speak of his assistance in the unfortunate matter of the bags, he writes us that should you, by using all possible dispatch, manage to bring the ship back early in the season he would be able to give us a good rate of freight. We have no doubt that your best endeavours ... etc. ... etc.'

I dropped the letter and sat motionless for a long time. Then I wrote my answer (it was a short one) and went ashore myself to post it. But I passed one letter-box, then another, and in the end found myself going up Collins Street with the letter still in my pocket – against my heart. Collins Street at four o'clock in the afternoon is not exactly a desert solitude; but I had never felt more isolated from the rest of mankind as when I walked that day its crowded pavement, battling desperately with my thoughts and feeling already vanquished.

There came a moment when the awful tenacity of Jacobus, the man of one passion and of one idea, appeared to me almost heroic. He had not given me up. He had gone again to his odious brother. And then he appeared to me odious himself. Was it for his own sake or for the sake of the poor girl? And on that last supposition the memory of the kiss which missed my lips appalled me; for whatever he had seen, or guessed at, or risked, he knew nothing of that. Unless the girl had told him. How could I go back to fan that fatal spark with my cold breath? No, no, that unexpected kiss had to be paid for at its full price.

At the first letter-box I came to I stopped and reaching into my breast-pocket I took out the letter – it was if I were plucking out my very heart – and dropped it through the slit. Then I went straight on board.

I wondered what dreams I would have that night; but as it turned out I did not sleep at all. At breakfast I informed Mr Burns that I had resigned my command.

He dropped his knife and fork and looked at me with indignation.

'You have, sir! I thought you loved the ship.'

'So I do, Burns,' I said. 'But the fact is that the Indian Ocean and everything that is in it has lost its charm for me. I am going home as passenger by the Suez Canal.'

'Everything that is in it,' he repeated angrily. 'I've never heard anybody talk like this. And to tell you the truth, sir, all the time we have been together I've never quite made you out. What's one ocean more than another? Charm, indeed!'

He was really devoted to me, I believe. But he cheered up when I told him that I had recommended him for my successor.

'Anyhow,' he remarked, 'let people say what they like, this Jacobus served your turn. I must admit that this potato business has paid extremely well. Of course, if only you had –'

'Yes, Mr Burns,' I interrupted. 'Quite a smile of fortune.'

But I could not tell him that it was driving me out of the ship I had learned to love. And as I sat heavy-hearted at my parting, seeing all my plans destroyed, my modest future endangered – for this command was like a foot in the stirrup for a young man – he gave up completely for the first time his critical attitude.

'A wonderful piece of luck!' he said.

C. J. Cutcliffe Hyne

THE 'PARADISE' COAL-BOAT

TO THOSE EXCELLENT PEOPLE who have travelled either largely or less in the mail steamers and the passenger liners of the ocean, Captain Ezra Pollard (as hereinafter set forth) will be a person of much incomprehensibleness. The skipper of a large passenger boat is a man apart: usually genial, more often than not a speaker of King's English, frequently signing himself RNR, and always accurately brass-edged in raiment. Pollard had none of these qualifications; he could not boast of having either a baronet or a shipowner for second cousin; and he possessed neither a smart uniform nor reputable reminiscences.

He had not started in the *Conway* or any of the other training ships. At the age of ten a parent had found him a nuisance ashore, and consequently had packed him off to sea as apprentice in a deep-water brigantine; and at sea, with very short intervals, he had remained ever since.

He had begun the business of the sea in the days when the spunyarn winch could be seen in the waist during fine weather, and skippers ran a piggery in a now obsolete craft called a long-boat, which rested on chocks between the masts. Until he was able seaman, he always signed on ship's articles with a X, his mark; and in his younger days he still came across a man here and there who went to sea with a greasy pigtail dangling over the coat collar. He learned to read, write, and add up tavern accounts in several currencies after this date; but he was thirty-two, and boatswain of a full-rigger, before it occurred to him that there were other heights still within reach.

His wife first put this into his head. He had married a barmaiden with ambition, and she had mixed enough drinks for seafaring men to understand to a nicety the exact value of the different grades. Ezra did not take rank as an officer at all; and when the first romance of marriage was over, this struck her as bad. So she used some blarney with one of her old admirers, got her husband a berth as third mate, and when she had hustled him off to sea again with a *Norie's Epitome* in his pocket, she went back to a situation herself to earn more money. A splendid seaman Ezra was already; and passable navigator he had got to be; and to this end she conjured him to save every farthing he could, and inwardly digest *Norie*, till, with a little coaching, he could pass his mate's examination.

Now, it is all very well to be a barmaid, because, if you have your head screwed on right, you may pick up knowledge from customers upon many points; and moreover, it is an excellent thing to be fired with ambition; but neither of these conditions of necessity make a mathematician out of a deck-hand. Ezra was willing, desperately, earnestly willing, but (by reason of his bringing up) he was the veriest bungler with the utensils of navigation. The fingers that could handle a steam winch like a toy were utterly clumsy when it came to working logarithms; and though he could with pains correct a compass and hammer out a day's dead-reckoning with clock and taffrail log, the sextant in his massive hands was always coy and chary about rendering up its secrets.

At the end of a voyage Mrs Pollard would meet him with a smile, draw his pay and her own, and take him off to some obscure nautical school where a retired master mariner taught the theories of his craft to those who aspired to command. And here Ezra would labour with slate, notebook, chart and instrument, to the irritation of his pedagogue and the muddlement of himself. Then the money would come to an end, and the pair of them would go off to their labours to earn more.

It may be understood, then, how it came to pass that Ezra Pollard was forty before he got his master's certificate, and how he found it necessary to serve four years more as mate before anyone saw fit to entrust him with a ship. By this time also Mrs Pollard had been forced to give up barmaiding (whether she liked it or not), as three children had occurred and these required looking after.

They lived in a narrow, ugly street in South Shields, and the home was poor: for one reason because the income was less than £100 a year, and for another because an excellent barmaid does not of necessity make a thrifty domestic manager; and Ezra knew what it was to have terror in his heart lest the supplies should break down altogether. Consequently, when one Gedge offered him command of the *Paradise*, a screw-collier of 900 tons burden, his joy at the step was almost keen enough to make him faint. Even men at forty-four can sometimes dazzle themselves with visions of future prosperity.

The *Paradise* was not an ideal craft. She was old and ramshackle. She groaned and complained so much in a seaway that no crew was ever known to sign on for a second run in her. She had coaldust and cockroaches in every fibre of her being, and her load line was so cunningly contrived that, when she had a full cargo under hatches, and there was anything of a sea running, she showed remarkably little of herself above water save two grimy mast-trucks and the top of a brine-whitened funnel. Indeed, it was owing to this little idiosyncrasy that Ezra got command. She had made a vacancy for him by kindly washing her last skipper overboard in a heavy run of sea off Flamboro' Head.

His wife came to see him off. 'Good-bye, old fellow!' she said. 'Don't forget me and the kids.'

'No,' said Ezra. 'I'll take care of the boat.' And two hours afterwards he was doing it, in a fog like a blanket outside Tyne pier-heads. He carried that fog with him to Dover, and drove the grimy coal-boat at a slow half-speed, and made the wet air hideous with his siren, as the Board of Trade directs. Moreover, he kept the upper bridge himself the entire time, and as the Channel also was full of shipping, he did not go below till he had berthed the collier outside Southampton. He went back in ballast, with the screw racing half its time, and consequently made another very slow passage.

He had a foreboding that there woud be trouble over the trip, but had no idea of the extent of it. He went up to the grimy Newcastle office with an uneasy mind, and after some delay was shown into the owner's private room.

Young Mr Gedge's face was sour. 'Let's see, Captain Pollard,' he said, 'it's ten pounds a month we're paying you, isn't it, because we thought we'd got a smart man? I'll give you an order for what's due to you at once, and you can get it cashed in the outer office. We shan't want any more of your work after this performance.'

Ezra was fairly startled. 'Good God, sir!' he burst out, 'you can't mean to sack me?'

'We do, though.'

'But I don't see how any man could have served you better. I know I've made slow passages, but look at the weather we've had. In Southampton I heard of ten ships reported in collision during the fog, and the Lord only knows what other damage has been done and not spoken about; and coming North again, there was a hard head wind blowing and a hell of a sea, and she wouldn't look at it. She was kicked about just like a cork in a gutter.'

Gedge picked up two newspapers and marked them with blue pencil. 'Look here,' he said. 'That's what the *Susan Potter* has done. She cleared two hours after you, she's got a quarter of a knot less speed, she'd take the same time to work cargo at the other end, and she's back here thirty hours ahead of you.'

'Then her skipper's been risking his boat, and risking the lives of his crew, that's all I can say.'

Gedge shrugged his shoulders. 'I'm not going to argue with you. I'm not a sailor, and I don't understand sailoring, and I don't intend to try. I'm a shipowner, and have to make my living as such. I've pulled in a profit over the *Susan Potter* – a small profit – and I've lost over the *Paradise*. I reckon I've lost two days' coal for her, two days' wear and tear, two days' interest on capital, and two days' wages and grub for her manning. That means somewhere about forty pounds. You quite grasp my way of looking at it?'

'Yes, sir,' said Ezra, 'and I'm very sorry. I see how it is, and I think I could do better another time. I know I could. I would. I'll drive that coal-boat, sir, full-speed through the thickest fog God ever threw down over the North Sea.'

'Yes?' said Gedge. 'But the great thing is, you're not going to get that chance. You may take your pay, Captain, and clear out of this office. If you can find another berth I should advise you to climb into it. If you can't, you may come back to me in a month's time and give me news of how you look at matters then.'

Which, being interpreted, meant that Ezra was given a month's dismissal by way of fine (as under the circumstances there was not the remotest probability of anyone else taking him on), with the vague chance of getting back to his old job if the man who stepped into his shoes did not do it better. Mrs Pollard had not much to say when the matter was reported, her looks and her actions being sufficiently expressive. She gave up going to chapel because there was no spare threepenny-bit for the collection, and also because she could not afford to wear out her Sunday dress. The family dinners were reduced in size and quality, and the new oilcloth which had been ordered for the best room was returned to the shop before the roll was untied. The eldest girl, too, was taken away from the Young Ladies' Seminary, where she had been learning gentility (and remarkably little else), and sent to the Board School, which was the hardest confession of *res angustae* of all of them. Without being directly told so, Captain Pollard distinctly understood that he was taking the bread out of his children's mouths, and cursed himself for a hound accordingly.

At the end of his month he turned up again at the shipowner's office, and, after waiting two shivering hours, was shown into the inner room. 'Hullo!' said Gedge, 'you here again, Captain? Not got command of a nice comfortable passenger boat yet? Anything I can do for you?'

'May I have her back, sir? I'd promise you to make good quick runs if you'd only give me another trial, sir.'

'What, is this the *Paradise* you're talking about? Well, I've another skipper in her now, and I should have to sack him if I gave you the berth. Would you like to have another fellow turned adrift for your convenience, Captain?'

Ezra mopped his face with a white pocket handkerchief. 'I've a wife and kids, Mr Gedge, and I've got to think of them first. I don't think you'd find a master anywhere to drive your steamboat harder than me.'

'You think you could push her along if you had a second try at the job, eh?'

'By God,' said Ezra. 'I'd go round no corners that weren't land! I'd stick on my course and not budge from it for a battleship. I'd drive her full ahead through any weather that is sent down to cover the sea, and if there's others gets in my road it's their look-out. I neither shift my hellum nor slow down for anything that swims.'

Gedge glanced at the man queerly. 'That's the right principle; only don't you go away with any reckless idea that I want you to blunder along, and run vessels down, and – bring – the crews back here – to make claims on me.'

Ezra mopped with the handkerchief. 'I'd like you to make it a bit clearer, sir. I don't think I quite – '

'What I have said is sufficiently clear already. I intend to have my steamers driven. I don't want accidents. And I won't have accidents that they can call me to account for afterwards. Now, it's no use saying you don't understand. There's the berth waiting for you, and you know what's required. Take it or leave it; only don't take it and handle the boat as you did before, or you'll get no third chance from me, and I don't think my recommendation will go far to find you another billet anywhere else.'

II

That Captain Ezra Pollard did accept the post, and did understand what was required of him, may be gathered from the statement that when the *Paradise* ran down an unknown smack, just south of the Spurn, Captain Ezra was in command. The air that night was thick with driving rain and spindrift; the sea was thick with homing smacks and the other traffic; and the collier, under two black trysails and a full head of steam, was going through it at the best of her speed. The skipper was not on the upper bridge at the time, but he rushed out of the charthouse at the shock of the collision, and rated his mate most violently for daring to ring off the engines without orders. With his own hand he telegraphed for 'full speed ahead', and called the mate a liar for suggesting that cries of help were coming up through the darkness. The mate retorted by calling him a murderer, and in the subsequent scuffle most of the crew took part. But in the meanwhile the grimy collier had been surging southward across Humber mouth at nine knots, and by the time the matter had been fought through, the cries had died out in the wet, windy night; and though wild threats of reporting were made in the heat of the moment, these were forgotten whilst the steamer waddled up the muddy waters of London river. A sailor-man at sea speaks big about the law; on shore he avoids it as much as may be.

Captain Ezra Pollard, however, did not forget the incident; in fact the memory of it stayed by him so persistently that it took all the sweetness out of his life, and he called himself much worse names as a daily exercise than his mate had called him in the heat of the moment. But he did not desist from driving the *Paradise* at her accustomed pace (which was as hard as she would go on a given coal consumption), come sunshine, come fog. He had four reasons for doing this, and they all dwelt in a small house in South Shields. And he was quite satisfied that one deviation from the course he had set down would cause the excellent Mr Gedge to dismiss him without mercy, and plunge the household in the Tyneside town into destitution. He did not blame Gedge, because he quite understood that a shipowner who has a living to make cannot afford, under any circumstances, to run coal-boats at a loss; but he very much wished that he (Ezra) followed any occupation other than the sea, and (being a sailor) his mind naturally turned on agriculture. As a farmer his life would be idyllic. With clay on his boots and a straw in his mouth, he would not be called upon to murder fishermen under any circumstances whatever; and he could go to chapel on Sundays, and sing noisily and with a clear conscience.

But meanwhile the *Paradise* kept him ferrying coals from the Tyne to London river, between which places there exists one of the best used steam-lanes in the world; and his owner decreed that he should not slow down for even the thickest fog that the weather-fiends could spin. Ezra never left port without a sinking beneath his waistcoat and a sense of impending misfortune in every grain of his person. And on thick nights the voices of the smacksmen he had run down off Humber mouth (and not carried home to claim damages) came and chatted to him out of the sea-smoke which drove from the wave-crests.

But though he had many close shaves – some of them desperately close – on the wild, thick nights along that crowded sea-road, for the next six years Ezra managed to keep out of actual collision; and so valuable a servant did he prove, that Gedge increased his pay by one pound a month, making it now eleven pounds in all; on the strength of which Mrs Pollard clanked whole sixpences into the plate at chapel, and bought a gilt clock with a glass shade for the best room.

Still, the evil fates could not let so promising a chance slip by for always. A night came, a bleak December night, thick with snow and heavy with gale. The iron lower decks of the *Paradise* were a mask of ice. On the upper bridge, ashes were strewn twice a watch to give foothold, and the canvas dodgers were thick glistening walls. Captain Pollard, who looked like a barrel of clothes, stumped athwart the bridge beating together his fingerless woollen gloves, and behind him the steam siren did its best to hoot above the booming of the gale and the clash of the racing seas. It was not much use looking ahead. With difficulty one could make out the loom of the foremast, and beyond that was a blanket of drifting snow and driving sea-smoke. Ezra had not picked up a light since he left the Tyne pier-heads, and his dead reckoning told him that he would have to port his helm soon to hit off London river. When he got in there and picked up his pilot, then for the first time since leaving home he would be able to go below and turn in.

Of a sudden a row of white lights shone out through the snow clouds, a green light dimly showing above them, a single white light topping all. Then the outline of a great steamer loomed out, and then *Crash!* and a noise as of ten thousand boiler-riveters all working at once.

The helm of the *Paradise* had been shoved hard-a-port, the stranger's to hard-a-starboard; the engines of each ship had been rung off, but not yet reversed. The time was too short. The stranger took the *Paradise's* stem a little aft of 'midships, and when the two ships broke apart from that horrible wrestle, there was a big passenger liner sinking rapidly in a freezing North Sea gale.

The *Paradise* backed off and lay to, rolling like a black drainpipe in the trough, and drifting rapidly to leeward. She carried no carpenter, but the skipper himself went forward to inspect, and found that, saving for a few plates bent, no damage had been done. It was a wonderful escape and it need never be reported. The skipper returned to deck with a grim, set face. If he steamed on to the river, he could slip into dock, and no questions would be asked. The crew could be easily silenced. But if he went back to the assistance of the other steamer, everything would be known; there would be a Board of Trade inquiry; Gedge would be mulcted in damages; he (Ezra) would probably 'lose his ticket', and certainly lose his berth for good and always. And of course, Mrs Pollard and the children would taste their due share of the disaster by being permitted either to starve or go to the deuce.

The ghosts of the smacksmen he had drowned off Humber mouth gave him advice from the darkness. 'A man can only be damned once,' they said, 'and you've been damned for us already. Think of the missis and the kids, you fool, and shove her for Gravesend at once. You've lost sight of the other steamer already, and you'll never find her again in a devil of a night like this. Besides, she's probably gone down by now.'

A dead rocket-stick dropped down like an arrow out of the night above, and fell on the ice of the upper bridge at his feet.

Ezra apostrophized the absent Gedge. 'No,' he said, 'curse you, I can't do it this time. A smack's different; there's only old sailors on her, who are made to be drowned. But there's women on that blasted steamer, and kids, who have lived soft all their lives and wanted for nothing; and I don't believe even you could leave them yourself.' He rung on his engines to 'full ahead' once more, and gave the quartermaster a course. And then he indulged in fluent profanity, because he was merely the master of a coasting collier, and expected to lose his only means of livelihood; and also because he saw in imagination his wife and children first shunned by the congregation of the chapel, and then begging crumbs in the public streets of South Shields.

The siren of the other steamer sent over the charging seas a sound like the bellow of a wounded bull, and Ezra followed it up with a new eagerness. ' "One may as well be hanged for a sheep as a lamb," says the proverb; and,' said Ezra to himself, 'If I'm going to crack myself up for good over pulling a parcel of petticoats out of the mess, hang me if I mightn't just as well take off the sailormen, yes, and even the brutes in the stokehold whilst I'm about it.' So he exhorted the weak crew of the collier in a language which they entirely understood, and swung his boat-davits outboard as he steamed through the snowy darkness.

III

The story of the actual rescuing of the three hundred human lives need not be retold here, as it was printed quite recently, with riotous amplitude of details, by all the newspapers of the civilized globe. Parliament was not sitting at the time; the world was gnawing for a sensation; and they had the story of the rescue served up to them in double-leaded type, with all the unpicturesque details and swear-words omitted. They learnt how by savage effort and reckless daring the master of an undermanned coal-boat had saved every soul on a swamping liner during a gale which had already made itself historical for casualties. All, that is, excepting the few who out of sheer contrariness chose to die from exposure to the bitter cold. Two of the *Paradise*'s men were killed during the transhipment, and one got injured for life; but these received only trivial mention. It was Ezra whom the freakish public in its never-to-be-reckoned-on way, set up for its week's hero; and Ezra, when he grasped the fact that ruin might be evaded after all, saw the one chance of his life ahead, and used all the small wit which God had given him to squeeze profit out of it to the uttermost ooze.

He could have laughed aloud at the fuss which was being made over the fact that he had risked his life – he who had risked life a thousand times before without comment. But he remembered Mrs Pollard, and the children, and the chapel, and he did not laugh. He posed as the massive, modest, guileless shipmaster, and made what he could out of the situation. The passengers he had picked up gave him a purse of two hundred guineas (showing that they were folks of no pride by assessing themselves low); the owners of the liner, by way of making a suitable present, gave him a watch which was worth his year's income; the dreaded Board of Trade let him off with flying colours; and, last of all, Gedge did not turn him adrift. On the contrary, he advanced him. The excellent Gedge had recently made a new investment. He had bought (by help of a mortgage) one of those delightful colliers that they build by the mile in the Tyneside yards, and cut off by the fathom as they are wanted; and (on selling the original of that name to a Norwegian) he christened her the *Paradise*, and put Ezra in command at the unheard-of wage of thirteen pounds a month. Mr Gedge knew luck when he saw it, and had a theory that fortunes are made by backing luck or buying its influence when it comes in one's way.

But Mrs Pollard had less of an eye for details than results. Her increased affluence suggested so many possibilities. She was able to take a tray now when the chapel gave tea-parties, and on Sunday nights she was frequently in a position to ask the minister in for supper, to the envy of her neighbours. She now also could afford to pay the premium for her eldest daughter to the genteelest milliner in all South Shields. She had, moreover, the satisfaction of hearing Ezra spoken of (by everyone who did not understand the true inwardness of the business) as the smartest coal-boat skipper who ever went out of Tyne pier-heads.

Still Ezra himself was not entirely happy. The new *Paradise* is a ten-knot boat, and has to be driven as such whatever weather may betide. Moreover, when loaded, there are two thousand tons of her altogether, so that her momentum is large, and the blow she could strike correspondingly heavy. The ambitious Mr Gedge will hear of extension of time between ports for no reason whatever, come fog come gale; and Ezra frequently spends fifty consecutive hours on the bridge, so as to be ready to act as circumstances should direct, should another of those unavoidable collisions be thrust upon him. Gedge warned him on the subject.

'Better not shove luck too hard, Captain,' he said, as he handed him over the new command. 'It's dangerous having those collisions at all; but it's a heap more dangerous to bring survivors home. Don't get nervous about driving her through. She's well insured.'

So the *Paradise* coal-boat still exists as a danger to navigators along certain tracks in the North Sea, and probably in the due course of events she will some day furnish the newspapers with another 'shipping disaster'. I only hope I am not in the other craft, that is all. I do not fancy Ezra is the man to stop and pick up human flotsam a second time. Mrs Pollard has such an assured position in the chapel circle now, that Ezra quite understands it would be death to her for him to lose his berth and pay.

Roald Dahl

DIP IN THE POOL

ON THE MORNING OF THE THIRD DAY, the sea calmed. Even the most delicate passengers – those who had not been seen around the ship since sailing time – emerged from their cabins and crept on to the sun deck where the deck steward gave them chairs and tucked rugs around their legs and left them lying in rows, their faces upturned to the pale, almost heatless January sun.

It had been moderately rough the first two days, and this sudden calm and the sense of comfort that it brought created a more genial atmosphere over the whole ship. By the time evening came, the passengers, with twelve hours of good weather behind them, were beginning to feel confident, and at eight o'clock that night the main dining-room was filled with people eating and drinking with the assured, complacent air of seasoned sailors.

The meal was not half over when the passengers became aware, by the slight friction between their bodies and the seats of their chairs. that the big ship had actually started rolling again. It was very gentle at first, just a slow, lazy leaning to one side, then to the other, but it was enough to cause a subtle, immediate change of mood over the whole room. A few of the passengers glanced up from their food, hesitating, waiting, almost listening for the next roll, smiling nervously, little secret glimmers of apprehension in their eyes. Some were completely unruffled, some were openly smug, a number of the smug ones making jokes about food and weather in order to torture the few who were beginning to suffer. The movement of the ship then became rapidly more and more violent, and only five or six minutes after the first roll had been noticed, she was swinging heavily from side to side, the passengers bracing themselves in their chairs, leaning against the pull as in a car cornering.

At last the really bad roll came, and Mr William Botibol, sitting at the purser's table, saw his plate of poached turbot with hollandaise sauce sliding suddenly away from under his fork. There was a flutter of excitement, everybody reaching for plates and wineglasses. Mrs Renshaw, seated at the purser's right, gave a little scream and clutched that gentleman's arm.

'Going to be a dirty night,' the purser said, looking at Mrs Renshaw. 'I think it's blowing up for a very dirty night.' There was just the faintest suggestion of relish in the way he said it.

A steward came hurrying up and sprinkled water on the tablecloth between the plates. The excitement subsided. Most of the passengers continued with their meal. A small number, including Mrs Renshaw, got carefully to their feet and threaded their ways with a kind of concealed haste between the tables and through the doorway.

'Well,' the purser said, 'there she goes.' He glanced around with approval at the remainder of his flock who were sitting quiet, looking complacent, their faces reflecting openly that extraordinary pride that travellers seem to take in being recognized as 'good sailors'.

When the eating was finished and the coffee had been served, Mr Botibol, who had been unusually grave and thoughtful since the rolling started, suddenly stood up and carried his cup of coffee around to Mrs Renshaw's vacant place, next to the purser. He seated himself in her chair, then immediately leaned over and began to whisper urgently in the purser's ear. 'Excuse me,' he said, 'but could you tell me something, please?'

The purser, small and fat and red, bent forward to listen. 'What's the trouble, Mr Botibol?'

'What I want to know is this.' The man's face was anxious and the purser was watching it. 'What I want to know is will the captain already have made his estimate on the day's run – you know, for the auction pool? I mean before it began to get rough like this?'

The purser, who had prepared himself to receive a personal confidence, smiled and leaned back in his seat to relax his full belly. 'I should say so – yes,' he answered. He didn't bother to whisper his reply, although automatically he lowered his voice, as one does when answering a whisperer.

'About how long ago do you think he did it?'

'Some time this afternoon. He usually does it in the afternoon.'

'About what time?'

'Oh, I don't know. Around four o'clock I should guess.'

'Now tell me another thing. How does the captain decide which number it shall be? Does he take a lot of trouble over that?'

The purser looked at the anxious frowning face of Mr Botibol and he smiled, knowing quite well what the man was driving at. 'Well, you see, the captain has a little conference with the navigating officer, and they study the weather and a lot of other things, and then they make their estimate.'

Mr Botibol nodded, pondering this answer for a moment. Then he said, 'Do you think the captain knew there was bad weather coming today?'

'I couldn't tell you,' the purser replied. He was looking into the small black eyes of the other man, seeing the two single little sparks of excitement dancing in their centres. 'I really couldn't tell you, Mr Botibol. I wouldn't know.'

'If this gets any worse it might be worth buying some of the low numbers. What do you think?' The whispering was more urgent, more anxious now.

'Pehaps it will,' the purser said. 'I doubt whether the old man allowed for a really rough night. It was pretty calm this afternoon when he made his estimate.'

The others at the table had become silent and were trying to hear, watching the purser with that intent, half-cocked, listening look that you can see also at the race track when they are trying to overhear a trainer talking about his chance: the slightly open lips, the up-stretched eyebrows, the head forward and cocked a little to one side – that desperately straining, half-hypnotized, listening look that comes to all of them when they are hearing something straight from the horse's mouth.

'Now suppose *you* were allowed to buy a number, which one would *you* choose today?' Mr Botibol whispered.

'I don't know what the range is yet,' the purser patiently answered. 'They don't announce the range till the auction starts after dinner. And I'm really not very good at it anyway. I'm only the purser, you know.'

At that point Mr Botibol stood up. 'Excuse me, all,' he said, and he walked carefully away over the swaying floor between the other tables, and twice he had to catch hold of the back of a chair to steady himself against the ship's roll.

'The sun deck, please,' he said to the elevator man.

The wind caught him full in the face as he stepped out on to the open deck. He staggered and grabbed hold of the rail and held on tight with both hands, and he stood there looking out over the darkening sea where the great waves were welling up high and white horses were riding against the wind with plumes of spray behind them as they went.

'Pretty bad out there, wasn't it, sir?' the elevator man said on the way down.

Mr Botibol was combing his hair back into place with a small red comb. 'Do you think we've slackened speed at all on account of the weather?' he asked.

'Oh my word yes, sir. We slackened off considerable since this started. You got to slacken off speed in weather like this or you'll be throwing the passengers all over the ship.'

Down in the smoking-room people were already gathering for the auction. They were grouping themselves politely around the various tables, the men a little stiff in their dinner jackets, a little pink and overshaved and stiff beside their cool white-armed women. Mr Botibol took a chair close to the auctioneer's table. He crossed his legs, folded his arms, and settled himself in his seat with the rather desperate air of a man who has made a tremendous decision and refuses to be frightened.

The pool, he was telling himself, would probably be around seven thousand dollars. That was almost exactly what it had been the last two days with the numbers selling for between three and four hundred apiece. Being a British ship they did it in pounds, but he liked to do his thinking in his own currency. Seven thousand dollars was plenty of money. My goodness, yes! And what he would do he would get them to pay him in hundred-dollar bills and he would take it ashore in the inside pocket of his jacket. No problem there. And right away, yes right away, he would buy a Lincoln convertible. He would pick it up on the way from the ship and drive it home just for the pleasure of seeing Ethel's face when she came out the front door and looked at it. Wouldn't that be something, to see Ethel's face when he glided up to the door in a brand-new pale-green Lincoln convertible! Hello, Ethel, honey, he would say, speaking very casual. I just thought I'd get you a little present. I saw it in the window as I went by, so I thought of you and how you were always wanting one. You like it, honey? he would say. You like the colour? And then he would watch her face.

The auctioneer was standing up behind his table now. 'Ladies and gentlemen!' he shouted. 'The captain has estimated the day's run, ending midday tomorrow, at five hundred and fifteen miles. As usual we will take the ten numbers on either side of it to make up the range. That makes it five hundred and five to five hundred and twenty-five. And of course for those who think the true figure will be still farther away, there'll be "low field" and "high field" sold separately as well. Now, we'll draw the first numbers out of the hat . . . here we are . . . five hundred and twelve?'

The room became quiet. The people sat still in their chairs, all eyes watching the auctioneer. There was a certain tension in the air, and as the bids got higher, the tension grew. This wasn't a game or a joke; you could be sure of that by the way one man would look across at another who had raised his bid – smiling perhaps, but only the lips smiling, the eyes bright and absolutely cold.

Number five hundred and twelve was knocked down for one hundred and ten pounds. The next three or four numbers fetched roughly the same amount.

The ship was rolling heavily, and each time she went over, the wooden panelling on the walls creaked as if it were going to split. The passengers held on to the arms of their chairs, concentrating upon the auction.

'Low field!' the auctioneer called out. 'The next number is low field.'

Mr Botibol sat up very straight and tense. He would wait, he had decided, until the others had finished bidding, then he would jump in and make the last bid. He had figured that there must be at least five hundred dollars in his account at the bank at home, probably nearer six. That was about two hundred pounds – over two hundred. This ticket wouldn't fetch more than that.

'As you all know,' the auctioneer was saying, 'low field covers every number *below* the smallest number in the range, in this case every number below five hundred and five. So, if you think this ship is going to cover less than five hundred and five miles in the twenty-four hours ending at noon tomorrow, you better get in and buy this number. So what am I bid?'

It went clear up to one hundred and thirty pounds. Others besides Mr Botibol seemed to have noticed that the weather was rough. One hundred and forty . . . fifty . . . There it stopped. The auctioneer raised his hammer.

'Going at one hundred and fifty. . . .'

'Sixty!' Mr Botibol called, and every face in the room turned and looked at him.

'Seventy!'

'Eighty!' Mr Botibol called.

'Ninety!'

'Two hundred!' Mr Botibol called. He wasn't stopping now – not for anyone.

There was a pause.

'Any advance on two hundred pounds?'

Sit still, he told himself. Sit absolutely still and don't look up. It's unlucky to look up. Hold your breath. No one's going to bid you up so long as you hold your breath.

'Going for two hundred pounds. . . .' The auctioneer had a pink bald head and there were little beads of sweat sparkling on top of it. 'Going. . . .' Mr Botibol held his breath. 'Going . . . Gone!' The man banged the hammer on the table. Mr Botibol wrote out a cheque and handed it to the auctioneer's assistant, then he settled back in his chair to wait for the finish. He did not want to go to bed before he knew how much there was in the pool.

They added it up after the last number had been sold and it came to twenty-one hundred-odd pounds. That was around six thousand dollars. Ninety per cent to go to the winner, ten per cent to seamen's charities. Ninety per cent of six thousand was five thousand four hundred. Well – that was enough. He could buy the Lincoln convertible and there would be something left over, too. With this gratifying thought he went off, happy and excited, to his cabin.

When Mr Botibol awoke the next morning he lay quite still for several minutes with his eyes shut, listening for the sound of the gale, waiting for the roll of the ship. There was no sound of any gale and the ship was not rolling. He jumped up and peered out of the porthole. The sea – Oh Jesus God – was smooth as glass, the great ship was moving through it fast, obviously making up for time lost during the night. Mr Botibol turned away and sat slowly down on the edge of his bunk. A fine electricity of fear was beginning to prickle under the skin of his stomach. He hadn't a hope now. One of the higher numbers was certain to win it after this.

'Oh, my God,' he said aloud. 'What shall I do?'

What, for example, would Ethel say? It was simply not possible to tell her that he had spent almost all of their two years' savings on a ticket in the ship's pool. Nor was it possible to keep the matter secret. To do that he would have to tell her to stop drawing cheques. And what about the monthly instalments on the television set and the

Encyclopaedia Britannica? Already he could see the anger and contempt in the woman's eyes, the blue becoming grey and the eyes themselves narrowing as they always did when there was anger in them.

'Oh, my God. What *shall* I do?'

There was no point in pretending that he had the slightest chance now – not unless the goddam ship started to go backwards. They'd have to put her in reverse and go full speed astern and keep right on going if he was to have any chance of winning it now. Well, maybe he should ask the captain to do just that. Offer him ten per cent of the profits. Offer him more if he wanted it. Mr Botibol started to giggle. Then very suddenly he stopped, his eyes and mouth both opening wide in a kind of shocked surprise. For it was at this moment that the idea came. It hit him hard and quick, and he jumped up from his bed terribly excited, ran over to the porthole and looked out again. Well, he thought, why not? Why ever not? The sea was calm and he wouldn't have any trouble keeping afloat until they picked him up. He had a vague feeling that someone had done this thing before, but that didn't prevent him from doing it again. The ship would have to stop and lower a boat, and the boat would have to go back maybe half a mile to get him, and then it would have to return to the ship, the whole thing. An hour was about thirty miles. It would knock thirty miles off the day's run. That would do it. 'Low field' would be sure to win it then. Just so long as he made certain someone saw him falling over; but that would be simple to arrange. And he'd better wear light clothes, something easy to swim in. Sports clothes, that was it. He would dress as though he were going up to play some deck tennis – just a shirt and a pair of shorts and tennis-shoes. And leave his watch behind. What was the time? Nine-fifteen. The sooner the better, then. Do it now and get it over with. Have to do it soon, because the time limit was midday.

Mr Botibol was both frightened and excited when he stepped out on to the sun deck in his sports clothes. His small body was wide at the hips, tapering upwards to extremely narrow sloping shoulders, so that it resembled, in shape at any rate, a bollard. His white skinny legs were covered with black hairs, and he came cautiously out on deck, treading softly in his tennis shoes. Nervously he looked around him. There was only one other person in sight, an elderly woman with very thick ankles and immense buttocks who was leaning over the rail staring at the sea. She was wearing a coat of Persian lamb and the collar was turned up so Mr Botibol couldn't see her face.

He stood still, examining her carefully from a distance. Yes, he told himself, she would probably do. She would probably give the alarm just as quickly as anyone else. But wait one minute, take your time, William Botibol, take your time. Remember what you told yourself a few minutes ago in the cabin when you were changing? You remember that?

The thought of leaping off a ship into the ocean a thousand miles from the nearest land had made Mr Botibol – a cautious man at the best of times – unusually advertent. He was by no means satisfied yet that this woman he saw before him was *absolutely certain* to give the alarm when he made his jump. In his opinion there were two possible reasons why she might fail him. Firstly, she might be deaf and blind. It was not very probable, but on the other hand it *might* be so, and why take a chance? All he had to do was check it by talking to her for a moment beforehand. Secondly – and this will demonstrate how suspicious the mind of a man can become when it is working through self-preservation and fear – secondly, it had occurred to him that the woman might herself be the owner of one of the high numbers in the pool and as such would have a sound financial reason for not wishing to stop the ship. Mr Botibol recalled that people had killed their fellows for far less than six thousand dollars. It was happening every day in the newspapers. So why take a chance on that either? Check on it first. Be sure of your facts. Find out about it by a little polite conversation. Then, provided that the woman appeared also to be a pleasant, kindly human being, the thing was a cinch and he could leap overboard with a light heart.

Mr Botibol advanced casualy towards the woman and took up a position beside her, leaning on the rail. 'Hullo,' he said pleasantly.

She turned and smiled at him, a surprisingly lovely, almost a beautiful smile, although the face itself was very plain. 'Hullo,' she answered him.

Check, Mr Botibol told himself, on the first question. She is neither blind nor deaf. 'Tell me,' he said, coming straight to the point, 'what did you think of the auction last night?'

'Auction?' she asked, frowning. 'Auction? What auction?'

'You know, that silly old thing they have in the lounge after dinner, selling numbers on the ship's daily run. I just wondered what you thought about it.'

She shook her head, and again she smiled, a sweet and pleasant smile that had in it perhaps the trace of an apology. 'I'm very lazy,' she said. 'I always go to bed early. I have my dinner in bed. It's so restful to have dinner in bed.'

Mr Botibol smiled back at her and began to edge away. 'Got to go and get my exercise now,' he said. 'Never miss my exercise in the morning. It was nice seeing you. Very nice seeing you. . . .' He retreated about ten paces, and the woman let him go without looking around.

Everything was now in order. The sea was calm, he was lightly dressed for swimming, there were almost certainly no man-eating sharks in this part of the Atlantic, and there was this pleasant kindly old woman to give the alarm. It was a question now only of whether the ship would be delayed long enough to swing the balance in his favour. Almost certainly it would. In any event, he could do a little to help in that direction himself. He could make a few difficulties about getting hauled up into the lifeboat. Swim around a bit, back away from them surreptitiously as they tried to come close to fish him out. Every minute, every second gained would help him win. He began to move forward again to the rail, but now a new fear assailed him. Would he get caught in the propeller? He had heard about that happening to persons falling off the sides of big ships. But then, he wasn't going to fall, he was going to jump, and that was a very different thing. Provided he jumped out far enough he would be sure to clear the propeller.

Mr Botibol advanced slowly to a position at the rail about twenty yards away from the woman. She wasn't looking at him now. So much the better. He didn't want her watching him as he jumped off. So long as no one was watching he would be able to say afterwards that he had slipped and fallen by accident. He peered over the side of the ship. It was a long, long drop. Come to thing of it now, he might easily hurt himself badly if he hit the water flat. Wasn't there someone who once split his stomach open that way, doing a belly flop from the high dive? He must jump straight and land feet first. Go in like a knife. Yes, sir. The water seemed cold and deep and grey and it made him shiver to look at it. But it was now or never. Be a man, William Botibol, be a man. All right then . . . now . . . here goes . . .

He climbed up on to the wide wooden top-rail, stood there poised, balancing for three terrifying seconds, then he leaped – he leaped up and out as far as he could go and at the same time he shouted *'Help!'*

'Help! Help!' he shouted as he fell. Then he hit the water and went under.

When the first shout for help sounded, the woman who was leaning on the rail started up and gave a little jump of surprise. She looked around quickly and saw sailing past her through the air this small man dressed in white shorts and tennis shoes, spreadeagled and shouting as he went. For a moment she looked as though she weren't quite sure what she ought to do: throw a lifebelt, run away and give the alarm, or simply turn and yell. She drew back a pace from the rail and swung half around facing up to the bridge, and for this brief moment she remained motionless, tense, undecided. Then almost at once she seemed to relax, and she leaned forward far over the rail, staring at the water where it was turbulent in the ship's wake. Soon a tiny, round black head appeared in the foam, an arm was raised above it, once, twice, vigorously waving, and a small faraway voice was heard calling something that was difficult to understand. The woman leaned still farther over the rail, trying to keep the little bobbing black speck in sight, but soon, so very soon, it was such a long way away that she couldn't even be sure it was there at all.

After a while another woman came out on deck. This one was bony and angular, and she wore horn-rimmed spectacles. She spotted the first woman and walked over to her, treading the deck in the deliberate, military fashion of all spinsters.

'So *there* you are,' she said.

The woman with the fat ankles turned and looked at her, but said nothing.

'I've been searching for you,' the bony one continued. 'Searching all over.'

'It's very odd,' the woman with the fat ankles said. 'A man dived overboard just now, with his clothes on.'

'Nonsense.'

'Oh yes. He said he wanted to get some exercise and he dived in and didn't even bother to take his clothes off.'

'You better come down now,' the bony woman said. Her mouth had suddenly become firm, her whole face sharp and alert, and she spoke less kindly than before. 'And don't you ever go wandering about on deck alone like this again. You know quite well you're meant to wait for me.'

'Yes, Maggie,' the woman with the fat ankles answered, and again she smiled, a tender, trusting smile, and she took the hand of the other one and allowed herself to be led away across the deck.

'Such a nice man,' she said. 'He waved to me.'

Eugene Burdick

LOG THE MAN DEAD

IN THE HARBOUR OF PLYMOUTH, in England, the ship-building firm of Hawkins and Company was working day and night on the ship. During the day men, naked to the waist, chipped at huge raw logs, converting them into ribs and spars. At night, torches and cressets were lit and, in the fitful light, hot creosote and tallow were poured over the caulking which had been pounded into the seams. In the sail shops, yards of bright-red cloth were converted into sails. The great, gaunt ribs of the ship grew higher than the shops and were finally planked over and sanded into a slick surface. The masts were inserted into their locks and the long task of fitting the sails begun.

Crimping crews began to drive impressed crewmen aboard the ship. Among these was a tall, slim boy named Simon Jonson, from Devonshire. This was the first time he had ever seen salt water. As he filed aboard he looked up at the masts, their tips vanishing into the mist. The ship seemed enormous.

Finally a carpenter chiselled the letters TIGER into the overhanging stern of the vessel. The next day the ship slid down the ways, heaved gently in the quiet waters and then rested, ready for the sea.

Four months later the ship was six hundred miles off Africa and becalmed in a great, dead circle of water. Occasionally a ground swell would bulge the grey, hot surface and the ship would creak. Under the steady blast of unrelieved brightness, the sea began to smell like iodine, quenched iron and dead fish.

But the *Tiger* was taut with excitement. For a man was on trial for his life and the man was Simon Jonson. He stood on the quarter-deck in front of a table over which the officers of a court-martial eyed him. Behind him the entire crew was drawn up in three straight lines.

The men stood stiffly and sweat streaked their clothes black, poured down their faces, ran in trickles into their shoes. Simon Jonson, facing the sun, was almost blinded, so that the figures of the officers behind the table seemed to be tiny black figures, all identical and all very far away. Occasionally a salty drop of sweat ran into his eye, but he patiently blinked it away. He was thinking of an event that had occurred three weeks before. In exact and precise outlines, the memory came back to him. As the voice of the prosecutor droned on, endlessly and far away, Simon thought back to that rotten, irresistible memory.

It had started with a simple argument between Watson, the boatswain's mate, and Blake, the sailmaker. They had stood arguing by the hatch leading into the fo'c'sle and Simon had been listening. Suddenly, in one of those blinding seconds of action, the argument had grown heated and Blake had swung his sail needle at Martin. Quite by accident, the curved, ugly needle caught in Watson's shoulder muscle and jutted out, turning the shirt red as the blood seeped out. In a moment, Mr Galbraith, the second mate, was on the scene, and had arrested Blake for attacking another man.

'He didn't mean anything, Mr Galbraith,' Watson said through his clenched teeth. As to minimize his injury he reached up and jerked the needle out of his shoulder. The blood ran in a gush down his arm. 'We was just fooling around.'

'We'll let the captain decide that,' Mr Galbraith said coldly. 'There are regulations to govern such matters.'

Two days later the captain had called the crew together and read the verdict against Blake. The captain was a tall, thin, aristocratic man who wore immaculate white linen at his throat. He looked somehow like a preacher as his Adam's apple worked in his long neck. When he finished two men seized Blake and dragged him to a block situated in the middle of the quarter-deck. Blake screamed a long, quivering shriek and then stared with bulging eyes up at the sky.

One of the men forced the sail needle into Blake's open hand and then forced the hand down onto the block. At the same time another man stepped forward with a sharp hatchet. Simon had been standing numbly, hardly knowing what was happening. But as he saw the hatchet he guessed what was to come. With a quick, sliding jerk, he was out of the right ranks of the crew, had stepped across the deck and, tearing the hatchet from the man's hand, threw it over the side. Then, wheeling about, he swung accurately and powerfully at one of the men holding Blake's hand. The man fell and the other man let go. Blake stood frozen, staring up at the sky, paralysed with fear, unable to move.

In a moment Simon was subdued by a brace of seamen and was standing in front of the captain. He had not been excited when he left the ranks and he was not excited now, only impatient to explain to the captain the true story of the needle-stabbing episode.

'It was not a fight, sir,' Simon started to say in a deliberate voice. 'They were really only joking. It was not – '

The captain's already thin face had drawn sharp with anger. Two spots of colour burned in his cheeks.

'It states in the Rules for the Regulation of the Navy that any man who draws the blood of another shall have the hand that inflicted the damage chopped off,' the captain said in a crisp, rigidly controlled voice.

'But any rule that doesn't recognize that this was just a joke between friends is a bad rule,' Simon said. He could not conceive that the captain would not see the justice of this.

'The Regulations also state that anyone that interferes with the administrations of justice aboard a naval ship shall be confined to the bowsprit,' the captain said. His narrow red tongue came out, flicked at the corners of his mouth, left his lips moist. 'You shall stand court-martial for that offence.'

And then, as the crew held Simon back, although he was calm and cool, the two men again held Blake's hand on the block. With a swish a new hatchet cut the air. A dark spray of blood shot over the deck, the severed hand opened with a jerk, and the gleaming, bright needle rolled out on the deck. Blake shrieked once, then groaned and fainted. Simon watched the proceedings coldly, his eyes moving from the hand to the captain's face.

'And Seaman Jonson was, to your best knowledge, not suffering from sunstroke, brain fever or other disease when he interfered with the administration of justice on last June fifteenth?' Lieutenant Galbraith, the prosecuting officer, was asking the ship's surgeon.

The surgeon, a squat fat man, with a red face, shook his head. 'He was of sound mind and body.' He turned his bloodshot drunkard's eyes toward Simon and then glanced quickly away.

Simon still could not believe that he would not be able to explain his actions. To his methodical, Devonshire mind it seemed a simple case of righting a wrong. He waited patiently for the moment when he would be asked to explain what had happened.

In a few more moments Lieutenant Galbraith finished his interrogation. He turned to the captain saying, 'Sir, I have finished the presentation of the case for His Majesty's Navy.'

'In your opinion, Mr Galbraith, does this offence fall under those crimes which call for automatic confinement to the bowsprit until dead?' the captain asked casually, although he was watching Simon while he spoke.

'Well, sir, it might be interpreted in another manner if extenuating circumstances were found,' Lieutenant Galbraith hedged, unwilling to face the reality of such a sentence.

'What would such extenuating circumstances be?' the captain asked in an icy voice. Without waiting for an answer he stood up and announced, 'Gentlemen, the court-martial shall retire to my cabin to reach a verdict.'

So suddenly that he could scarcely comprehend what had happened, the officers had left the quarter-deck and Simon realized that he would never have a chance to plead his case; that the decision would be reached on the basis of the evidence that the court-martial had now taken. For the first time he thought seriously of 'bowspritting'. It was one of the most dreaded words in the navy and Simon had heard endless stories of former 'bowspritting' sentences in the crew's quarters.

This was the most hideous of punishments. A sailor sentenced to be 'spitted' was led to the bow of the ship where the powerful jutting beak of the ship, reaching far out over the cut-water, constituted the bowsprit. At the foot of the bowsprit he was given a ration of beer, a half-loaf of bread and sharp sail knife. Then two boatswain mates tied his body to the bowsprit, leaving his arms free. There, after finishing the bread and beer, he had three alternatives.

First, he could kill himself with the knife and have a speedy death. Or he could cut himself loose and fall into the ocean, where he would either drown or fall victim to the shark or the sharp slashing teeth of the barracuda. Or, finally, he could starve to death on the bowsprit. The thing he could not do was to come back off the bowsprit onto the ship. Five yards behind the victim the ship was going about its normal life, but he could only eye that life as his own existence was slowly squeezed out.

If the man stayed on the bowsprit and died, his body was not removed, and for months there would be the thick, rotten odour of death about the bowsprit as the elements and the sharp, pecking beaks of sea birds reduced the body. Finally there would be nothing left but a jiggling, clean-picked skeleton, held to the spar by the few remaining lines. And no man would, or could, touch the lines on the skeleton. They must wait until the line rotted off and the skeleton slipped loose and fell into the sea.

'They won't spit you, Simon,' one of the crew members murmured to him. 'You did nothing wrong.'

'Quiet there,' the sergeant snarled.

The crew fell silent and then, after a pause, began to whisper among themselves. From the sound of their whispers Simon knew they thought he would get the bowsprit. He began to feel as if he were involved in a hot, steaming nightmare which had gripped him in some strange way, but which would release him before it was too late. The sun suddenly seemed to increase in size and warmth. His head felt empty and burned out. He knew he was afraid.

In ten minutes the officers filed back out of the cabin. The surgeon licked a smear of Demerara rum off his lips, the captain touched his hands to the linen at his neck, Lieutenant Galbraith looked deliberately past Simon. They assembled quickly around the table and Lieutenant Galbraith stood up. He cleared his throat and spoke.

'We find Apprentice Seaman Jonson guilty of obstructing the administration of justice and under the Regulations of the Navy we order him confined to the bowsprit, never to return. God rest his soul. Ship's Clerk, strike his name from the record. Boatswain, carry out the sentence. All hands splice the main brace.'

Simon heard the crew stiffen in anger behind him, even before he realized what the sentence was. Then Simon felt his cheeks burn hot; behind his eyes he felt blackness loom up; the table and officers angled before his eyes and then vanished. He had fainted.

The captain turned and walked into his cabin. The officers walked slowly toward the limp, unconscious body of the boy. They picked him up and carried him to the bowsprit and bound him to the long spar. It was a hot, sultry day and Simon did not regain consciousness for some time. An officer was stationed at the foot of the bowsprit to make sure that Jonson did not return to the ship. As far as the British Navy was concerned, Simon Jonson was already dead. The ship's clerk drew a line through his name on the roster and put these words after it: 'Died at sea.'

Simon had been on the bowsprit only a half hour when the whole aspect of the sea suddenly altered. The bottle-green colour changed, a flat, black bank of clouds came bustling down out of the middle distance, and, with a sudden jerk, the sails filled, the frigate heeled over and began to scud across the ocean. The Canaries dropped away and the ship lurched swiftly toward the equatorial seas. The shock of the cool wind brought young Simon back to consciousness and as soon as he looked around he could see what happened. He glanced at the sea, down the bowsprit to where the officer stood. Then he glanced at the worsening sea. He tucked the bread, the bottle of beer and the knife into his shirt, tightened the ropes around his chest and waist and locked his arms around the bowsprit.

Simon was tough, intelligent and determined to live. When he looked over his shoulder at the men, who gathered at the foot of the bowsprit to shout encouragement to him, his eyes bulged slightly with fear, but his jaw was strong and tight. As the seas got higher the bowsprit would occasionally dip deep into the green water, lurch back, and Simon would come to the surface dripping water, his fingers biting into the smooth, tough wood of the bowsprit.

The storm lasted six days. During that time Simon drank and ate nothing. His only refreshment was the shock of the seas passing over his body as the bowsprit lunged into the tropical waters. When it rained, he turned his head toward the sky, stuck his tongue out and caught a pitiful few drops of water. With his hands, he scooped the thin, slick layer of rainwater off the surface of the spar and obtained a few more drops. Meanwhile the *Tiger* pitched and wallowed down the length of Africa, passed Dakar, and finally began to head south-east to swing in under the great belly of Africa and to run along the Gold Coast.

On the seventh day the winds died and the sun came up hot and clear. The sails began to flap again, the ship rolled listlessly. They were within a hundred miles of the equator. The bowl of the sea and sky became brassy with heat, the ocean steamed. The sun burned the salt water off of Simon's skin, leaving streaks of pure-white salt behind. In the storm his cap and shoes washed away, and now the exposed skin on his feet, hands and face turned pink, then red, and as blisters formed, a painful white.

By the tenth day the boy's tongue began to protrude from his mouth and he chewed on a small piece of the bread, trying to work up some saliva. On the eleventh day Martin advised him to take some of the beer, and for the first time the boy uncorked the bottle and took a mouthful of the rich bitter stuff. Martin was the boatswain of the *Tiger* and although he had spent twenty years at sea he was bitterly opposed to the navy method of discipline. A tough, wizened, sun-blackened man, he had much admired Simon's calm performance before the court-martial. The beer revived Simon at once and he waved a hand at the crew members who stood at the foot of the bowsprit. The crew roared support back to him.

'Just a mouthful, Simon. That's all you can have today,' Martin called to him. 'Cork up the bottle and put it back in your shirt.'

The boy obeyed reluctantly, his bleary, bloodshot eyes fastened on the bottle of beer. Martin now spent his nights sleeping at the foot of the bowsprit, awakening throughout the night to give the boy encouragement and, occasionally, to pray with him.

On the thirteenth day two things happened. The lines holding Simon had become loose because of the weight he had lost. It took him six hours to untie the knots and tighten up the lines around his shrunken body. The second thing that happened was that he began to moan – an occasional desolate, low scream of pain that hung over the ship like a curse before the tropical winds swept it away.

By now the ship had swung under the great overhanging belly of Africa and was heading toward the tiny island of Sao Thomé, which was almost exactly on the equator. Each day the sun came up hot and clear and beat down on the boy on the unprotected bowsprit. During the hottest part of the day the helmsman tried to steer so that the sails made a shadow over Simon, but the captain insisted relentlessly that they hold to the true compass course.

By now the boy's tongue was black and swollen. The exposed skin of his feet and neck had formed into hard brown scabs of burnt flesh. He lay like a sack of rags, only his hands, clinging like claws to the bowsprit, seemed alive. He gave a cry of despair two or three times a day. Once a day he took a single mouthful of beer from the bottle. He could no longer chew the bread. Several times when the members of the crew were swabbing down decks they would throw a bucket of cool sea-water over his dry body. This would revive him and he would wave a thin hand in thanks. The crew members cheered wildly whenever this happened. The officer on watch would beat the offending crew member, but it went on despite this.

On the seventeenth day, Sao Thomé was sighted and the ship steadied on a direct course for the island. The boy had not stirred for a day now and the crew feared he was dead. As the ship threaded its way through the channel the crew stood watching him. The ship was finally warped alongside the dock.

'Boy, you've made it, you're safe,' Martin said in a low voice.

'Come on, boy, wake up. Cut yourself loose. We've made a port.'

Nothing happened, and a groan went up from the crew. Martin's voice went higher, a note of despair in it, as he repeated the words.

Then the bundle of rags stirred, the boy's head, now balancing on an incredibly thin neck, came up. Through the puffed and lacerated eyelids there was a gleam of light. Thick, swollen fingers laced with blood reached into his shirt, took out the knife. With weak, grotesque motions he sawed at the ropes, cutting through a thread at a time. He finished one rope and then collapsed, unconscious. In a half hour he revived and doggedly cut through the last rope. Then he turned and looked dully at the crew without speaking.

'You can't come back down the bowsprit,' Martin shouted. 'It's against the King's Regulations. Drop into the water.'

The words slowly worked through to Simon's mind. He let go of the knife, half-turned on the bowsprit and fell into the still water alongside the dock with a loud splash.

The boatswain, Martin, and two other sailors dived over the side. They collared Simon and swam over to the pier with him. Two other sailors had sprinted off down the dock. They came back with oranges, sugar lumps and a beaker of water. They squeezed the juice of several oranges into his mouth, past the swollen, blackened tongue; then gradually and slowly they gave him water. By that afternoon the tough fibre of the boy's body was already knitting and he was asking for meat. He was going to live. But the seventeen days on the bowsprit had changed Simon Jonson. He was no longer a boy. He had become a hard and bitter man. Although he recovered quickly from the ravages of exposure, lines remained about his mouth and eyes. Whenever the *Tiger* was mentioned his face became a flat, implacable mask in which his eyes glittered with a cold hatred.

Martin explained that it had never been contemplated that a man would return alive from the trip to the bowsprit. In the eyes of the captain, Simon was now dead. In the eyes of the Navy and of England, Simon was also dead, and his family would be notified that he had died at sea. He was without passport, nationality, money, family or profession. Simon nodded grimly as Martin talked, his eyes occasionally wandering down the dock to the black, empty outline of the bowsprit on which he had lived for so many days.

'I'll live somehow,' Simon said flatly. 'Can you teach me how to build a boat before the *Tiger* sails? If you can, I'll have a trade that I can work at. Then I won't starve to death on this miserable island.'

'I'll try, my boy,' Martin said. 'But it is a difficult craft. It takes time.'

Eighteen hours a day, for the time the Tiger remained in port, Martin taught Simon the craft. Simon's gaunt hands were weak at first, but they were sure and deft. He learned quickly. In all that time, however, Simon did not once talk of England and he would not permit Martin to mention the Royal Navy or the humiliation of his bowspritting. Martin was disturbed by the steel-hard bitterness he found in Simon. Once he began to talk of Christian forgiveness, but Simon only stared at him with glazed and cynical eyes. Martin's voice trailed off inconclusively, disconcerted by the hardness in Simon's face which appeared to intensify.

Finally the *Tiger* sailed. Everyone on the island was on the docks to watch it leave – except Simon Jonson. He was on the far side of the island cutting a rosewood tree into spars for a sloop he had already started to build. He had his trade, and was hard at work.

During the next year Simon built furniture, homes, canoes – anything to keep alive. In his spare time he worked on his sloop. It took two years to finish it.

The day it was finished he took on a crew of four Gold Coast Negroes and began to roam the under part of Africa. He bought hardwoods, spices, gold, pearls, and an occasional diamond. These goods he then resold to European merchants. He gained a reputation for being a fair and honest dealer and he worked at a grinding pace. He confided in no one, made no friends, was never known to smile. Within five years he was one of the richest men to be found along the Gold Coast.

Four times a year he wrote long letters to Martin. In these letters his furious, raging hatred of the British Navy was put into words. Martin, now retired to his cottage in Oxford, wrote Simon to soften his attitude, to let bygones be bygones. Each reply was the same: a restatement of Simon's quiet, deadly hatred for the men who had tortured him and whom he would never forget.

Finally, seven years after the bowspritting of Simon, Martin wrote a letter in which he offered to send his youngest daughter, Nancy, to Sao Thomé in the hopes that she and Simon would be married. The girl was eighteen, tall, clean-limbed and cheerful. Martin wrote that she was the only thing that could save Simon from the cancerous hate that was eating inside him.

For six months there was no response to his letter.

Then, suddenly and unexpectedly, Simon Jonson was given his revenge. He was in a dirty, hot anchorage north of Cape Lopez, negotiating for the purchase of six huge pearls that had been passed from one native hand to another halfway around the globe. He had almost completed the sale when a canoe with three natives in it came flying across the anchorage. They reported that they had seen an English man-of-war drifting hopelessly with the current, far out at sea. And, they reported, there was a man tied to the bowsprit.

Simon completed his sale, gathered his crew and set sail in the direction the natives indicated. After two days of sailing he located the ship. As soon as he saw it, he knew what had happened. It was the victim of what was called a line hurricane.

Line hurricanes are short-lived storms of a terrible intensity. The horizon is suddenly obscured by a black, solid line of clouds that is laced with lightning flashes around the surface of the sea, the sea in front of the storm becomes flat, the whole universe seems to stop and to wait dully for a few seconds. The hurricane strikes like a coiled snake. In a matter of seconds the wind rises to enormous velocities and pulls the tops of the waves after it, so that there is a flat, flying sheet of water a few feet off the surface. Beneath this, great combers of green-and-white water crash insanely against one another. For several minutes the whole ocean turns dark, and the hissing of water and wind is so great that normal voices are utterly lost. Then it is suddenly over. The sea falls flat, the sun reappears, a few wounded fish lie gasping and dying on the surface. But if a sailing vessel is caught in such a storm with sail on, either its sails will be ripped to shreds or its masts snapped. A poorly handled ship will simply vanish and a well-handled one will be badly damaged at the very best.

As Simon approached the ship, he saw it was a large man-of-war. It carried thirty-three guns and the name *India* was on its stern. All the masts had been broken, the decks were a tangle of broken spars and lines, there were gaping holes in the gun decks where the guns had come adrift and smashed their way overboard, the rails were splintered and torn, bits of sail, mattresses, shattered casks, wet powder were scattered over everything.

And the natives had been right . . . from the bowsprit dangled the body of a man.

As Simon bore down on the *India*, the desultory activity of the men aboard the ship stopped. Men staggered to the rails, looked with bleary eyes at Simon's sloop. A hatch opened and the captain walked out on deck. Simon hove-to a hundred feet from the damaged ship.

'What happened to you?' he shouted to the captain.

'Hit by a line hurricane,' the captain said in a rasping voice. 'No time to batten down or secure. Our guns came adrift and smashed half the crew before they went overboard. Compass ruined. All our water kegs smashed into pieces.'

The captain ran a dry tongue over even drier lips. Simon realized that all of the men along the rail were half dead with thirst.

'You are a hundred and fifteen miles south-west of Calbar. I advise you to make for it at once,' Simon said. He motioned for his black crew to set sail and he began to veer away from the *India*.

'Wait, man,' the captain cried. 'Do you have water? My God, we are dying of thirst. We can never make land in this condition. If you have water, in the name of mercy give it to us.'

'Yes, I have five large kegs of fresh water,' Simon said.

'Look, you talk English; you must be an Englishman,' the captain croaked. 'I order you to come alongside and give us water and supplies. I further order you – '

'I am no English subject,' Simon said coldly. 'I am a citizen of the seas. I am under no obligation to obey your orders.'

He ran back alongside the ship, but carefully stayed out of gunshot. The captain, reeling slightly under the impact of the tropical sun, stared down at him unbelievingly.

'Then I request you to aid us in the name of common humanity,' the captain said.

'Ah, common humanity, that is another thing,' Simon said, but his voice was colder and more deadly than before. 'Then, in the name of common humanity, I order you to take that man down from the bowsprit.'

'That is impossible,' the captain said. 'That man was sentenced to the bowsprit several days ago under the authority of His Majesty's Regulations for the Government of the Royal Navy. It is impossible for me or anyone else to order him cut loose.'

The men on the rail, the captain and Simon all looked down the ship towards the bowsprit. The poor wretch tied there raised his head, his eyes glittering with hope. The captain turned and looked down at Simon.

There was a long silence while all the vast and massive authority of the British Navy matched wills with a single individual in a small sloop.

'It is impossible for me to aid you as long as that man is tied to the bowsprit,' Simon said deliberately and slowly. He gestured to his crew and the sails of his sloop went up. As the canvas ballooned slowly, the sloop picked up way and began to move away from the *India.*

'No man was ever allowed to come down off the bowsprit to the ship,' the captain screamed.

Simon did not reply. He merely glanced once at the captain, then at the man on the bowsprit. Then he turned his back to the ship.

The captain's tongue came out, his hot, dry breath whistled out through the dry passages of his nose. Then he threw back his head and shouted after Simon, suddenly afraid that he could not be heard.

'Cut the man loose from the bowsprit. I pardon him unconditionally.'

The crew began a ragged cheer. Men stumbled down the deck toward the bowsprit, clambered over the debris to set their shipmate free. The man on the bowsprit waved his hands feebly, unable to realize fully what had happened.

Simon heard the command and put his tiller hard over. The sloop bore down on the shattered hulk of the *India.* As lines came from the ship and were tied to huge water casks in the sloop, Simon did something he had not done in seven years. He put his head back and smiled up at the crew. As the men stove in the end of the first cask and stuck their heads into the fresh water he continued to smile at them.

Two weeks later when he returned to Sao Thomé, after aiding the *India* to make port, he sat down to answer the last letter of his friend Martin.

'My dear and only friend Martin,' he began. 'Since you wrote, something has happened which has much changed my former attitude. You will now find that I am more kindly disposed toward His Majesty's Navy in particular and the English people in general. I would now be most grateful if you would send your youngest daughter Nancy to Sao Thomé as you proposed in your last letter. She will not have an easy life here, but she can be assured that I shall give her all the love and care and devotion of which I am capable . . .'

H. G. Wells

IN THE ABYSS

THE LIEUTENANT STOOD in front of the steel sphere and gnawed a piece of pine splinter. 'What do you think of it, Steevens?' he asked.

'It's an idea,' said Steevens, in the tone of one who keeps an open mind.

'I believe it will smash – flat,' said the lieutenant.

'He seems to have calculated it all out pretty well,' said Steevens, still impartial.

'But think of the pressure,' said the lieutenant. 'At the surface of the water it's fourteen pounds to the inch, thirty feet down it's double that; sixty, treble; ninety, four times; nine hundred, forty times; five thousand, three hundred – that's a mile – it's two hundred and forty times fourteen pounds; that's – let's see – thirty hundredweight – a ton and a half, Steevens; *a ton and a half* to the square inch. And the ocean where he's going is five miles deep. That's seven and a half – '

'Sounds a lot,' said Steevens, 'but it's jolly thick steel.'

The lieutenant made no answer, but resumed his pine splinter. The object of their conversation was a huge ball of steel, having an exterior diameter of perhaps nine feet. It looked like the shot for some Titanic piece of artillery. It was elaborately nested in a monstrous scaffolding built into the framework of the vessel, and the gigantic spars that were presently to sling it overboard gave the stern of the ship an appearance that had raised the curiosity of every decent sailor who had sighted it, from the Pool of London to the Tropic of Capricorn. In two places, one above the other, the steel gave place to a couple of circular windows of enormously thick glass, and one of these, set in a steel frame of great solidity, was now partially unscrewed. Both the men had seen the interior of this globe for the first time that morning. It was elaborately padded with air cushions, with little studs sunk between bulging pillows to work the simple mechanism of the affair. Everything was elaborately padded, even the Myers apparatus which was to absorb carbonic acid and replace the oxygen inspired by its tenant, when he had crept in by the glass manhole, and had been screwed in. It was so elaborately padded that a man might have been fired from a gun in it with perfect safety. And it had need to be, for presently a man was to crawl in through that glass manhole, to be screwed up tightly, and to be flung overboard, and to sink down – down – down, for five miles, even as the lieutenant said. It had taken the strongest hold of his imagination; it made him a bore at mess; and he found Steevens, the new arrival aboard, a godsend to talk to about it, over and over again.

'It's my opinion,' said the lieutenant, 'that that glass will simply bend in and bulge and smash, under a pressure of that sort. Daubrée has made rocks run like water under big pressures – and, you mark my words – '

'If the glass did break in,' said Steevens, 'what then?'

'The water would shoot in like a jet of iron. Have you ever felt a straight jet of high-pressure water? It would hit as hard as a bullet. It would simply smash him and flatten him. It would tear down his throat, and into his lungs; it would blow in his ears – '

'What a detailed imagination you have!' protested Steevens, who saw things vividly.

'It's a simple statement of the inevitable,' said the lieutenant.

'And the globe?'

'Would just give out a few little bubbles, and it would settle down comfortably against the day of judgement, among the oozes and the bottom clay – with poor Elstead spread over his own smashed cushions like butter over bread.'

He repeated this sentence as though he liked it very much. 'Like butter over bread,' he said.

'Having a look at the jigger?' said a voice, and Elstead stood between them, spick and span in white, with a cigarette between his teeth, and his eyes smiling out of the shadow of his ample hat-brim. 'What's that about bread and butter, Weybridge? Grumbling as usual about the insufficient pay of naval officers? It won't be more than a day now before I start. We are to get the slings ready today. This clean sky and gentle swell is just the kind of thing for swinging off a dozen tons of lead and iron, isn't it?'

'It won't affect you much,' said Weybridge.

'No. Seventy or eighty feet down, and I shall be there in a dozen seconds, there's not a particle moving, though the wind shriek itself hoarse up above, and the water lifts half-way to the clouds. No. Down there – ' He moved to the side of the ship and the other two followed him. All three leant forward on their elbows and stared down into the yellow-green water.

'*Peace,*' said Elstead, finishing his thought aloud.

'Are you dead certain that clockwork will act?' asked Weybridge presently.

'It has worked thirty-five times,' said Elstead. 'It's bound to work.'

'But if it doesn't?'

'Why shouldn't it?'

'I wouldn't go down in that confounded thing,' said Weybridge, 'for twenty thousand pounds.'

'Cheerful chap you are,' said Elstead, and spat sociably at a bubble below.

'I don't understand yet how you mean to work the thing,' said Steevens.

'In the first place, I'm screwed into the sphere,' said Elstead, 'and when I've turned the electric light off and on three times to show I'm cheerful, I'm slung out over the stern by that crane, with all those big lead sinkers slung below me. The top lead weight has a roller carrying a hundred fathoms of strong cord rolled up, and that's all that joins the sinkers to the sphere, except the slings that will be cut when the affair is dropped. We use cord rather than wire rope because it's easier to cut and more buoyant – necessary points, as you will see.

'Through each of these lead weights you notice there is a hole, and an iron rod will be run through that and will project six feet on the lower side. If that rod is rammed up from below, it knocks up a lever and sets the clockwork in motion at the side of the cylinder on which the cord winds.

'Very well. The whole affair is lowered gently into the water, and the slings are cut. The sphere floats – with the air in it, it's lighter than water – but the lead weights go down straight and the cord runs out. When the cord is all paid out, the sphere will go down too, pulled down by the cord.'

'But why the cord?' asked Steevens. 'Why not fasten the weights directly to the sphere?'

'Because of the smash down below. The whole affair will go rushing down, mile after mile, at a headlong pace at last. It would be knocked to pieces on the bottom if it wasn't for that cord. But the weights will hit the bottom, and directly they do the buoyancy of the sphere will come into play. It will go on sinking slower and slower; come to a stop at last, and then begin to float upward again.

'That's where the clockwork comes in. Directly the weights smash against the sea bottom, the rod will be knocked through and will kick up the clockwork, and the cord will be rewound on the reel. I shall be lugged down to the sea bottom. There I shall stay for half an hour, with the electric light on, looking about me. Then the clockwork will release a spring knife, the cord will be cut, and up I shall rush again, like a soda-water bubble. The cord itself will help the flotation.'

'And if you should chance to hit a ship?' said Weybridge.

'I should come up such a pace, I should go clean through it,' said Elstead, 'like a cannon-ball. You needn't worry about that.'

'And suppose some nimble crustacean should wriggle into your clockwork – '

'It would be a pressing sort of invitation for me to stop,' said Elstead, turning his back on the water and staring at the sphere.

They had swung Elstead overboard by eleven o'clock. The day was serenely bright and calm, with the horizon lost in haze. The electric glare in the little upper compartment beamed cheerfully three times. Then they let him down slowly to the surface of the water, and a sailor in the stern chains hung ready to cut the tackle that held the lead weights and the sphere together. The globe, which had looked so large on deck, looked the smallest thing conceivable under the stern of the ship. It rolled a little, and its two dark windows, which floated uppermost, seemed like eyes turned up in round wonderment at the people who crowded the rail. A voice wondered how Elstead like the rolling. 'Are you ready?' sang out the commander. 'Ay, Ay, sir!' 'Then let her go!'

The rope of the tackle tightened against the blade and was cut, and an eddy rolled over the globe in a grotesquely helpless fashion. Someone waved a handkerchief, someone else tried an ineffectual cheer, a middy was counting slowly, 'Eight, nine, ten!' Another roll, then with a jerk and a splash the thing righted itself.

It seemed to be stationary for a moment, to grow rapidly smaller, and then the water closed over it, and it became visible, enlarged by refraction and dimmer, below the surface. Before one could count three it had disappeared. There was a flicker of white light far down in the water, that diminished to a speck and vanished. Then there was nothing but a depth of water going down into blackness, through which a shark was swimming.

Then suddenly the screw of the cruiser began to rotate, the water was crickled, the shark disappeared in a wrinkled confusion, and a torrent of foam rushed across the crystalline clearness that had swallowed up Elstead. 'What's the idea?' said one AB to another.

'We're going to lay off about a couple of miles, 'fear he should hit us when he comes up,' said his mate.

The ship steamed slowly to her new position. Aboard her almost everyone who was unoccupied remained watching the breathing swell into which the sphere had sunk. For the next half-hour it is doubtful if a word was spoken that did not bear directly or indirectly on Elstead. The December sun was now high in the sky, and the heat very considerable.

'He'll be cold enough down there,' said Weybridge. 'They say that below a certain depth sea water's always just about freezing.'

'Where'll he come up?' asked Steevens. 'I've lost my bearings.'

'That's the spot,' said the commander, who prided himself on his omniscience. He extended a precise finger south-eastward. 'And this, I reckon, is pretty nearly the moment,' he said. 'He's been thirty-five minutes.'

'How long does it take to reach the bottom of the ocean?' asked Steevens.

'For a depth of five miles, and reckoning – as we did – an acceleration of two feet per second, both ways, is just about three-quarters of a minute.'

'Then he's overdue,' said Weybridge.

'Pretty nearly,' said the commander. 'I suppose it takes a few minutes for that cord of his to wind in.'

'I forgot that,' said Weybridge, evidently relieved.

And then began the suspense. A minute slowly dragged itself out, and no sphere shot out of the water. Another followed, and nothing broke the low oily swell. The sailors explained to one another that little point about the winding-in of the cord. The rigging was dotted with expectant faces. 'Come up, Elstead!' called one hairy-chested salt, impatiently, and the others caught it up, and shouted as though they were waiting for the curtain of a theatre to rise.

The commander glanced irritably at them.

'Of course, if the acceleration's less than two,' he said, 'he'll be all the longer. We aren't absolutely certain that was the proper figure. I'm no slavish believer in calculations.'

Steevens agreed concisely. No one on the quarter-deck spoke for a couple of minutes. Then Steevens' watchcase clicked.

When, twenty-one minutes after the sun reached the zenith, they were still waiting for the globe to reappear, not a man aboard had dared to whisper that hope was dead. It was Weybridge who first gave expression to that realization. He spoke while the sound of eight bells still hung in the air. 'I always distrusted that window,' he said quite suddenly to Steevens.

'Good God!' said Steevens; 'you don't think – '

'Well!' said Weybridge, and left the rest to his imagination.

'I'm no great believer in calculations myself,' said the commander dubiously, 'so that I'm not altogether hopeless yet.' And at midnight the gunboat was steaming slowly in a spiral round the spot where the globe had sunk, and the white beam of the electric light fled and halted and swept discontentedly onward again over the waste of phosphorescent waters under the little stars.

'If his window hasn't burst and smashed him,' said Weybridge, 'then it's a cursed sight worse, for his clockwork has gone wrong, and he's alive now, five miles under our feet, down there in the cold and dark, anchored in that little bubble of his, where never a ray of light has shone or a human being lived, since the waters were gathered together. He's there without food, feeling hungry and thirsty and scared, wondering whether he'll starve or stifle. Which will it be? The Myers apparatus is running out, I suppose. How long do they last?'

'Good heavens!' he exclaimed, 'what little things we are! We daring little devils! Down there, miles and miles of water – all water, and all this empty water about us and this sky. Gulfs!' He threw his hands out, and as he did so, a little white streak swept noiselessly up the sky, travelled more slowly, stopped, became a motionless dot, as though a new star had fallen up into the sky. Then it went sliding back again and lost itself amidst the reflections of the stars and the white haze of the sea's phosphorescence.

At the sight he stopped, arm extended and mouth open. He shut his mouth, opened it again, and waved his arms with an impatient gesture. Then he turned, shouted 'El-stead ahoy!' to the first watch, and went at a run to Lindley and the search-light. 'I saw him,' he said. 'Starboard there! His light's on, and he's just shot out of the water.

Bring the light round. We ought to see him drifting, when he lifts on the swell.'

But they never picked up the explorer until dawn. Then they almost ran him down. The crane was swung out and a boat's crew hooked the chain to the sphere. When they had shipped the sphere, they unscrewed the manhole and peered into the darkness of the interior (for the electric light chamber was intended to illuminate the water about the sphere, and was shut off entirely from its general cavity).

The air was very hot within the cavity, and the india-rubber at the lip of the manhole was soft. There was no answer to their eager questions and no sound of movement within. Elstead seemed to be lying motionless, crumpled up in the bottom of the globe. The ship's doctor crawled in and lifted him out to the men outside. For a moment or so they did not know whether Elstead was alive or dead. His face, in the yellow light of the ship's lamps, glistened with perspiration. They carried him down to his own cabin.

He was not dead, they found, but in a state of absolute nervous collapse, and besides cruelly bruised. For some days he had to lie perfectly still. It was a week before he could tell his experiences.

Almost his first words were that he was going down again. The sphere would have to be altered, he said, in order to allow him to throw off the cord if need be, and that was all. He had had the most marvellous experience. 'You thought I should find nothing but ooze,' he said. 'You laughed at my explorations, and I've discovered a new world!' He told his story in disconnected fragments, and chiefly from the wrong end, so that it is impossible to re-tell it in his words. But what follows is the narrative of his experience.

It began atrociously, he said. Before the cord ran out, the thing kept rolling over. He felt like a frog in a football. He could see nothing but the crane and the sky overhead, with an occasional glimpse of the people on the ship's rail. He couldn't tell a bit which way the thing would roll next. Suddenly he would find his feet going up, and try to step, and over he went rolling, head over heels, and just anyhow, on the padding. Any other shape would have been more comfortable, but no other shape was to be relied upon under the huge pressure of the nethermost abyss.

Suddenly the swaying ceased, the globe righted, and when he had picked himself up, he saw the water all about him greeny-blue, with an attenuated light filtering down from above, and a shoal of little floating things went rushing up past him, as it seemed to him, towards the light. And even as he looked, it grew darker and darker, until the water above was as dark as the midnight sky, albeit of a greener shade, and the water below black. And little transparent things in the water developed a faint glint of luminosity, and shot past him in greenish streaks.

And the feeling of falling! It was just like the start of a lift, he said, only it kept on. One has to imagine what that means, that keeping on. It was then of all times that Elstead repented of his adventure. He saw the chances against him in an altogether new light. He thought of the big cuttle-fish people knew to exist in the middle waters, the kind of things they find half digested in whales at times, or floating dead and rotten and half eaten by fish. Suppose one caught hold and wouldn't let go. And had the clockwork really been sufficiently tested? But whether he wanted to go on or go back mattered not the slightest now.

In fifty seconds everything was as black as night outside, except where the beam from his light struck through the waters, and picked out every now and then some fish or scrap of sinking matter. They flashed by too fast for him to see what they were. Once he thinks he passed a shark. And then the sphere began to get hot by friction against the water. They had underestimated this, it seems.

The first thing he noticed was that he was perspiring, and then he heard a hissing growing louder under his feet, and saw a lot of little bubbles – very little bubbles they were – rushing upward like a fan through the water outside. Steam! He felt the window, and it was hot. He turned on the minute glow-lamp that lit his own cavity, looked at the padded watch by the studs, and saw he had been travelling now for two minutes. It came into his head that the window would carck through the conflict of temperatures, for he knew the bottom water is very near freezing.

Then suddenly the floor of the sphere seemed to press against his feet, the rush of bubbles outside grew slower and slower, and the hissing diminished. The sphere rolled a little. The window had not cracked, nothing had given, and he knew that the dangers of sinking, at any rate, were over.

In another minute or so he would be on the floor of the abyss. He thought, he said, of Steevens and Weybridge and the rest of them five miles overhead, higher to him than the very highest clouds that ever floated over land are to us, steaming slowly and staring down and wondering what had happened to him.

He peered out of the window. There was no more bubbles now, and the hissing had stopped. Outside there was a heavy blackness – as black as black velvet – except where the electric light pierced the empty water and showed the colour of it – a yellow-green. Then three things like shapes of fire swam into sight, following each other through the water. Whether they were little and near or big and far off he could not tell.

Each was outlined in a bluish light almost as bright as the lights of a fishing smack, a light which seemed to be smoking greatly, and all along the sides of them were specks of this, like the lighter port-holes of a ship. Their phosphorescence seemed to go out as they came into the radiance of his lamp, and he saw then that they were little fish of some strange sort, with huge heads, vast eyes, and dwindling bodies and tails. Their eyes were turned towards him, and he judged they were following him down. He supposed they were attracted by his glare.

Presently others of the same sort joined them. As he went on down, he noticed that the water became of a pallid colour, and that little specks twinkled in his ray like motes in a sunbeam. This was probably due to the clouds of ooze and mud that the impact of his leaden sinkers had disturbed.

By the time he was drawn down to the lead weights he was in a dense fog of white that his electric light failed altogether to pierce for more than a few yards, and many minutes elapsed before the hanging sheets of sediment subsided to any extent. Then, lit by his light and by the transient phosphorescence of a distant shoal of fishes, he was able to see under the huge blackness of the super-incumbent water an undulating expanse of greyish-white ooze, broken here and there by tangled thickets of a growth of sea lilies, waving hungry tentacles in the air.

Farther away were the graceful, translucent outlines of a group of gigantic sponges. About this floor there were scattered a number of bristling flattish tufts of rich purple and black, which he decided must be some sort of sea-urchin, and small, large-eyed or blind things having a curious resemblance, some to woodlice, and other to lobsters, crawled sluggishly across the track of the light and vanished into the obscurity again, leaving furrowed trails behind them.

Then suddenly the hovering swarm of little fishes veered about and came towards him as a flight of starlings might do. They passed over him like a phosphorescent snow, and then he saw behind them some larger creature advancing towards the sphere.

At first he could see it only dimly, a faintly moving figure remotely suggestive of a walking man, and then it came into the spray of light that the lamp shot out. As the glare struck it, it shut its eyes, dazzled. He stared in rigid astonishment.

It was a strange vertebrated animal. Its dark purple head was dimly suggestive of a chameleon, but it had such a high forehead and such a braincase as no reptile ever displayed before; the vertical pitch of its face gave it a most extraordinary resemblance to a human being.

Two large and protruding eyes projected from sockets in chameleon fashion, and it had a broad reptilian mouth with horny lips beneath its little nostrils. In the position of the ears were two huge gill-covers, and out of these floated a branching tree of coralline filaments, almost like the treelike gills that all young rays and sharks possess.

But the humanity of the face was not the most extraordinary thing about the creature. It was a biped; its almost globular body was poised on a tripod of two frog-like legs and a long thick tail, and its fore limbs, which grotesquely caricatured the human hand, much as a frog's do, carried a long shaft of bone, tipped with copper. The colour of the creature was variegated; its head, hands, and legs were purple; but its skin, which hung loosely upon it, even as clothes might do, was a phosphorescent grey. And it stood there blinded by the light.

At last this unknown creature of the abyss blinked its eyes open, and, shading them with its disengaged hand, opened its mouth and gave vent to a shouting noise, articulate almost as speech might be, that penetrated even the steel case and padded jacket of the sphere. How a shouting may be accomplished without lungs Elstead does not profess to explain. It then moved sideways out of the glare into the mystery of shadow that bordered it on either side, and Elstead felt rather than saw that it was coming towards him. Fancying the light had attracted it, he turned the switch that cut off he current. In another moment something soft dabbed upon the steel, and the globe swayed.

Then the shouting was repeated, and it seemed to him that a distant echo answered it. The dabbing recurred, and the whole globe swayed and ground against the spindle over which the wire was rolled. He stood in the blackness and peered out into the everlasting night of the abyss. And presently he saw, very faint and remote, other phosphorescent quasi-human forms hurrying towards him.

Hardly knowing what he did, he felt about in his swaying prison for the stud of the exterior electric light, and came by accident against his own small glow-lamp in its padded recess. The sphere twisted, and then threw him down; he heard shouts like shouts of surprise, and when he rose to his feet he saw two pairs of stalked eyes peering into the lower window and reflecting his light.

In another moment hands were dabbing vigorously at his steel casing, and there was a sound, horrible enough in his position, of the metal protection of the clockwork being vigorously hammered. That, indeed, sent his heart into his mouth, for if these strange creatures succeeded in stopping that, his release would never occur. Scarcely had he thought as much when he felt the sphere sway violently, and the floor of it press hard against his feet. He turned off the small glow-lamp that lit the interior, and sent the ray of the large light in the separate compartment out into the water. The sea-floor and the man-like creatures had disappeared, and a couple of fish chasing each other dropped suddenly by the window.

He thought at once that these strange denizens of the deep sea had broken the rope, and that he had escaped. He drove up faster and faster, and then stopped with a jerk that sent him flying against the padded roof of his prison. For half a minute, perhaps, he was too astonished to think.

Then he felt that the sphere was spinning slowly, and rocking, and it seemed to him that it was also being drawn through the water. By crouching close to the window, he managed to make his weight effective and roll that part of the sphere downward, but he could see nothing save the pale ray of his light striking down ineffectively into the darkness. It occurred to him that he would see more if he turned the lamp off, and allowed his eyes to grow accustomed to the profound obscurity.

In this he was wise. After some minutes the velvety blackness became a translucent blackness, and then, far away, and as faint as the zodiacal light of an English summer evening, he saw shapes moving below. He judged these creatures had detached his cable and were towing him along the sea bottom.

And then he saw something faint and remote across the undulations of the submarine plain, a broad horizon of pale luminosity that extended this way and that way as far as the range of his little window permitted him to see. To this he was being towed, as a balloon might be towed by men out of the open country into a town. He approached it very slowly, and very slowly the dim irradiation was gathered together into more definite shapes.

It was nearly five o'clock before he came over this luminous area, and by that time he could make out an arrangement suggestive of streets and houses grouped about a vast roofless erection that was grotesquely suggestive of a ruined abbey. It was spread out like a map below him. The houses were all roofless enclosures of walls, and their substance being, as he afterwards saw, of phosphorescent bones, gave the place an appearance as if it were built of drowned moonshine.

Among the inner caves of the place waving trees of crinoid stretched their tentacles, and tall, slender, glassy sponges shot like shining minarets and lilies of filmy light out of the general glow of the city. In the open spaces of the place he could see a stirring movement as of crowds of people, but he was too many fathoms above them to distinguish the individuals in those crowds.

Then slowly they pulled him down, and as they did so, the details of the place crept slowly upon his apprehension. He saw that the courses of the cloudy buildings were marked out with beaded lines of round objects, and then he perceived that at several points below him, in broad open spaces, were forms like the encrusted shapes of ships.

Slowly and surely he was drawn down, and the forms below him became brighter, clearer, more distinct. He was being pulled down, he perceived, towards the large building in the centre of the town, and he could catch a glimpse ever and again of the multitudinous forms that were lugging at his cord. He was astonished to see that the rigging of one of the ships, which formed such a prominent feature of the place, was crowded with a host of gesticulating figures regarding him, and then the walls of the great building rose about him silently, and hid the city from his eyes.

And such walls they were, of water-logged wood, and twisted wire-rope, and iron spars, and copper, and the bones and skulls of dead men. The skulls ran in zigzag lines and spirals and fantastic curves over the buildings; and in and out of their eye-sockets, and over the whole surface of the place, lurked and played a multitude of silvery little fishes.

Suddenly his ears were filled with a low shouting and a noise like the violent blowing of horns, and this gave place to a fantastic chant. Down the sphere sank, past the huge pointed windows, through which he saw vaguely a great number of these strange ghostlike people regarding him, and at last he came to rest, as it seemed, on a kind of altar that stood in the centre of the place.

And now he was at such a level that he could see these strange people of the abyss plainly once more. To his astonishment, he perceived that they were prostrating themselves before him, all save one, dressed as it seemed in a robe of placoid scales, and crowned with a luminous diadem, who stood with his reptilian mouth opening and shutting, as though he led the chanting of the worshippers.

A curious impulse made Elstead turn on his small glow-lamp again, so that he became visible to these creatures of the abyss, albeit the glare made them disappear forthwith into night. At this sudden sight of him, the chanting gave place to a tumult of exultant shouts; and Elstead, being anxious to watch them, turned his light off again, and vanished from before their eyes. But for a time he was too blind to make out what they were doing, and when at last he could distinguish them, they were kneeling again. And thus they continued worshipping him, without rest or intermission, for a space of three hours.

Most circumstantial was Elstead's account of his astounding city and its people, these people of perpetual night, who have never seen sun or moon or stars, green vegetation, nor any living, air-breathing creatures, who know nothing of fire, nor any light but the phosphorescent light of living things.

Startling as is his story, it is yet more startling to find that scientific men, of such eminence as Adams and Jenkins, find nothing incredible in it. They tell me they see no reason why intelligent, water-breathing, vertebrated creatures inured to a low temperature and enormous pressure, and of such a heavy structure that neither alive nor dead would they float, might not live upon the bottom of the deep sea, and quite unsuspected by us, descendants like ourselves of the great Theriomorpha of the New Red Sandstone age.

We should be known to them, however, as strange, meteoric creatures, wont to fall catastrophically dead out of the mysterious blackness of their watery sky. And not only we ourselves, but our ships, our metals, our appliances, would come raining down out of the night. Sometimes sinking things would smite down and crush them, as if it were the judgement of some unseen power above, and sometimes would come things of the utmost rarity or utility, or shapes of inspiring suggestion. One can understand, perhaps, something of their behaviour at the descent of a living man, if one thinks what a barbaric people might do, to whom an enhaloed, shining creature came suddenly out of the sky.

At one time or another Elstead probably told the officers of the *Ptarmigan* every detail of his strange twelve hours in the abyss. That he also intended to write them down is certain, but he never did, and so unhappily we have to piece together the discrepant fragments of his story from the reminiscences of Commander Simmons, Weybridge, Steevens, Lindley, and the others.

We see the thing darkly in fragmentary glimpses – the huge ghostly building, the bowing, chanting people, with their dark chameleonlike heads and faintly luminous clothing, and Elstead, with his light turned on again, vainly trying to convey to their minds that the cord by which the sphere was held was to be severed. Minute after minute slipped away, and Elstead, looking at his watch, was horrified to find that he had oxygen only for four hours more. But the chant in his honour kept on as remorselessly as if it was the marching song of his approaching death.

The manner of his release he does not understand, but to judge by the end of cord that hung from the sphere, it had been cut through by rubbing against the edge of the altar. Abruptly the sphere rolled over, and he swept up, out of their world, as an ethereal creature clothed in a vacuum would sweep through our own atmosphere back it its native ether again. He must have torn out of their sight as a hydrogen bubble hastens upward from our air. A strange ascension it must have seemed to them.

The sphere rushed up with even greater velocity than, when weighted with the lead sinkers, it had rushed down. It became exceedingly hot. It drove up with the windows uppermost, and he remembers the torrent of bubbles frothing against the glass. Every moment he expected this to fly. Then suddenly something like a huge wheel seemed to be released in his head, the padded compartment began spinning about him, and he fainted. His next recollection was of his cabin, and of the doctor's voice.

But that is the substance of the extraordinary story that Elstead related in fragments to the officers of the *Ptarmigan*. He promised to write it all down at a later date. His mind was chiefly occupied with the improvement of his apparatus, which was effected at Rio.

It remains only to tell that on 2 February 1896, he made his second descent into the ocean abyss, with the improvements his first experience suggested. What happened we shall probably never know.

He never returned. The *Ptarmigan* beat about over the point of his submersion, seeking him in vain for thirteen days. Then she returned to Rio, and the news was telegraphed to his friends. So the matter rests for the present. But it is hardly probable that no further attempt will be made to verify his strange story of these hitherto unsuspected cities of the deep sea.

Richard Middleton

THE GHOST SHIP

FAIRFIELD IS A LITTLE VILLAGE lying near the Portsmouth Road about half-way between London and the sea. Strangers who find it by accident now and then, call it a pretty, old-fashioned place; we, who live in it and call it home, don't find anything very pretty about it, but we should be sorry to live anywhere else. Our minds have taken the shape of the inn and the church and the green, I suppose. At all events we never feel comfortable out of Fairfield.

Of course the Cockneys, with their vasty houses and their noise-ridden streets, can call us rustics if they choose, but for all that Fairfield is a better place to live in than London. Doctor says that when he goes to London his mind is bruised with the weight of the houses, and he was a Cockney born. He had to live there himself when he was a little chap, but he knows better now. You gentlemen may laugh – perhaps some of you come from London way – but it seems to me that a witness like that it worth a gallon of arguments.

Dull? Well, you might find it dull, but I assure you that I've listened to all the London yarns you have spun tonight, and they're absolutely nothing to the things that happen at Fairfield. It's because of our way of thinking and minding our own business. If one of your Londoners were set down on the green of a Saturday night when the ghosts of the lads who died in the war keep tryst with the lasses who lie in the churchyard, he couldn't help being curious and interfering, and then the ghosts would go somewhere where it was quieter. But we just let them come and go and don't make any fuss, and in consequence Fairfield is the ghostiest place in all England. Why, I've seen a headless man sitting on the edge of the well in broad daylight, and the children playing about his feet as if he were their father. Take my word for it, spirits know when they are well off as much as human beings.

Still, I must admit that the thing I'm going to tell you about was queer even for our part of the world, where three packs of ghost-hounds hunt regularly during the season, and blacksmith's great-grandfather is busy all night shoeing the dead gentlemen's horses. Now that's a thing that wouldn't happen in London, because of their interfering ways, but blacksmith he lies up aloft and sleeps as quiet as a lamb. Once when he had a bad head he shouted down to them not to make so much noise, and in the morning he found an old guinea left on the anvil as an apology. He wears it on his watch-chain now. But I must get on with my story; if I start telling you about the queer happenings at Fairfield I'll never stop.

It all came of the great storm in the spring of '97, the year that we had two great storms. This was the first one, and I remember it very well, because I found in the morning that it had lifted the thatch of my pigsty into the widow's garden as clean as a boy's kite. When I looked over the hedge, widow – Tom Lamport's widow that was – was prodding for her nasturtiums with a daisy-grubber. After I had watched her for a little I went down to the Fox and Grapes to tell landlord what she had said to me. Landlord he laughed, being a married man and at ease with the sex. 'Come to that,' he said, 'the tempest has blowed something into my field. A kind of a ship I think it would be.'

I was surprised at that until he explained that it was only a ghost-ship and would do no hurt to the turnips. We argued that it had been blown up from the sea at Portsmouth, and then we talked of something else. There were two slates down at the parsonage and a big tree in Lumley's meadow. It was a rare storm.

I reckon the wind had blown our ghosts all over England. They were coming back for days afterwards with foundered horses and as footsore as possible, and they were so glad to get back to Fairfield that some of them walked up the street crying like little children. Squire said that his great-grandfather's great-grandfather hadn't looked so dead-beat since the battle of Naseby, and he's an educated man.

What with one thing and another, I should think it was a week before we got straight again, and then one afternoon I met the landlord on the green and he had a worried face. 'I wish you'd come and have a look at that ship in my field,' he said to me; 'it seems to me it's leaning real hard on the turnips. I can't bear thinking what the missus will say when she sees it.'

I walked down the lane with him, and sure enough there was a ship in the middle of his field, but such a ship as no man has seen on the water for three hundred years, let alone in the middle of a turnip-field. It was all painted black and covered with carvings, and there was a great bay window in the stern for all the world like the Squire's drawing-room. There was a crowd of little black cannon on deck and looking out of her port-holes, and she was anchored at each end to the hard ground. I have seen the wonders of the world on picture-postcards, but I have never seen anything to equal that.

'She seems very solid for a ghost-ship,' I said, seeing the landlord was bothered.

'I should say it's a betwixt and between,' he answered, puzzling it over, 'but it's going to spoil a matter of fifty turnips, and missus she'll want it moved.' We went up to her and touched the side, and it was as hard as a real ship. 'Now there's folks in England would call that very curious,' he said.

Now I don't know much about ships, but I should think that that ghost-ship weighed a solid two hundred tons, and it seemed to me that she had come to stay, so that I felt sorry for landlord, who was a married man. 'All the horses in Fairfield won't move her out of my turnips,' he said, frowning at her.

Just then we heard a noise on her deck, and we looked up and saw that a man had come out of her front cabin and was looking down at us very peaceably. He was dressed in a black uniform set out with rusty gold lace, and he had a great cutlass by his side in a brass sheath. 'I'm Captain Bartolomew Roberts,' he said, in a gentleman's voice, 'put in for recruits. I seem to have brought her rather far up the harbour.'

'Harbour!' cried landlord; 'why, you're fifty miles from the sea.'

Captain Roberts didn't turn a hair. 'So much as that, is it?' he said coolly. 'Well, it's of no consequence.'

Landlord was a bit upset at this. 'I don't want to be unneighbourly,' he said, 'but I wish you hadn't brought your ship into my field. You see, my wife sets great store on these turnips.'

The captain took a pinch of snuff out of a fine gold box that he pulled out of his pocket, and dusted his fingers with a silk handkerchief in a very genteel fashion. 'I'm only here for a few months,' he said; 'but if a testimony of my esteem would pacify your good lady I should be content,' and with the words he loosed a great gold brooch from the neck of his coat and tossed it down to landlord.

Landlord blushed as red as a strawberry. 'I'm not denying she's fond of jewellery,' he said, 'but it's too much for half a sackful of turnips.' And indeed it was a handsome brooch.

The captain laughed. 'Tut, man,' he said, 'it's a forced sale, and you deserve a good price. Say no more about it'; and nodding good-day to us, he turned on his heel and went into the cabin. Landlord walked back up the lane like a man with a weight off his mind. 'That tempest has blowed me a bit of luck,' he said; 'the missus will be main pleased with that brooch. It's better than the blacksmith's guinea any day.'

Ninety-seven was Jubilee year, the year of the second Jubilee, you remember, and we had great doings at Fairfield, so that we hadn't much time to bother about the ghost-ship, though anyhow it isn't our way to meddle in things that don't concern us. Landlord, he saw his tenant once or twice when he was hoeing his turnips and passed the time of day, and landlord's wife wore her new brooch to church every Sunday. But we didn't mix much with the ghosts at any time, all except an idiot lad there was in the village, and he didn't know the difference between a man and a ghost, poor innocent! On Jubilee Day, however, somebody told Captain Roberts why the church bells were ringing, and he hoisted a flag and fired off his guns like a royal Englishman. 'Tis true the guns were shotted, and one of the round shot knocked a hole in Farmer Johnstone's barn, but nobody thought much of that in such a season of rejoicing.

It wasn't till our celebrations were over that we noticed that anything was wrong in Fairfield. 'Twas shoemaker who told me first about it one morning at the Fox and Grapes. 'You know my great great-uncle?' he said to me.

'You mean Joshua, the quiet lad,' I answered, knowing him well.

'Quiet!' said shoemaker indignantly. 'Quiet you call him, coming home at three o'clock every morning as drunk as a magistrate and waking up the whole house with his noise.'

'Why, it can't be Joshua!' I said, for I knew him for one of the most respectable young ghosts in the village.

'Joshua it is,' said shoemaker; 'and one of these nights he'll find himself out in the street if he isn't careful.'

This kind of talk shocked me, I can tell you, for I don't like to hear a man abusing his own family, and I could hardly believe that a steady youngster like Joshua had taken to drink. But just then in came butcher Aylwin in such a temper that he could hardly drink his beer. 'The young puppy! the young puppy!' he kept on saying; and it was some time before shoemaker and I found out that he was talking about his ancestor that fell at Senlac.

'Drink?' said shoemaker hopefully, for we all like company in our misfortunes, and butcher nodded grimly.

'The young noodle,' he said, emptying his tankard.

Well, after that I kept my ears open, and it was the same story all over the village. There was hardly a young man among all the ghosts of Fairfield who didn't roll home in the small hours of the morning the worse for liquor. I used to wake up in the night and hear them stumble past my house, singing outrageous songs. The worst of it was that we couldn't keep the scandal to ourselves, and the folk at Greenhill began to talk of "sodden Fairfield" and taught their children to sing a song about us:

Sodden Fairfield, sodden Fairfield, has no use for bread-and-butter,
Rum for breakfast, rum for dinner, rum for tea, and rum for supper!

We are easy-going in our village, but we didn't like that.

Of course we soon found out where the young fellows went to get the drink, and landlord was terribly cut up that his tenant should have turned out so badly, but his wife wouldn't hear of parting with the brooch, so that he couldn't give the Captain notice to quit. But as time went on, things grew from bad to worse, and at all hours of the day you would see those young reprobates sleeping it off on the village green. Nearly every afternoon a ghost-waggon used to jolt down to the ship with a lading of rum, and though the older ghosts seemed inclined to give the Captain's hospitality the go-by, the youngsters were neither to hold nor to bind.

So one afternoon when I was taking my nap I heard a knock at the door, and there was parson looking very serious, like a man with a job before him that he didn't altogether relish. 'I'm going down to talk to the Captain about all this drunkenness in the village, and I want you to come with me,' he said straight out.

I can't say that I fancied the visit much myself, and I tried to hint to parson that as, after all, they were only a lot of ghosts, it didn't very much matter.

'Dead or alive, I'm responsible for their good conduct,' he said, 'and I'm going to do my duty and put a stop to this continued disorder. And you are coming with me, John Simmons.' So I went, parson being a persuasive kind of man.

We went down to the ship, and as we approached her I could see the Captain tasting the air on deck. When he saw parson he took off his hat very politely, and I can tell you that I was relieved to find that he had a proper respect for the cloth. Parson acknowledged his salute and spoke out stoutly enough. 'Sir, I should be glad to have a word with you.'

'Come on board, sir, come on board,' said the Captain, and I could tell by his voice that he knew why we were there. Parson and I climbed up an uneasy kind of ladder, and the Captain took us into the great cabin at the back of the ship, where the bay-window was. It was the most wonderful place you ever saw in your life, all full of gold and silver plate, swords with jewelled scabbards, carved oak chairs, and great chests that looked as though they were bursting with guineas. Even parson was surprised, and he did not shake his head very hard when the Captain took down some silver cups and poured us out a drink of rum. I tasted mine, and I don't mind saying that it changed my view of things entirely. There was nothing betwixt and between about that rum, and I felt that it was ridiculous to blame the lads for drinking too much of stuff like that. It seemed to fill my veins with honey and fire.

Parson put the case squarely to the Captain, but I didn't listen much to what he said; I was busy sipping my drink and looking through the window at the fishes swimming to and fro over landlord's turnips. Just then it seemed the most natural thing in the world that they should be there, though afterwards, of course, I could see that that proved it was a ghost-ship.

But even then I thought it was queer when I saw a drowned sailor float by in the thin air with his hair and beard all full of bubbles. It was the first time I had seen anything quite like that at Fairfield.

All the time I was regarding the wonders of the deep, parson was telling Captain Roberts how there was no peace or rest in the village owing to the curse of drunkenness, and what a bad example the youngsters were setting to the older ghosts. The Captain listened very attentively, and only put in a word now and then about boys being boys and young men sowing their wild oats. But when parson had finished his speech he filled up our silver cups and said to parson, with a flourish, 'I should be sorry to cause trouble anywhere where I have been made welcome, and you will be glad to hear that I put to sea tomorrow night. And now you must drink me a prosperous voyage.' So we all stood up and drank the toast with honour, and that noble rum was like hot oil in my veins.

After that Captain showed us some of the curiosities he had brought back from foreign parts, and we were greatly amazed, though afterwards I couldn't clearly remember what they were. And then I found myself walking across the turnips with parson, and I was telling him of the glories of the deep that I had seen through the window of the ship. He turned on me severely. 'If I were you, John Simmons,' he said, 'I should go straight home to bed.' He has a way of putting things that wouldn't occur to an ordinary man, has parson, and I did as he told me.

Well, next day it came on to blow, and it blew harder and harder, till about eight o'clock at night I heard a noise and looked out into the garden. I dare say you won't believe me, it seems a bit tall even to me, but the wind had lifted the thatch of my pigsty into the widow's garden a second time. I thought I wouldn't wait to hear what widow had to say about it, so I went across the green to the Fox and Grapes, and the wind was so strong that I danced along on tip-toe like a girl at the fair. When I got to the inn landlord had to help me shut the door; it seemed as though a dozen goats were pushing against it to come in out of the storm.

'It's a powerful tempest,' he said, drawing the beer. 'I hear there's a chimney down at Dickory End.'

'It's a funny thing how these sailors know about the weather.' I answered. 'When Captain said he was going tonight, I was thinking it would take a capful of wind to carry the ship back to sea, but now here's more than a capful.'

'Ah, yes,' said landlord, 'it's tonight he goes true enough, and, mind you, though he treated me handsome over the rent, I'm not sure it's a loss to the village. I don't hold with gentrice who fetch their drink from London instead of helping local traders to get their living.'

'But you haven't got any rum like his,' I said to draw him out.

His neck grew red above his collar, and I was afraid I'd gone too far; but after a while he got his breath with a grunt.

'John Simmons,' he said, 'if you've come down here this windy night to talk a lot of fool's talk, you've wasted a journey.'

Well, of course, then I had to smooth him down with praising his rum and Heavens forgive me for swearing it was better than Captain's. For the like of that rum no living lips have tasted save mine and parson's. But somehow or other I brought landlord round, and presently we must have a glass of his best to prove its quality.

'Beat that if you can!' he cried, and we both raised our glasses to our mouths, only to stop half-way and look at each other in amaze. For the wind that had been howling outside like an outrageous dog had all of a sudden turned as melodious as the carol-boys of a Christmas Eve.

'Surely that's not my Martha,' whispered landlord; Martha being his great-aunt that lived in the loft overhead.

We went to the door, and the wind burst it open so that the handle was driven clean into the plaster of the wall. But we didn't think about that at the time; for over our heads, sailing very comfortably through the windy stars, was the ship that had passed the summer in landlord's field. Her portholes and her bay-window were blazing with lights, and there was a noise of singing and fiddling on her decks. 'He's gone,' shouted landlord above the storm, 'and he's taken half the village with him!' I could only nod in answer, not having lungs like bellows of leather.

In the morning we were able to measure the strength of the storm, and over and above my pigsty there was damage enough wrought in the village to keep us busy. True it is that the children had to break down no branches for the firing that autumn, since the wind had strewn the woods with more than they could carry away. Many of our ghosts were scattered abroad, but this time very few came back, all the young men having sailed with Captain; and not only ghosts, for a poor half-witted lad was missing, and we reckoned that he had stowed himself away or perhaps shipped as cabin-boy, not knowing any better.

What with the lamentations of the ghost-girls and the grumblings of families who had lost an ancestor, the village was upset for a while, and the funny thing was that it was the folk who had complained most of the carryings-on of the youngsters, who made most noise now that they were gone. I hadn't any sympathy with shoemaker or butcher, who ran about saying how much they missed their lads, but it made me grieve to hear the poor bereaved girls calling their lovers by name on the village green at nightfall. It didn't seem fair to me that they should have lost their men a second time, after giving up life in order to join them, as like as not. Still, not even a spirit can be sorry forever, and after a few months we made up our mind that the folk who had sailed in the ship were never coming back, and we didn't talk about it any more.

And then one day, I dare say it would be a couple of years after, when the whole business was quite forgotten, who should come trapesing along the road from Portsmouth but the daft lad who had gone away with the ship, without waiting till he was dead to become a ghost. You never saw such a boy as that in all your life. He had a great rusty cutlass hanging to a string at his waist, and he was tattooed all over in fine colours, so that even his face looked like a girl's sampler. He had a handkerchief in his hand full of foreign shells and old-fashioned pieces of small money, very curious, and he walked up to the well outside his mother's house and drew himself a drink as if he had been nowhere in particular.

The worst of it was that he had come back as soft-headed as he went, and try as we might we couldn't get anything reasonable out of him. He talked a lot of gibberish about keel-hauling and walking the plank and crimson murders – things which a decent sailor should know nothing about, so that it seemed to me that for all his manners Captain had been more of a pirate than a gentleman mariner. But to draw sense out of that boy was as hard as picking cherries off a crab-tree. One silly tale he had that he kept on drifting back to, and to hear him you would have thought that it was the only thing that happened to him in his life. 'We was at anchor,' he would say, 'off an island called the Basket of Flowers, and the sailors had caught a lot of parrots and we were teaching them to swear. Up and down the decks, up and down the decks, and the language they used was dreadful. Then we looked up and saw the masts of the Spanish ship outside the harbour. Outside the harbour they were, so we threw the parrots into the sea and sailed out to fight. And all the parrots were drownded in the sea and the language they used was dreadful.' That's the sort of boy he was, nothing but silly talk of parrots when we asked him about the fighting. And we never had a chance of teaching him better, for two days after he ran away again, and hasn't been seen since.

That's my story, and I assure you that things like that are happening at Fairfield all the time. The ship has never come back, but somehow as people grow older they seem to think that one of these windy nights, she'll come sailing in over the hedges with all the lost ghosts on board. Well, when she comes, she'll be welcome. There's one ghost-lass that has never grown tired of waiting for her lad to return. Every night you'll see her out on the green, straining her poor eyes with looking for the mast-lights among the stars. A faithful lass you'd call her, and I'm thinking you'd be right.

Landlord's field wasn't a penny the worse for the visit, but they do say that since then the turnips that have been grown in it have tasted of rum.

Harry E. Turner

THE SEA TRYST

If there were more pleasant ways to spend an evening, Salaman couldn't think of them right now.

He was sitting in the first class dining-room of the Cunard Liner RMS *Queen Elizabeth II* having lingered over a bottle of Château Lafite Rothschild '67 which had complemented a truly superb dinner. They were a day and a half into the Atlantic from Southampton and the weather was excellent. A gentle swell moved the giant liner but it was a soporific, comforting motion.

Salaman glanced out of the starboard window of the dining-room at the vast spread of ocean and watched the spume hiss along the flanks of the ship as she nosed forward at a steady twenty-five knots. Beneath his feet he could feel the rhythmic throb and judder of huge engines and all around were the faint creakings and groanings of 96,000 tons of steel, wood and aluminium in perpetual motion.

The wine steward poured the remainder of the Lafite Rothschild into Salaman's glass with the reverence of a priest and watched as Salaman drained it slowly.

'Stefan,' said Salaman addressing the steward directly, 'Who is that girl at Table 132?'

The steward smiled and leant forward confidentially.

'That's Miss Fiona Stuart, sir, she's a regular. Done two dozen crossings at least since I've been on the *QEII*.'

Salaman nodded. 'She's very beautiful,' he said, 'if a trifle old-fashioned. Tell me, Stefan, why hasn't she appeared for dinner before this evening?'

Stefan's eyes narrowed mysteriously. 'Ah, well, sir, that's her custom, see. Stays in her cabin until we're two days out. Funny girl. Doesn't eat a mortal thing until she surfaces for dinner on the third night. A bad sailor I shouldn't wonder.'

Salaman lit a Monte Cristo cigar and drew the smoke carefully.

'Send her a bottle of Krug with my compliments, Stefan, and ask her if she would do me the honour of joining me at my table.'

The wine steward nodded, happy to be associated with any shipboard seduction; such liaisons invariably threw up the most lavish tips at the end of the voyage.

Salaman waited patiently while Stefan went gliding off to obtain the champagne, allowing his gaze to settle on Miss Fiona Stuart, six tables away from where he sat.

She was a ravishing girl, probably twenty-three or -four at most with a peaches-and-cream complexion that could only be English. Her long eyelashes shielded huge chestnut eyes and her tawny hair was arranged in a curiously dated fashion, coiled in flat discs over each ear and held in place with tiny decorative flowers. Her dress was pure silk, flesh coloured, and it hung softly over her small breasts and exquisite shoulders. She had finished what appeared to be a modest supper and was lighting a cigarette fixed into a long, white holder.

Stefan reappeared and, balancing a silver tray on one palm, minced over to Table 132. The girl looked up in surprise as he uncorked the champagne with a flourish and poured it into a long stemmed glass. He leant towards her and spoke a few words in her ear. She nodded slowly in acknowledgement and then looked suddenly and directly across at Salaman, her face expressionless.

Salaman, who knew his style with women – and its success rate, smiled back at her from behind a wreath of cigar smoke. The girl hesitated for a moment and then handed her glass to Stefan. When she stood up Salaman could see that she was tall, probably five feet eight or nine and as slender as a wand.

She moved across towards his table like a gazelle in slow motion, soft hips gently pummelling the tight silk of her dress.

Salaman rose to greet her, and Stefan, a pace behind, drew back a chair for her to sit in. Salaman extended his hand and she took it in cool, satin-smooth fingers.

'My name is Salaman. I am delighted you could join me. Forgive me, but I have already taken the liberty of acquainting myself with your name, Miss Stuart.'

She smiled now, and it was radiant.

'Mr Salaman, how kind of you to invite me. Are you travelling alone?'

Salaman put his cigar in the ashtray and took a long, slow breath. 'I *was*. But not any longer.'

She stared at him for a moment, sizing him up. He was obviously rich, elegantly dressed in a white dinner jacket and ruffled. His face was bronzed and lean with the kind of dark, yet gleaming eyes that women's magazines sometimes describe as 'smouldering'.

He was tall, probably over six feet and she put his age in the mid-thirties. He smelled faintly of an elusive, clean fragrance.

'Are you a Frenchman?' she asked, picking up her glass of champagne. Salaman laughed, for she had a very direct way of looking at him.

'Partly,' he said, 'I'm actually a mongrel collection of French, Spanish, American and Jewish. My passport, however, is as English as yours.'

She nodded briefly, absorbing this scant intelligence. 'And you are single?' she asked. Salaman was faintly conscious that it was he who should be asking the questions and calling the shots in this early skirmishing.

'I am single,' he said. 'And you – ?'

She suddenly drained her champagne glass and let it roll across the tablecloth towards him.

'Mr Salaman,' she said in a low voice, 'We are at sea – in mid-Atlantic. We are suspended between two continents – two worlds even. Time slips effortlessly by – all too quickly perhaps. I deplore wasting my time, spending it needlessly on trivial niceties. You invited me to your table as the first manoeuvre in an attempt to seduce me. Let me make it quite plain – I am willing – even eager – to be seduced by you. Unless you have a particular penchant for prolonging delicious anticipation I suggest we meet in my cabin in ten minutes.'

She stood up, turned abruptly and walked away. It was several moments before Salaman had recovered sufficiently to re-light his cigar. His hands, he noticed with some irritation, was trembling slightly. My God, what a girl! He could still smell her perfume – and oddly enough it was stronger now than when she had been sitting opposite him.

Stefan came gliding over to the table with an expression like a bishop. He leant discreetly towards Salaman and cupped a hand to his mouth. 'Cabin 1250, sir,' he whispered, straightening the fallen champagne glass.

Salaman waved the man away impatiently. His own feelings were a cauldron of triumph, apprehension, lust and irritation.

She was his, if he wanted her – unless of course she was teasing.

He moistened his lips and recalled that slender, silk-clad body. No, she wasn't teasing. And he wanted her – my God, he wanted her more than any other woman he'd ever met in his life. But why were his feelings of lust tempered with this sense of unease? Perhaps it was because he enjoyed the old fashioned cat-and-mouse game with a woman – a game he had played with considerable aplomb over the years. It was, he had long ago concluded, the only game worth a candle in his life. He was rich, having inherited his father's bank in Zurich, and successful in his own right as a financier, winter sportsman and art gallery proprietor.

But beautiful women were his only real addiction – the administrators of his fabulous trust fund had once ventured the opinion that they – women that is – were his Achilles heel. An understandable viewpoint, from the constipated Swiss banking fraternity and one which the young Salaman had chosen to ignore.

He glanced around the dining-room at his fellow passengers. They tended to be at the very best, middle aged, although most of them were really very old. The women, with sagging skin, tightly crimped, iron grey hair and heavy jewellery, were escorted by paunchy, florid faced men with bulging shirt fronts. It was an irony of life that cruising was synonymous with senior citizens when in fact it was a life style that would enchant most young people – if only they could have afforded it.

He stood up and let his cigar drop into the ashtray. Whether Miss Fiona Stuart was an eager innocent or scheming Jezebel made little or no difference to him. She was young and she was beautiful – two cherished qualities that were doomed to flower but briefly – and then fade.

She was right. Time was precious and should not be wasted. He would go directly to Cabin 1250 and let fate take its course.

Outside the dining-room a little knot of men in evening clothes were clustered round a notice board. Cigar smoke hung like a mushroom cloud above their silver heads. A uniformed officer was talking to them in the manner of a lecturer or schoolteacher. The notice board had a huge nautical map of the Atlantic fixed to it and it was marked with coloured pins and flags.

'– historic date of April the fourteenth –' the officer was saying – 'twenty-six years ago almost to the hour shipping lanes have moved south, away from the hazard of ice floes since that time although this voyage is on the precise route of that now legendary voyage –'

Salaman shrugged and moved on. Armchair sea-dogs, the lot of them, he mused.

The inside of the *QEII* is a vast, floating hotel, honeycombed with corridors, shopping plazas, lounges and staircases, and it took several minutes for Salaman to find his way to the correct end of One Deck – where Cabin 1250 snuggled opposite a small breakfast galley.

The ship's engines sounded harsher here, and their vibrations were stronger. A faint smell of furniture wax, oil and air fresheners oozed along the panelled walls. Salaman hesitated for a few seconds and then rapped gently on the cabin door. He heard a creak of bunk springs and then the slither of footsteps, this was followed by the scrape of a lock being drawn and the door opened. The remains of a weak evening sun streaming through the porthole threw a halo of light around her hair. It was unpinned now and fell in great waves across her shoulders. Her face looked pale, accentuating the huge, luminous eyes. There was a brief moment of friendship as their hands touched and then the sex began.

She wrapped herself around him like a monkey clinging to a stick and dragged him onto the floor of the cabin. Her hunger was prodigious and she directed his own fevered movements with gasping cries and clawing nails.

His lips were bruised with her kissing and his shoulders scored with deep scratch marks. She climaxed with a scream and went limp in his arms. At first, in panic, he though she was dead, but the pounding of her heart reassured him. He picked her up like a doll and carried her to the bunk where they lay gasping like stranded fish. Minutes later she was astride him again, manical in her fury and lust. Salaman's body felt as if it had been flayed with whips and his lungs ached with exertion. He pushed her away, his hands slipping on the sheen of perspiration that glistened on her skin. The sun had melted away beyond the lip of the horizon and the ocean was a black, oily swell under dark clouds. Close to the side of the ship crescents of foam reared up and smashed themselves against the hull. Salaman extricated himself from her grip and switched on the table lamp. The cabin was small and luxurious with panelled walls and tapestry curtains. On the dressing-table were dozens of framed photographs in ancient, cracked frames. Fascinated, Salaman sat up and looked at them closely. Fiona lay back with her eyes closed breathing like an exhausted child.

The photographs themselves were brown with age, some of them crudely repaired with transparent tape. One was of a huge ocean liner tied up in dock. Workmen in cloth caps and old-fashioned clothes stood on the quayside looking towards the camera in self-conscious poses. Another picture showed the same liner at sea, still in sight of the docks, a 'V' shaped wake of foam spreading from her stern. Others showed groups of ships' officers assembled on the boat deck, most of them looked very young. Yet another wasn't a photograph at all but a framed fragment from an old and yellowing newspaper. Its headline proclaimed, 'Only 700 survive *Titanic* disaster.' One was a carefully pressed piece of parchment that looked like a log entry or page from a diary. It said, 'eleven-forty pm April 14. Forty-one degrees, forty-six minutes north, fifty degrees, fourteen minutes west.'

Salaman turned back to Fiona and she was watching him now. Her eyes had taken on a coldness that made him almost shudder.

'These pictures,' he said softly, 'and these clippings – are they yours?'

She made no reply but sighed deeply drawing breath it seemed from the deepest recesses of her soul. The cabin had an icy chill and above the faint throb of the engines he could hear big waves slashing high up the sides of the ship. He turned back to the photographs and picked up one that had fallen on its face. As he turned it over he felt his heart falter. It was an old, old photograph of a girl in a long silk dress with her hair fashioned in circular discs over her ears. She was very pretty and she clung to the arm of a young officer in a neat uniform. In the background was the liner, dwarfing them with its soaring hull. It bore the name *Titanic*. He felt her hand on his shoulder and it made him start.

'Do you understand?' she said, and he shook his head.

'He was my fiancé,' she whispered. 'We were to have been married in May. But he stayed with the Captain – Captain Smith.'

Salaman gasped. 'Your fiancé!' he said, 'but the *Titanic* went down sixty-six years ago!'

Fiona nodded and he saw a tear squeeze from the corner of her eyes and form a rivulet on her cheek.

'Sixty-six years ago tonight,' she said.

'In exactly two hours from now when we reach that fateful position at forty-one degrees, forty-six minutes north and fifty degrees, fourteen minutes west.'

Her voice had changed now, it sounded like a muted bell, chiming from some faraway place. Salaman took her in his arms as if acting out some dream that had overwhelmed him and he kissed her eyes and her lips and her cold as marble forehead.

'I had a premonition of the disaster,' she whispered, kissing him softly. 'I swore to him that if he were lost at sea I would never give myself to another. He laughed and said that if I did, *ever,* on an anniversary of his death – should it occur – he would return and claim me as his bride. A young lover's foolish tryst – but made with such conviction – such passion – such absolute certainty.'

Salaman felt her body stir against him and he held her closer. He understood now. He was an instrument of fate and nothing in heaven and earth could alter the inexorable roll of events that must happen now. He should have been terrified but instead he was elated, his body tingled with desire and compassion and he covered her face with wild, urgent kisses.

For two hours their passion rose and fell like the dark ocean outside but he never tired, he grew stronger and she grew weaker, their bodies fused and arched until she felt like parchment and dust in his hands.

And then, for a brief moment, the moon scudded from behind a cloud, illuminating the darkened cabin and he saw the old, wrinkled body cradled in his arms with its ancient face and sparse white hair, the matchstick limbs spread uselessly on the sheets. The sea rose in a great roar although there was no storm and spray lashed the porthole in a frenzy. The ship rolled deeply, hung in the roll and then righted itself.

A terrible stench pervaded the cabin, a smell of cloying hideousness. A smell dredged up from the bowels of the ocean. The cabin door suddenly swung open, clattering against the panelled wall and a blast of cold air and icy spray swept into the cabin.

Salaman turned and looked towards the doorway, beyond fear now, but frozen in awe at what he saw standing there.

It was the form of a man, encrusted with barnacles and festooned with seaweed that hung from every part of him, obscuring features. Sea water oozed from his feet, spreading a dark strain on the carpet. Under the slime and the dense vegetation it was just possible to make out the faded insignia of a junior officer's uniform. The creature raised its arm – slowly – painfully – and beckoned. The old lady on the bunk, bent and frail, staggered to her feet and moved towards him, her old eyes shining, her lips moving in silent endearments.

Salaman turned away as they embraced and didn't look up again until he heard the cabin door close with a soft click.

When he raised his head the moon had escaped from the clouds and light flooded the cabin.

Outside the sea was calm and thousands of stars embroidered the purple of the sky right down to the edge of the horizon.

Gordon Meyer

THE STRAIT

THE NEWLY ARRIVED OFFICER left the Captain's cabin realizing the other man thought him a fraud, going back to sea after so many years; and accepted him less as his Fourth or Spare Officer than as a friend of the owners. And not liking it.

Yet had the Captain ever discarded, even temporarily, the notion of men having peculiar reasons for doing peculiar things in favour of the suggestion of their doing them sometimes for no reason?

He turned the corner by the little dining-saloon, and was ambushed from the pantry. Yubo, the steward long exiled from Yugoslavia (the Fourth Officer already knew this) led the way to the cabin. He took the newcomer's heavy portfolio, and its owner's eyes did not leave it once.

Immediately he was alone, the Spare Officer shot the door bolt. He unlocked the portfolio, glanced unemotionally at the contents, then, opening his jacket, unfastened his belt, and slipped off a holstered Brazilian copy of a short-barrelled .38 Smith and Wesson. He added the revolver to the contents of the portfolio, which he relocked and put at the bottom of one of the two clothes cupboards. He locked the cupboard door, tested it, slid the key carefully into his trouser ticket pocket, then noticed a second cupboard.

He took the key from the second cupboard, and made quite sure it did not fit the first.

Outside again, he hesitated, wanting to lock the door, aware he was under observation from the pantry – traditional news channel to the crew – and was relieved to hear the old refugee's heavily accented Spanish. 'Better lock it, sir, while we're in port.'

Of course the ship was full of longshoremen, stevedores and less explicable odds and ends of dock life, who slipped quietly aboard busy ships, to be found later in forbidden spaces.

He climbed the stairway terminating outside the Captain's cabin, and made his way through the chart-room to the enclosed bridge. His business was to discover what the Captain had called the new extent of his ignorance. But as soon as he looked through the wide plate glass sheets, he forgot about this. He felt he had picked up something laid down long ago.

They lay all round, and the complications of their masts and derricks appeared to him like those of a wood half-destroyed by shellfire; the meshwork of their standing and running riggings a huge plan of lines of force. In a holder on the forward bulkhead he found a pair of binoculars, and began reading off the names: *Salamanca, Cabo de Hornos, Rio Quinto, Vera Cruz, Cuba Maru, Official del Mar de Landa, Santa Fé*; and, made fast at right angles to the ship he had just joined, *Ithaca Island*. Next to these titles hung, like huge punctuation marks, iron claws weighing thousands of pounds.

They were grey and white, black and rust. Thick ropes of white water sluiced out of their sides, and through their long windpipes deep discoloured breaths floated off somewhere on that sodden air. Like captive princes, new arrivals were led in by long ropes, to be manacled unwillingly to their places of detention. They were prodded all the way by small, dirty insignificant things, from under whose counters water poured in long powerful horizontal streams, as after crashing from a height into a swift narrow river. More restraints were placed on them until their dignity, which lay in movement, was broken, and they resembled outsize Gullivers tied by minute Lilliputians.

Over all this lay a grey mist. Behind that the hidden capital. But sometimes twin towers or a cupola emerged just as the wind might blow colder; only almost immediately to withdraw and disappear.

This scene the man in the wheelhouse took in as one who reads poetry he does not quite understand, or in a language he has forgotten. Again he scrutinized the names, now with painful awareness they no longer struck inside him the theme-notes once learned so intimately – not even *Cabo de Hornos*. But yes, one sounded now, faint, far off, certainly long ago: *Ithaca Island*. Ithaca the Precipitous. There arose in him a not altogether exhausted vision; the secretive harbour (that careful turn to port) – oh, islands of goats, ravens, pomegranates, nightingales; where in summer each olive tree became an oasis in the aroma of slow-baking grasses, and embraces tasted of retzina and oil. . . .

One more of Europe's seductive, reproachful disguises.

Were he in Europe again, would he do what he was now intending to do? In Europe were shame and wrath – Camus had said it in a Brazilian story. The officer well understood the thought behind that: the wrath, in fact, that these two emotions found little or no field for action in this other continent. But to him, in the given context, it was merely one continent's exasperated criticism of another. Frustration at the impossibility of imposing its own concepts. After many winterless years in South America he recognized it as no more than saying: in Europe they drink tea, in South America, *maté*. Or making some other purely physical commonplace distinction. Would Europeans care to think of it that way? As originators of such judgements would they care to investigate *why* they needed so much shame and wrath?

He had done things here which in Europe (not everywhere in Europe) would arouse shame and wrath, or manifestations of them. The variation of concepts with latitude and longitude made the fact of ideological warfare for a moment intelligible.

Mere translated words could not carry over rootedly different concepts from one race to another. They often widened failures to understand. One's task was to rethink. That done, one found oneself divorced from one's original concepts, and exile thenceforth only a physical matter.

No, his present purpose created in him neither shame nor wrath. Perhaps an obscure exhilaration. In Europe had that exhilaration drained away, leaving a sediment that eventually oxidised the soul? Rust of old tastes and creeds. What wearied was the repetition. So the recurrent ache to return must be animal then....

He began to examine the instruments. They had the vague familiarity of relations not seen since youth: radar, indispensable in *Sea Otter's* proposed latitudes; gyroscope compass with two repeaters, one on each wing of the bridge; inclinometer, automatic pilot, and so on. As for *Sea Otter* herself: just over 1,000 tons registered nett, a mere 307 feet overall, a destroyer's length. She would be lively in the so-called Pacific.

She had been built some ten years ago by the Norwegians. That gave him confidence. He found her a pretty little ship, the officers' and crew's quarters pleasant and snug. Yet the Captain in their first conversation had shown the resentful conviction that Europeans built their ships to last ten years, with the intention of selling them thereafter to South American republics.

It was the intercontinental criticism in reverse. He had distinctly felt the Captain position him in the area of this criticism: he was

European, therefore responsible. Life in exile meant the worst of both worlds.

He had not found it possible to persuade the Captain that there might be another view of the matter, nor of various others on which the Captain had expressed his firm conclusions, punctuating these with the fall of his fist on his cabin desk.

The Captain, alone in his cabin, was in turn thinking of the new arrival. He sat at his desk in blue cotton shirt and trousers, a shortish man, wiry, with small head, well over sixty, sucking *maté* through a *bombilla* with a gold mouthpiece.

The thick white hair was parted boyishly to each side; at the forward end of the parting, over the forehead, the hair lifted, forming what the crew called his bow-wave. His very dark brown eyes sometimes glistened with mischief, and sometimes were moody and bitter, as when they had fixed on the new officer's gold watch. Thus, in one moment flashed out an endearing modesty as he confessed his shame at taking *maté* in front of the owners; and in the next his face would contract, darken as he levelled his hates at Europe, and certain countries in particular. The Spare Officer's was one of these.

He took another pull at the *bombilla*, his eyes on the defect list his First Officer had brought, his mind for a moment on the men under him. Schiuma, his First, was Argentine like himself – thank God. Villegas, the Second, a Spaniard, product of the Bilbao navigation school, would never get anywhere; had not the thrust of an Argentine. Baez, the Third, Paraguayan, had studied in the Argentine naval school, and it showed. As for Paraguay, like Uruguay, it was little more than an Argentine province.

His major-domo was a Canary Islander, the cook a Pole, his assistant Chinese, the steward Yugoslav, and all four, as he knew, had stowed away in ships bound for the Rio de la Plata, to enter Buenos Aires without papers. Men washed up with Europe. And how not, after two mass exterminations? His were good men, peaceful, not drunkards, glad of a steady job – all united by the flag of Panama. The Chief Engineer, also Argentine, was even religious.

Another advantage of the Panama flag, besides that of avoiding home taxes, was the privilege of picking one's crews without interference of the trouble-making syndicates. On the other hand, the owners could suddenly present him with a species of unclassifiable marine life: an English Spare Officer who had not been to sea since the age of Naupa, and would not have been able to join but for friendship with the owners.

He sucked reflectively at the *bombilla*: an 8,000-mile voyage should give occasions for turning that to account. For example, had the *Inglés* seen the captured English regimental flags in the church in Reconquista Street?

In his mind the list of forthcoming issues began to form. He rang his bell, had the steward send him the First. A deep-chested, tough-looking man with a wiry clump of ginger hair appeared in the doorway. 'Schiuma, the *Inglés* will be more of a passenger than watch-keeping officer. Put him in your watch, then we'll have a new face for lunch.'

'Very good, sir.'

'And some different conversation, Schiuma.'

'Yes, sir.' It was impossible to tell what the First was thinking; he just looked at his captain with a steady expressionless gaze.

'And when he's off watch, get him translating the instruction manuals for the radar, the Sperry gyroscope and the Kidder fire extinguisher system.'

'Yes, sir.'

'And anything else you can think of.'

The following afternoon, when no more frozen meat could be loaded into her forward refrigerator hold, and a thin drizzle was falling, *Sea Otter*, seeming to tire of it all, slipped her lines and departed.

Dismissing her tug with a noisy salute, she gained open water while the bos'n's party was still banging home the hatch clamps. She steered to within a degree or two of due south and, without helmsman, assisted by a northerly breeze and moderate phosphorescent sea, held to that course through the first night.

At sunrise the Spare Officer, sharing the morning watch with the First, took bearings. The ship was due east of Miramar, distance by radar twelve miles. Course was altered to 220 degrees. Now she rode comfortably into a head sea, headed for what was virtually the most easterly point of Patagonia.

The Spare Officer, before the beginning of the voyage, had learned the peculiarities of the Southern Ocean: that below the thirty-fifth parallel winds become more westerly, increasing with each mile a ship steams south, reaching their greatest force in winter. It was now mid-winter. They were leaving the quiet area of the ocean for that of cyclones, icebergs, loose ice. He balanced once more these hazards against another characteristic of the region: its utter loneliness.

He replaced the compass cover, looked seaward and caught his breath again at the light. In this incredible luminosity the *Panzerschiff Graf Spree* had sighted at sunrise the masts of three warships at over nineteen miles. And within eight minutes had, unfortunately for her, identified erroneously two of her opponents as destroyers. The same light had shone on Sturdee's pursuit of von Spee's cruisers with his own battle-cruisers *Invincible* and *Inflexible*, with their eight twelve-inch guns and twenty-five knots the only unchallengeable ships in the Southern Ocean. But the farther south *Sea Otter* steamed, the heavier grew the sensation of lifelessness, cold desolation and waste.

The table presided over by the Captain was attended, on his left side, by the Chief Engineer Officer and the First; on his right, by the Spare Officer and the Chilean Pilot. The talk at the first meal had been of the trivia of sailors' lives: freights, rates of pay, the incompetence and laziness of shore electricians, mechanics and engineers. When at one moment attention centred on utilising the space above *Sea Otter's* refrigerator holds and below hatches, the Spare Officer intervened with a question: how many tons of cargo could be carried there? About one hundred, the First told him, and the Captain looked at the Spare with a little surprise.

The Spare was generally unable to observe the person on whom so much was to depend for a few days, except on the rare occasions on which the Pilot spoke, for they sat next to each other. Then he saw a short, corpulent man with dark hair, moustache and eyes, and a face resembling, he thought, a large fruit, slowly rotting. The split was his smile. A pair of enormous heavy-folding eyelids would collapse from time to time over the eyes like theatre curtains, and it seemed nothing would ever raise them. It was to be hoped they would not be in that position while he was piloting the ship through the Strait. The others had the impression the Pilot was fighting against sleep; or even perhaps some drug. He hardly ever spoke without being spoken to, and then allowed himself only a word or two in a high feminine voice. With all this, and the special diet he commanded, to the amused disgust of the Captain who could eat anything, the Pilot seemed to convey that in his isolation he was destined for higher things than a seat at the dining-table of a small freighter he would have to pilot through one of the bleakest, coldest, most dangerous regions on the planet.

The Captain tolerated him; he did not like Chileans. Too nationalistic. (His own nation was in violent frontier dispute with the Pilot's.) Distastefully he watched the other man come to life, the conversation turning to copper. That great fruit of a head lifting from the plate: 'Yes (wagging a fat finger while the sleepy grin spilled over the rest of his large face), but it has to be *Chilean* copper!' The Captain did not like pilots in general. Moreover he did not need one down here; the Patagonian and Fuegian channels were to him as the streets round another man's house. He smiled his not altogether unpleasant, cynical smile, watching the Pilot following dutifully his steak, green salad and saccharine path.

'And you shouldn't drink, I suppose,' the Spare said by way of an overture.

'There are *many* things,' the other answered lethargically, the eyes uncovering, shooting at the Spare for much less than a second, 'that I shouldn't do.'

'Anyway, those are old topics in this ship.' The Captain had spread his elbows on the table as if a pleasant dish had been put there. The much-washed blue drill shirt, the wavy white hair, the spent face gave him the faded handsomeness of an ex-actor who is having more successes offstage than he had on. 'Let's concentrate on what really interests us.'

He looked down the table at the Spare; the latter looked back, waiting.

The Captain was smiling again; it had started like that last time. The Spare found that the smile coming and going on that hard face was compounded of cruelty and pleasantness; and he remembered the earlier exchanges. It was a pity. He had come to a certain affection for the Captain's country, spoke its language perfectly, knew its literature, history, music; had no friends of his own race there, but in the other race had had everything: friends, enemies, lovers, wives – the lot. What the Captain's compatriots enjoyed he enjoyed, what they suffered he suffered. Yet in an age in which people stuck labels on each other at first sight because it saved the pain of thought he could not ticket his distinctions. He knew what was coming; so did the others.

'Now tell us, Fourth (the mouth smiling, the eyes not), you say you're English; at least that's what it says on your *cédula*.'

'Yes, Captain.'

'But you also said (even the way a man's tongue went over his teeth could carry the theme) that you had Scottish blood in you.'

'That's right.' Was this the point of the compass from which the assault would come?

'Tell us now (the friendly glance raked in the support of the others); all those stories about the meanness of the Scots, are they true?'

'Captain, Scotland is where they invent them. . . .' Only the others began to laugh. 'In Aberdeen. . . .'

'And another thing; why do you have an Irish first name?' The Captain neglected marginal prey as a cheetah does.

'My mother is part Irish.'

'Well, what race *are* you?'

One could even wonder, thought the other. 'English.'

'Exactly. All of you are English.'

He paused; it was for the Spare to say, what do you mean? He did.

'What I say; you're *all* English. Why do Scotland and Wales indulge themselves in the caprice of calling themselves countries?'

'They are.'

'*Were*. Now they're provinces.'

The Captain was the only one in the saloon who did not notice his tone was changing.

'They even have their own languages, Captain.'

'That's nothing. Can they decide their own future?' He seemed to sense the other's impoverished political education.

'They've decided it; by becoming part of the United Kingdom; they're represented in Parliament.'

There was a perceptible jerk as the Captain selected top gear. 'Come, come, they have a few representatives, but not enough to change their destiny. We know far more about countries like yours than you know about ours. They're provinces, like Córdoba. . . .'

'No. . . .'

'San Juan, Mendoza. The other business is all theatre.'

The Englishman had not for a long time felt particularly English. But perhaps it was because there had been no need. For years what had ached in him was Europe. Now suddenly he was driven into areas long ago vacated. Ah, if he had never left them he would have kept his sense of humour now, as anyone intelligent, fresh out from

England, would have done. He suddenly found himself tied with the ropes of his own blood.

The Captain was taking his triumph silently. Everyone was waiting for the other man.

'Well, you must think of it as part of the English paradox, Captain.'

No remark of the Spare made the Captain pause. 'I've been in London many times. I served in the Flota Argentina seventeen years. London has the filthiest docks I ever saw.'

Still the ambiguous smile accompanying the knife-work. The Spare tried to make this one glance off; none of the others, he noticed, had said one word; they did not approve.

'What were your other impressions of London, Captain?' He kept his voice level, ignorant that it was this that provided the challenge.

'Neither the hotels nor the houses had so much as one bidet! How can you keep clean, *mi querido señor*, if you don't have the proper sanitation?'

The triumphant backlash sent the laughter ricocheting round the entire table, which shook to the fall of the fist. 'Well, gentlemen. . . .' The fist opened, flattened on the cloth, everybody rose; one trembling.

Of course, one had to expect it, if one did not shelter behind the English palisades. It was endurable also because he was going to need the Captain.

During the middle watch, Cabo Blanco light was raised. By dawn the cape had been left astern. In sight a long, low coast exhibiting total absence of humanity. A stiff gale blew from the west in a clear sky.

The shoreline rose; soon the tiny settlement could be made out, crouching under the long, low bluff, away from the westerlies tearing their passage from the cordilleras across the Patagonian wastes. The Captain came up to the bridge, had the ship stand on until she bore south-west from Puerto Deseado. It was about eight-thirty when she altered course and entered the river. The cold made the heads of the fo'c'sle party ache.

The Captain's ship-handling, the Spare admitted, was first class. Clearing the narrow, he positioned the ship expertly, letting go the off-shore anchor, to take her in stern first alongside a couple of hundred feet of badly thrown together stone and concrete under the name of the National Mole. Only the longshoreman spoiled it, dropping most of the heaving lines, then arguing as to which bollard to make fast to, as if to emphasise they had a choice. Yes, one had to admit it; a perfect manoeuvre.

The ship now quiet, the crew looked out on a port of brief call for sailors and explorers. A place of cloudy green water and desolate shingles. Otherwise, simply not to be known.

Soon *Sea Otter's* after hold was filling with the small sheep carcasses from the local *frigorifico*. Each fell with a dull wooden sound as of empty boxes, and it seemed they must crack. The men worked well in the intense cold, and with good will.

It was after lunch that the Spare Officer felt the first symptoms: an inexplicable malaise, racking pains in the legs, fever and desire to vomit. He went ashore, to breathe what he hoped would be a more healthy air than that of the ship, where, just outside his cabin, paint, oil, food and hot engine exhausts had concentrated a nauseous mixture.

He walked slowly past the edge of the ink-blot of civilization, wondering at his strange weakness. With difficulty he reached the top of a low height, and collapsed. For a time he lay full length on the ground. When, coming to again, he realized the extent of his feebleness, he gave way for a moment to panic. He struggled back to the ship, got on his bunk, and in a few minutes was vomiting up what seemed to be his very soul. Some time later he was woken by loud bangings on the door.

It was Baez, the Third. 'The Captain says would you translate these. Some corrections to the Sailing Directions.' He stared at the man on the bunk. 'What's the matter? You're almost yellow.'

The Spare struggled into a sitting position. 'Just a touch of seasickness.'

Baez regarded him sceptically. 'We've been in port all day, and haven't had any dirty weather yet.' He disappeared, and in a few minutes had returned. 'Captain says you must go ashore and see the doctor.'

'But I'm all right.'

'Maybe, but we'll see what the doctor says. This is your last chance to see one. I've ordered transport from the agent.'

The lorry racketed through the dirt streets lined with flat-roofed one-storey buildings. 'I don't know whether we'll catch him; it's Saturday.' The Spare looked at one of the rough pleasant men who was making his country out of the rounding wastes, and with little help from the capital, which kept its stranglehold on the rest of the republic.

'If we miss him it doesn't matter, I'll get something from a chemist.'

The doctor was just leaving; the examination was brief. 'Really I need analyses, but you've probably got a touch of hepatitis; that means you should be in bed for two months.'

The Spare Officer stared, managing to say nothing.

'And with special diet, and above all, no movement and no cold.'

It was unnecessary to add that these conditions could not be fulfulled in a ship, especially where *Sea Otter* was going.

'You'd better explain to the Captain, meanwhile I'll prescribe something.' He was in a hurry.

At the chemist's the Spare also brought a bottle of pills for kidney trouble. He entered the Captain's cabin.

'Well?'

'Dose of kidney trouble, Captain; he's given me some pills.' He held the bottle up. 'Should be all right in two or three days.'

The Captain studied the other man a moment. 'Your colour's very bad. There's no doctor until Valparaiso. I don't want sick men in my ship.'

'I'm already feeling better.' He was trembling. The Captain could put him ashore, to be flown back to Buenos Aires. The next few seconds took a long time to pass.

'Well, we sail tomorrow morning as soon as I have customs clearance.'

Back in his cabin, the Spare locked the door. He looked for a moment out of the port at the vast panorama, the brilliant lowering sun, the wild exuberant clarity; then got on his bunk, yielding more with relief than weakness. He fixed his eyes on the dirty rectangle of thick glass, until the passing, repassing and hovering gulls were slowly stained orange in the setting sun, and swore that nothing would stop him.

Soon strange stars flickered over the polar horizons, and seabirds ghosted by in the dusk. The strange ambiguous peace of the empty southern nights spread over everything. Ambiguous because it was the peace such as a coma gave.

To the Spare's relief, the day dawned less cold. Sky partly concealed by films of light cloud, wind still westerly, but weaker. The Captain, since rising, had been impatiently awaiting the Customs Officer, and gave the order to single up before the latter was fairly off the ship.

Clearing Penguin Island, *Sea Otter* stood out to sea until a direct course could be laid for Cape Virgins, some 320 miles south-west.

The Spare went up to the chartroom to attend to the translations; but used most of his time persuading the Second to talk about himself. Villegas, a short thick-set man with a moustache, was only too pleased. Without company on his long watches, he was morose and melancholy. He had, it emerged, finished the naval school in Bilbao in 1938, then served in the fruit trade – Mediterranean, Canaries, Channel – and subsequently in the Argentine oil-tanker fleet for five years.

'And you left because . . .'

'Because the Argentines would not recognize my title.' It had the swiftness of a reply often made.

'And you find opportunities under the Panama flag?'

At that, Villegas turned away. With bitter humour he repeated it to the man at the wheel. The two of them shared the sour joke before Villegas came back to the Spare. They resumed their staring at the glaring bow-wave. 'There are no chances; this is the only ship the company owns. Why is that? You know the owners.'

The Spare turned this away with a joke, then asked the other how well he knew the channels.

The Second took his eye off the fo'c'sle where the deck party was scraping hatch covers. 'Like the back of my hand,' he said, showing it. He looked forward again. 'All those cold empty channels. And in Valparaiso, after all that desolation, we only anchor, to let the Pilot off. It always reminds me of the Mediterranean: the houses climbing the hills, the trees, the sun, the colours. And then I calculate that the distance of this voyage in another direction would take in Santos, Rio, Lisboa, Cadiz, Barcelona, Genoa, Naples. . . .'

No need to finish. In the ensuing silence two continents fought another round for the final ownership of two souls.

'To think we might have passed each other in the street in Bilbao.'

Villegas turned his head quickly towards the other man; it was his turn to request information.

'I had just spent six years at boarding school,' answered the Spare. 'I had learned a great deal about very little, and my instinct clearly told me I was being slowly fitted out for everything except life.'

To the First Officer, too, the Spare's continual questioning about the Strait appeared a natural enough way of passing the tedious hours.

In the dark part of the morning watch, only when they entered the chart-room together, or in the momentary glow of their cigarettes, could Schiuma and the Spare see each other's faces. Then Schiuma saw a long-boned dark face, with dark eyes neither devious nor frank – a face he would not have known could be an Englishman's.

'Yes,' he said, 'navigation *is* dangerous.'

The other man waited.

'The weather's always terrible, they haven't finished surveying yet, and the aids are poor: the lights are only powered by gas, in tanks. Sometimes it runs out. The buoys are small, and in the dirty weather we always have it's sometimes difficult to see them, and in any case they are always being dragged by the terrific currents and gales.'

'Anchorages, what are they like?'

'Few and far between. But we won't be anchoring.'

He was vaguely surprised when the other man persisted.

'Well, the holding ground is poor, for one thing. The bottom is uneven or consists of small stones and gravel. Then the currents, as I was saying. Those anchorages look safe because they appear to be landlocked, but there isn't one without a gully or cliff from which the williwaws rebound.'

'Yes, I've heard of those.' The Spare noticed the other's amusement, and in the growing light saw it was shared by the man at the wheel. 'Is there much room to manoeuvre?'

'In many parts none.'

'But there's deep water.'

'Thirty to forty fathoms. In the western part of the Strait the rise is over forty feet.'

The First stared through the binoculars for a long moment before speaking again. 'Cape Virgins. Cape of the Eleven Thousand Virgins, as Magellan named it on the holy day he found the Strait. That's where we go in.'

Approaching the Cape, *Sea Otter* was struck by a sudden furious westerly gale. This and the heavy sea it raised, in what was to the Spare an unbelievably short time, she took squarely on the beam. She stood on, however, until the entrance could be made on a westerly course. It was a relief to everyone when the moment came.

At the entrance a short spiteful green sea was charging out, but preferable to the beam sea. The Captain prophesied foul weather on the Pacific side. He turned to the First. 'Have you given him a run-down on the Strait?'

'Yes, and he had a surprising number of questions.'

The Captain turned, looked at the Spare. 'Nothing to it when you know it. Like driving a car; you've got to keep a good look-out, and know your landmarks. That one over there should have a name familiar to you.'

The Spare trained the glasses on a tongue of sand and shingle running for a few miles south-west of the Cape.

'Dungeness. Two miles north of the light is the hull of the English steamer *Hungost*, and a quarter-mile north-west of that is the English frigate *Innes*.'

The Captain was never so instructional as when recounting English disasters, thought the Spare. But the Strait made its strongest propaganda in its wrecks.

In the Captain's eyes there was a glitter as he surreptitiously recorded his contempt of the Pilot's appearance. *Sea Otter* now in the Strait, the Pilot had come into his own: in plum-covered velvet corduroys, fur-collared gaberdine wind-cheater, cloth cap and his usual black suede shoes. Except for the shoes, thought the Captain, he could have been going racing. Equipped with binoculars, the fat Chilean oscillated between bridge and chartroom in a nimbus of self-importance, taking the ship through the second Narrows. Pilots on this passage, the Captain reminded himself, were obligatory.

His annoyance increased on his finding his lunch table attended only by the First and his Chief Engineer. It was almost a silent meal, for the Spare was again prostrate in his bunk, wishing for the first time that it was sea-sickness. But there was nothing to produce that, and up on the bridge the Pilot was now taking the ship between Magdalena and Quartermaster Islands in perfect sunny weather.

The Captain called the steward. 'Tell the Spare Officer I would like to see his face for supper.'

Then, between one moment and the next, the ship was in one of those terrific squalls which could blow a sailing ship, even without sail on, over on her beam ends. The sea was whipped into solid fury, whole sheets of water blowing over the side as the wind slammed down the mountains. In an hour it was over; the Spare with difficulty roused himself for his watch.

The ship was beginning the long approach to the southern-most point of the South American continent. As dusk came on, the mountain appeared spread across the line of advance, black or piebald. A meeting place, he thought, for the extremes of beauty and ugliness; both epithets were valid for this stark region. As the light was drained off, the mountains became terrifying. The ship was doubling Cape Froward, and the cross on its black summit did nothing to redeem the sterile gloom. The Pilot made the big alteration to 298 degrees, to take the ship up to the north-west. Fine on the starboard bow appeared Cape Holland, conical and black in the eclipsing daylight. But later, along the starboard hand, the piebald crests blazed fantastically in a supranormal, almost sickening moonlight.

Daylight revealed something altogether different: *Sea Otter* folded away among the mountains as though in the pages of a half-shut book. The word 'rock' had taken on a new, deeper significance. The phrase 'a wall of rock' lost its acquired commonplaceness, to take up again something of its ancient horror, because in those terrifying fjords, through which they were winding for 600 miles, the men actually *felt* the wall. Too near, too high, relieved by nothing, it became for them the physical frontier of the universe.

Sea Otter's speed never slackened, she was now steaming almost due north in a narrow channel past Cutler Island, an islet of some 250 feet in height. The surrounding heights were all snow covered. Forest, beginning at the waterline, rose to about a third of the height of the small mountains. There was always some part of the sky clear, but sunrise had not been observable, and each new entrance to be navigated was curtained in mist or cloud.

Everything being momentarily well under control, the Pilot went below to lunch in the saloon. He was alone there when the Spare Officer entered.

The two men greeted each other. None of the others had entered; in a quick low voice the Spare said, 'We're all right, aren't we?'

The Pilot acknowledged this in a way typical of him, with a profound operative reverence, bowing low, sweeping his hand across the body, so that the other man looked for the wide-brimmed cocked and plumed hat. He supposed this sort of theatre resolved in the Pilot some obscure insincerity – unless it was intended as symbolic of their curious and provisional relationship.

At lunch time the Chilean disseminated an air of profound and secret importance; then at one moment, seeing a spectacular line of snow-covered heights through the ports, squeaked, '*¡Linda la nievecita!*' and the Spare realized he was nervous and excited.

The Captain entered the saloon. 'Good Mor Ning!' He addressed the Spare as though the others were not there.

The Spare, recognizing the other's mock-modest reference to his interest in learning English, replied in his own tongue. Everyone took his place, feeling the atmosphere flowing off the two men as they came again into each other's presence.

Yubo the steward put the Captain's special Swiss cheese before him; the Captain ate with relish as the others took their soup. He took no liquids with his meals, it was that which seemed to hone the edge of his barbs.

When he turned to the Spare, as everyone knew he would, lights were flashing on and off in his eyes. 'I'll bet you what you like we'll have the Malvinas within three years. And you know why?'

'No, Captain. You'll take them?'

'The English will sell them to us.' Four, five, six times his hard finger-tips hit the table. 'They'll take a good price.' In this last sentence was the new indictment.

'Every transaction has a buyer for the seller, Captain.'

'The thing is, we don't want your Falkland Islands.' His face was triumphant with the surprise he knew he had caused.

'Oh, surely. . . .' The Spare was laughing.

'No, you're wrong!' The cutlery jumped as the fist hit the table. The others did not intervene; they waited.

'Then why does your government claim them every year?'

'To maintain the right to claim, and it keeps the people's attention off other things. What do we want the Malvinas for?'

'Every year the wool sells for I don't know how many millions sterling. Wouldn't that pay a few bills?' He had been unable to prevent the sly tone entering his voice.

'What's that to our total production?' The contemptuous reply shot out with the finality of a degree. Suddenly the speaker looked at the Spare with one of his most charming smiles. The latter recognized the generosity a victor considered he could show. Yet it was impossible not to return the smile.

'You see (the Captain beckoned to the steward, pointed to the dish), I'm a man who likes to get to the bottom of things. And I intend going on! So you'd better arm yourself with patience for the rest of the voyage. Forty-five days, my friend.' He took a huge second helping of lentil stew, which in the Spare's present state turned his stomach. Indeed, the few mouthfuls he took were sickening. He no longer touched wine; never stood if there was a chance of sitting, and felt apathetic and irritable. A small ship resembled a monastery: its miniature hierarchy fed off the day's trivial departures from established order; and his had been observed.

'Why don't you eat, man? Look at me, I eat anything!' The Captain suited the action to the word. The Spare looked elsewhere, found the other three doing the same. 'Your colour's worse. There's something I don't understand. How could the doctor not have examined your eyes? For me you've got hepatitis.' He turned to the steward. 'Put the Fourth Officer on the same diet as the Pilot. And you (turning back to the Spare), you'd better take your night watches below. We don't really need you.'

The other man was too far gone to refuse the contemptuous kindness.

'But why the hell didn't you go ashore in Puerto Deseado?' The Captain, Pilot, Chief Engineer had gone. Schiuma was finishing off a litre of red wine in huge gulps. The question was sharp, not idle; he might have been interrogating a seaman. The Spare was forced to meet his inquiring gaze. He took refuge in a gesture of resignation, and with relief saw the incisiveness fade before other thoughts.

'Don't mind the Captain (his look was neither condolatory nor callous); he says whatever he likes and sometimes it's rougher than we want it, we're all set to tell him he's a *viejo de mierda*. He's all right.'

'Of course he'd retired, hadn't he? And then couldn't make out ashore.' Immediately he regretted having revealed his knowledge.

The First said sharply: 'You knew that, then?'

The Spare did not answer. Schiuma wiped his mouth vigorously, and they left the saloon. The Spare managed to time his collapse with the moment of gaining his bunk.

It must be that chair at the head of the table, he thought. It imposed on the Captain a pattern of judgement and authenticity. It had arms, and ordained the placing of men at his right and his left. Furthermore, owing to the fore-and-aft slope of the saloon deck (the table being in that plane), the chair's occupant was higher than the others. To defeat delusions of chairmanship, a person of perfect equilibrium would be needed: a sort of moderator, or someone of a Socratic turn of mind, who would let the argument blow where it listed instead of forcing a lot of boring conclusions. Unfortunately, as the ship had begun knocking off the longitudes and now the latitudes, that fist had crashed ever harder on the table.

He fell asleep congratulating himself that for once he had stopped himself from saying what he thought.

'That's your station.' The Pilot made a last adjustment to the knob, and sat back from the wireless in the officers' saloon. 'The news comes on in fifteen minutes.'

He rose, ambled slowly, portentously out, leaving the Spare Officer alone.

He settled back in his chair, which could not be seen from the door. He felt feverish, but the chair was comfortable, and he had to concentrate. He listened carefully to the Chilean International News bulletins, then the home news, the weather reports, and finally the police reports. It was when he was copying down the numbers of reported stolen cars that the First Officer came quietly into the saloon, and stood watching him.

'You think they'll find the cars down here?'

The Spare's notebook shut; he looked up. 'Playing about with numbers; an old habit. I have systems for remembering them.'

'Are you coming to do the four till eight with me? Don't if you're not feeling up to it.'

By the time they were on the bridge, the weather had deteriorated; sunlight broke through for minutes at a time. Frequent rainbows ended the rain squalls, and violent gales ricochetted off the mountains. Steadily the peaks repeated themselves, sliding in and out of each other.

Navigation was now done on Chilean charts which were of very large scale, but with little or no detail. On these the ship negotiated the six-mile-long Guia Narrows, between Hanover and Chatham Islands. It required vigilance; there was an eight-knot current running. Steadily the peaks grew in size and splendour, but none on board had seen a more primeval, inhuman landscape.

The only relief was the untidy green and yellow forest – mostly Antarctic beech, so thick that the ground was invisible – covering the lower parts of the islands. Above the forest-line the water foamed white down into the trees. Nevertheless, the last hours of daylight were indescribably gloomy; huge black cloud masses convulsed slowly about the heights, which when visible were black or piebald. Steely water, tasteless air, and always the intense penetrating cold. Every perceptible phenomenon, and there were many, insisted on desolation. True, the charts named every island, islet, bay, point, summit, but these were as abstract as the parallax tables; were nothing but the first phrases of a feeble rejoinder which would never be completed. For humanity to establish itself here, the Spare thought, it would have to be equipped as for another planet.

He went into the chart-room alone, opened the long drawer, selected the chart covering the most critical part of the whole Strait; and here he was surprised by the Captain.

'What are you looking at English Narrows for? We don't need that chart until tomorrow.'

The Spare looked up, smiling: 'Just interest. More dramatic part of the trip, isn't it?'

Several times the Captain nodded: he was studying the Spare.

'Very narrow,' said the Spare.

'At one part, two hundred yards.' His professional interest deflected his other thoughts. 'That's not so much trouble, though. The chief worry is the S-bend.'

'Where there's a special procedure for going through.'

'Which you've studied, I hope.'

'Yes, Captain, I've studied it.' He put the chart back in the drawer as the Pilot entered. 'So we won't be going through tonight,' the Spare said loudly.

'We go through only in slack water and daylight.'

'Because of the tides.'

'At springs they're very strong; also the channel is very winding. Isn't that so, Pilot?'

With mock drama the Pilot said: 'Very dangerous!'

The Captain did not notice it, he was watching the Spare curiously, because in the other's face showed something he could not at first quite identify. He went through into the wheelhouse, and chatted with the First; suddenly it occurred to him that it was relief. He went below.

The Spare went into the wheelhouse and stood beside Schiuma.

'The procedure for vessels approaching English Narrows is always observed?'

'Always. A vessel coming from the north or Pacific side must sound a long blast when she's abreast of Maude Point and Lamaora Island, and can only continue her passage if there's no answer. A ship arriving from this side must do the same when abreast of Nickoll Point and Chinook Island.'

'And if the two arrive at the critical point simultaneously and on opposite courses, the ship from the northward must wait.'

'Correct. The ship from the northward must wait.'

'And they must broadcast.'

'One hour before arriving in the vicinity, every ship must keep radio watch, and transmit every ten minutes her estimated time of passing.'

'Thorough!'

'You'll see why.'

'And what about warships, do they conform?'

'Yes, but instead of sounding their sirens they fire a gun.' Schiuma turned, and went into the chart-room. After hesitating a moment, the Spare Officer followed. He watched the other man at work for a while, and noticed that no course had been laid off after Mason Island, a rocky island with a light.

'Is that where the Captain intends stopping tonight?'

'Yes. About a mile and a half due south of the island. As you see, it's a comparatively wide stretch of water, and curiously enough there's no current.'

He put down the dividers; the Spare picked them up, measured off the run on the latitude scale. 'Be there about six.'

When they returned to the wheelhouse, they talked of other things until the Spare asked permission to go below for a few moments.

He returned to the chart-room, went out through the after door, closing it behind him. At the head of the stairway, at the foot of which was situated the Captain's cabin, he paused, and took from his wallet an envelope.

The Captain, at his desk, his lips to the *bombilla*, hearing the knock, raised only his eyes towards the open door. The Spare was glad to see in them the pleasanter, more mischievous expression; he noticed the eyes go straight to the envelope.

'Come in, come in. What's that, my translations?'

The Spare approached the desk. 'Captain, excuse the way this is done. I'm only the messenger.' He handed over the envelope.

The Captain put down his *maté*; mingled with his habitual wary, distrustful look was something of astonishment. 'You want me to read this now?'

'If you would.'

Ripping open the envelope, the Captain pulled out the single sheet. The Spare Officer watched the expressions passing one after another over the small, half charming, half irritated features, and was not surprised to see that the one repeating itself mostly was irritation. He waited patiently, noticing that the Captain had not shaved, and that the wiry grey stubble insisted on his age more than the hair on his head.

The Captain put down the sheet, smoothed it several times with his hand; he did not pick up his *maté*. 'You had better shut the door.'

The Spare Officer shut the cabin door.

'You know what it says?' The Captain tapped the sheet twice with his fingers.

'I was there when it was composed, Captain.'

'Why don't you sit down?'

'Thank you.'

'You had better tell what it very carefully doesn't say.'

'The owners couldn't take any chances, Captain.'

'Of course I don't have to do this, even if it is signed by the owners.'

'Captain,' the Spare spoke resignedly, openly showing that everything was in the other man's hands, 'this is your ship. It's not for me to tell you you can do what you like.'

A few days ago, in one of their many discussions, the Captain had said: 'In my ship I can do absolutely whatever I like.' The reply that had risen to the Spare's lips was, 'That would make you a pirate.' He was glad at not having released it.

'If it's drugs I won't touch it.'

'Nor would I, Captain.'

'What is it then?'

'Guns and ammunition.'

Only one question could follow this. The Spare Officer named the port.

For a little while the Captain was at a loss; too many questions were forming simultaneously inside him. 'Why couldn't the owners have told me?' was the first that issued from him.

It was said in a level enough voice, but the other man guessed at the resentment behind it. 'Only because it was left to me as the agent for the ultimate receivers, and because I have the money to pay the suppliers, and also because I wasn't sure until this afternoon that delivery would be made.'

This at one stroke multiplied the number of questions the Captain still had to ask; it was getting to be too much for him. The Spare saw he must do all he could to involve the Captain as quickly as possible, and remove the impression of his total ignorance.

'How could you possibly discover such a thing while at sea in my ship?' He switched off the portable stove on which his *maté* kettle had been boiling.

Wanting the other man's goodwill, the Spare accepted that one question must lead to many others. 'Oh, the usual way, Captain. You know.... Passing messages over the commercial radio; all that sort of nonsense.' He skimmed over it rapidly. 'As soon as the shipment is aboard I have to pay, and as you have seen I have to pay you ten thousand dollars if you are agreeable to the whole thing. I'm sure the crew will be glad to get their bonus at the end of the voyage. You've got a damn fine crew, if I may say so.'

'They may talk.'

'The cases will be marked "Electrical Equipment", with the name of the port, and the words "In transit". I think the crew are more interested in keeping their jobs. And, after all, it isn't exactly the first little irregularity the company and this ship will have committed.'

A curious expression had settled on the Captain's face; it had become illumined, the eyes had brightened. A word sprang into the Spare's mind. No, he thought, it would be unfair to call it that. To want more than anything to be able to pay off the mortgage on one's fruit farm, tell the bank to go to hell, and then enjoy undisturbed the rest of a hard life was not greed.

'I can guess where it's for,' the Captain said, to hide his thoughts.

It was also a question; the Spare did not answer it.

'Are you mixed up politically in this?'

'No, Captain, I keep out of politics. I'm just someone my friends knew they can trust. After this trip I go home, I have a wife waiting for me. She's still very attractive.'

The Captain was a man who found a '*gato encerrado*' in everything; that is to say, he always melt a rat. Now there were too many rats for him.

'Crazy.... And you mean to tell me you have all that money with you?'

'Yes.'

The Captain looked at the man in his cabin in a way he had not done yet. 'Cash?'

'Part in cash, part in drafts.'

Something in his tone told the Captain that in this area he had no right to enter further. He just said, 'You really are crazy,' very softly, and the Spanish was highly idiomatic.

The Spare Officer was happy to find at last a point of agreement on their personal matters; he drew up his chair a little, not taking his eyes off the other man's. Time was getting short.

'It *is* a deal, isn't it, Captain? And you'll forgive the way it had to be done?'

The air in the cabin became slightly electrified, because in that moment the Captain, although he had not realized it, was being won over. When he realized, he would resist. Not that there was insufficient inducement, the Spare reflected, his eyes still on the other man's face; but there was that prickly matter: Soza, the Captain, had not been consulted in the first place. That baroque pride had to be assuaged in more ways than one.

As so often, then, it was reduced to a matter of personalities. The pause was very noticeable.

At the end of it the two men were beginning to smile at each other in a way they had never done. Soza said: 'If we don't get caught. . . .'

The Spare breathed deeply. 'At the port everything's fixed, even to dummy bills of lading.'

'And what do they show?'

'Trans-shipment in Buenos Aires.'

With increasing pressure the Captain slowly rubbed his grey stubble. 'Two things could mess it up: dirty weather and a Chilean warship.'

The Spare thought: 'So you still haven't said it?'

'Yes, I believe there are two modern-type destroyers in Punta Arenas.'

The Captain was looking at him; it was just somewhere to put his eyes. A screen had come down over his face; he had retreated behind it, leaving only a meaningless exterior. He was busy with his own calculations.

'We'd have one hour from receiving another ship's first transmission that she's going through.'

'One of the additional beauties of English Narrows!'

A mistake. Not by a joke either would the other allow the thing to be clinched. He endured the gaze of the Captain, who still said nothing. He had recognized the moment in which, with a man like Soza, one generally said the wrong thing. He was capricious, then. And he himself was in that torturing position of needing something from a capricious person. Trying to show that not even his silence was expectation, he looked away, out through the wide ports at the nocturnal granite peaks reeling by in the dusk.

But when he looked back again the Captain was waiting for him. '*Muy bien* . . . only let's hope there are no accidents.'

And the other thought: 'My God, but you make one sweat for it.'

'Shut it.' The Captain nodded to the wireless cabin door. He put his head through the bridge door. 'First, I don't want to be disturbed for a few minutes.'

The First turned round from the bridge windows, curious. 'Very good, sir.' The Captain pulled the door shut.

They were alone in the warm little room. The Captain approached the chart-table. 'Now it's all clear, eh?' He threw up his head in a succession of little jerks; this and the half smile said, 'Now we know your little game.' The Spare had got out again the chart he had been studying when interrupted earlier by the Captain.

He indicated the area of Mason Island. 'This is where you normally like to lie at night, Captain, isn't it?'

'Yes. No need even to anchor. But it won't do for you, will it?' He regarded the younger man as an old man amusedly watches a pupil make the first mistakes with gun or horse.

The other smiled. 'Too far from the scene of the crime. We must be on the other side as early as possible after daybreak. They won't hang around.'

'With all that stuff on them, they won't dare to lose you.'

A flash of the old pin-pricking. He was trying to make him nervous again. He would do it even if the lifeboats were being lowered. The Spare got himself under control.

'Could we continue to the north end of Indian Reach? And stop here (he pointed with the dividers)? We could then go through at first light.'

The Captain reflected for only a moment. 'It's not so comfortable, and we'll have to anchor, but (he straightened up) there's no other remedy. Open the doors. And tell the First to come in; I'll have to tell him something.'

'Of course.'

But before the Spare could move, the Captain spoke again. 'And the Pilot?'

'Taken care of.'

The Captain waited for details; he did not get them. Finally: 'Personally I wouldn't trust him as far as I could spit. After his last trip with us two of the navigation manuals were missing.'

'This is one case where he can be trusted.' The little enigmatic smile was the only thing the Spare would add. As he left the chartroom, he was struck by the sight of the Captain, head down, tapping the dividers reflectively on the chart, as if studying a navigational problem. He believed he understood all that was passing through the other man's mind in that moment.

A murmur of curiosity went round the crew when at six pm Mason Island was left astern. The wits offered the kind of explanation to be expected; others were thoughtful.

The sensation of being completely enclosed grew. Steep snow-capped granite and slate sides, relieved only by white streams shooting from rock to rock, to plunge into the thick moss and arctic beech covering the lower slopes. Glaciers. Tall cascades volleying straight into woody bays. All fugitive impressions of a fictitious fertility. The narrow forest had merely been granted a tenuous usufruct near the waterline.

There was no wind. The black water was oil-smooth. The sky became overcast again, threw unwanted glooms on an already gloomy scene. The feeling was of having arrived at the end of the world. And in another sense the beginning: a vast, unintelligible and utterly inhuman procreation.

It was nearly seven o'clock when *Sea Otter* entered the south end of Indian Reach, the southern section of the Messier Channel, running for about twenty miles between Saumarez Island and the Narrows. A little late in the day to be negotiating this section of the Strait. Steadily the reach narrowed until the pressure of the rock wall was felt as a palpable thing. In the black lacquer of the water the outlines of the peaks were no longer copied. But it was still possible to see the horrible chasms succeeding one another. And impossible to imagine man ever settling in such a ruin, since not even his cupidity would find anything to fasten on.

Soon the ship was up on the Covadonga group, a few small islands lying in mid-channel, and the Spare Officer's pulse beat above normal as he sighted the first human being seen since *Sea Otter* had entered the Strait: a small scow manned by five men; four standing, working long sweeps, a fifth steering.

The Captain had noticed his reaction. 'Nothing to worry about. They're Alacalufe Indians. Not more than forty or fifty left. They fish for *cholgas* – big mussels – which they trade for clothes and victuals. They probably want to come aboard.' He went out on to the starboard wing of the bridge, shouted, 'Today, no!'

Later the Spare, looking through the binoculars, saw smoke ashore, fine on the port bow. He turned to the Captain. 'Aren't those wireless masts?'

The Captain smiled again. 'You're getting nervous. It's a small settlement known as Eden Harbour, and it's masked by those thickly wooded islands.'

But it was difficult not to be nervous; they were approaching the most critical moment of the whole voyage. He was relieved now to see no further indication of humanity.

'Slow ahead.'

'Slow ahead, sir.' The rest of the familiar sequence followed until *Sea Otter* lay quietly at anchor. For a few moments everyone remained in silence in the dark wheelhouse.

The Captain moved first. 'Call me if we start dragging, First. Or if anything unusual occurs.' Schiuma looked at him; this the Captain had never said, it was always understood. 'And have the wireless operator start keeping watch an hour before first light.' He went below, followed by the Pilot.

Silent the ship lay, surrounded by black water, in turn contained by black mountains. In the primeval scene she looked as strange as perhaps a space-ship on an undiscovered planet. Presently the night cleared. The glacial cold was now more intense and penetrating than ever. A half moon rode at the zenith. In its light and the glare of the snow, the water rippled a deeper black. The Spare, checking bearings on the wing of the bridge, was struck by the scene: the water, mountain ranges, the night itself under the fantastic moonlight all folded in a phantom calm. Looking down the narrow strait, he could believe that at any moment would appear, slowly adding substance to ghostly form, one of those first caravels that for thirty-eight days sought and finally found the famous loophole in the continent. It was only too easy, down here on the scene, to imagine her, stealing over the glassy jet surface, nearer, nearer, until there became audible the slow creaking of her blocks and yards, the voices of the men on deck, using the same language as *Sea Otter*'s crew, and at last the soft rush of water curling round her forefoot. Then gone from sight, vanished into her own immortal century. It was to them the Strait belonged.

First light. Loudly the surrounding gullies and clefts re-echoed with the long siren blast. The only answer *Sea Otter* got was from long flights of duck streaming low over the water, and the convolutions of the flightless Steamboat duck, whirring over the water like old side-wheelers. Welcome sights, where every growing and moving thing relieved the ache of the lifeless black and white solitudes.

Sea Otter steamed ahead, keeping over to the western shore to offset the powerful current setting on Zealous Islet from the opposite side of the channel. In a few minutes she began negotiating the famous S-Bend.

The width was not more than about two hundred yards, the sides draped in the same thick, lifeless looking forest of *ñires* and yellowy moss. The Pilot, in complete charge, never faltered, nor even reduced speed; and speed was important now. Everyone who had a right was on the bridge, and did not speak. The only words heard were those of the Pilot's cryptic litany to the helmsman, and the latter's confirmations.

Now in the most tortuous part of the whole Strait, the peaks, islands, rocks, forest rushed upon the ship. She turned. They came at her again. Then at last she turned again to port, a full 90 degrees, completing the second half of the S. Suddenly she was in open water, and everyone saw the black hull of the strange freighter.

'Stop engines.'

Silently *Sea Otter* rushed towards the ship ten times her side.

'Slow astern. Switch on the loud-hailer. Take the microphone, Fourth Officer.' And a few moment later: 'Stop engines.'

All way was now off the ship, the Spare switched on the microphone. He spoke in English. 'How much fresh water can you spare us?'

There was silence at first. A stir could be seen in the other wheelhouse. Then: 'One hundred tons precisely.' It was not an Englishman's English.

The Spare, standing immediately next to the Captain, hardly moved his head. 'It's all in order.' No one else caught the words.

From the fo'c'sle-head the First was looking up to the bridge like a small boy kept out of a secret. The loud-hailer buzzed again. 'We're coming alongside.'

From the big freighter came a heavy splash, a long roaring rattle;

her cable began to pile up on the bottom. At intervals a bell tolled on her fo'c'sle.

'Touch ahead,' said Soza.

'Touch ahead, sir.'

'Fenders!' shouted the First.

'I'll have to inspect each case, Captain.'

'Be quick about it.' Captain Soza went to the wing of the bridge: 'Schiuma!'

'Sir!'

'Get the hatch covers off. Just the top covers. The cargo is to go in the between spaces. Be quick about it!'

There came a gentle bump, felt through the two ships. The Spare disappeared in the direction of his cabin. The Captain, still on the wing of the bridge, would not show his curiosity; he shouted again to the First: 'I don't want to see one cigarette.' He was a little too far off to see the faint smile on Schiuma's face. Now, surreptitiously, his eyes raked the other ship from masthead to waterline, from stem to stern, where in that moment the impotent dirty cloth at her jack-staff stirred nervously in the almost windless air, to reveal the four quarters, the two white containing a star. A ripple ran along the Captain's thin bow-mouth as he saw the same flag as his own.

From *Sea Otter*'s deck those not working looked up at the knife-edged narrow-angled bows leaning against the clouds like a leaning tower. The loop-holed structure on her soared like the keep of a tall castle, and her side threw up against *Sea Otter* a sheer iron wall of immense height; it was now being scaled by the Spare Officer, a bulky portfolio locked to his wrist.

Presently the first of the long crates swung out in the claws of the freighter's huge derrick.

Soza looked at his watch: 'Seventy-five minutes. Not bad. Slow astern!'

The quartermaster repeated it, grasped the telegraph handles, bells clanged in the wheelhouse and in the ship's steel heart. No sirens were sounded, but silent salutes were exchanged between the two Captains who would probably never see each other again.

Sea Otter soon gained wider water. The peaks drew back, grew in height. Round them the blackness had gathered once again. Up there the convulsions could be seen as snow-curtains suddenly lifted were flung across the mountain tops. The bulletin the wireless operator pushed through the door was no surprise to the Captain.

'Just in time.' He looked at the Spare, as though the latter had narrowly escaped disgrace. 'San Pedro forecast: Force nine gale, force nine sea. You know what that means.'

At lunch the Captain gave no one an opening. Anyway, there was now a new worry. The worn orders were repeated, and the First left early.

Soon the weather had darkened and the first squalls had hit the ship. The first williwaws shrieked down the mountainsides.

By mid-afternoon little *Sea Otter* was punching her small tonnage into a short violent head sea and pounding rain. Water began forcing through even secured ports, visibility dropped to 1,000 yards, then to less than 500. The barometer rushed round to 990, retreated a little, remained quivering violently, in the space of half a minute.

The upper decks were empty. Everyone not on watch was below. In the chart-room the Second was staring at a speedometer which under some of the blows dropped as much as three knots for several seconds. And in the principal cabin sat the two men who had each in his way, one willingly, antagonized the other throughout the voyage so far. There was a week to go in the Pacific before the first port of call, but the moment in which each was to define himself to the other was now.

The Captain had got out a bottle. 'Scotch?'

'How I wish I could!'

'Of course. In your condition the worst thing.'

He poured himself a long shot; it would be his only one. He drank before speaking. The other man knew what lay in the offing was another interrogation. Nothing new in itself, but to contain something new.

They felt now a change in the ship's movement; the sea had lengthened. It was also growing in height and ugliness, and the charcoal sky ahead showed not one glimmer. No one could have told the time of day, but it was late afternoon. The violent wind, always westerly, heaped the seas up into black hills which disintegrated over the ship.

'Of course, it's now clear why you couldn't afford to remain in Puerto Deseado, although you knew you had this illness.'

The other said nothing, he made a non-committal gesture.

'You did know it, didn't you?' Soza's face wore again – or had put on, the other wondered – that brilliant glittery look, charming and shrewd, as of one who pardons all.

'Thought I might perhaps have a touch.' The vessel shook to a tremendous blow as a huge solid sea smashed its way over the small bows, pouring over the fo'c'sle-head, to race away, a roaring flood, to the lee scuppers, to carry overboard anyone foolish enough to be there.

The Captain did not even notice the shock; he said: '*¡Vamos!*'

He added nothing; he let the mocking disbelief hang in the silence.

It was, however, a silence only between the two men. Its context was everything cosmic that boiled and detonated outside. The ship now shuddered as though shaken as a maraca is shaken. In better visibility they could have calculated the fantastic arcs the vessel was describing through sky, mountain and water. Arcs lengthening as the pounding increased. But they distinctly heard her joints begin to scream.

'So you won't be making the return trip with us?' He was impervious.

'No, Captain.' He kept his chair with difficulty.

'Pity, we could have had some more discussions! I hope you've enjoyed them as much as I.' A little slyly he had loosed this off.

'Yes, indeed,' the other lied. He was waiting for the Captain to reveal what really intrigued him.

It came.

'Now that everything's settled, you can tell me, in confidence of course, what *you* get out of it!'

The other at last felt relaxed, amused at the older man's face.

'My expenses, Captain.'

The Captain had stiffened. The other had spoken tranquilly, and it would not do. There was a '*gato encerrado*', there always was with these people. Come to that, one could smell a rat anywhere. If he himself had been paid off so handsomely, what would they be paying their agent?

It was the twist in the Captain's mouth that told the Spare he was considered a liar.

'Captain (he was very patient), when we get to port and I've done what I have to, I shall fly back to the Rio de la Plata, visiting friends on the way. (He did not miss the look of amused omniscience). Every luxury. For this I'm drawing one thousand dollars.' He paused. 'I'm afraid you'll have to believe it. No "*gato encerrado*".'

But the Captain was again regarding him as he would a madman. It irritated him to take an explanation upsetting to the values he had constructed for the other man's race. From habit his eyes narrowed, he nodded his head as if he understood.

'But *why* do you do it?'

At last. It was more than another question in the interrogatory; it was a cry of incomprehension, a recoil before the suspected presence of something that could upset a whole philosophy.

The difficulty for the Spare Officer was to formulate a variation of what could only be the same answer. '*Porque sí,*' he said finally.

'What do you mean? There's a reason for everything, man.'

Of course. Some liked to get to the bottom of things; that was why they never understood when they found neither bottom nor top. But he knew there could still be a better explanation.

It was when he began to grope in his own language that he was able to give it. 'I don't know if it can be said in *castellano*.'

All the muscles in the Captain's face had hardened. Their relationship had veered back for a moment to the old ambiguous equilibrium between tolerance and hostility. The Captain dominated himself, at once felt better, perhaps against his will. He unsheathed his best weapon, and the other thought, 'Why don't you smile like that more often?'

'Tell me in English then, if it's simple.'

'Oh it's simple enough.'

'Well then?'

'For the hell of it, Captain, just for the hell of it.'

George G. Toudouze

THREE SKELETON KEY

MY MOST TERRIFYING EXPERIENCE? Well, one does have a few in thirty-five years of service in the Lights, although it's mostly monotonous routine work – keeping the light in order, making out the reports.

When I was a young man, not very long in the service, there was an opening in a lighthouse newly built off the coast of Guiana, on a small rock twenty miles or so from the mainland. The pay was high, so in order to reach the sum I had set out to save before I married, I volunteered for service in the new light.

Three Skeleton Key, the small rock on which the light stood, bore a bad reputation. It earned its name from the story of the three convicts who, escaping from Cayenne in a stolen dugout canoe, were wrecked on the rock during the night, managed to escape the sea but eventually died of hunger and thirst. When they were discovered, nothing remained but three heaps of bones, picked clean by the birds. The story was that the three skeletons, gleaming with phosphorescent light, danced over the small rock, screaming. . . .

But there are many such stories and I did not give the warnings of the old-timers at the *Isle de Sein* a second thought. I signed up, boarded ship and in a month I was installed at the light.

Picture a grey, tapering cylinder, welded to the solid black rock by iron rods and concrete, rising from a small island twenty-odd miles from land. It lay in the midst of the sea, this island, a small, bare piece of stone, about one hundred and fifty feet long, perhaps forty wide. Small, barely large enough for a man to walk about and stretch his legs at low tide.

This is an advantage one doesn't find in all lights, however, for some of them rise sheer from the waves, with no room for one to move save within the light itself. Still, on our island, one must be careful, for the rocks were treacherously smooth. One misstep and down you would fall into the sea – not that the risk of drowning was so great, but the waters about our island swarmed with huge sharks who kept an eternal patrol around the base of the light.

Still, it was a nice life there. We had enough provisions to last for months, in the event that the sea should become too rough for the supply ship to reach us on schedule. During the day we would work about the light, cleaning the rooms, polishing the metalwork and the lens and reflector of the light itself, and at night we would sit on the gallery and watch our light, a twenty-thousand-candle-power lantern, swinging its strong, white bar of light over the sea from the top of its hundred-and-twenty-foot tower. Some days, when the air would be very clear, we could see the land, a thread-like line to the west. To the east, north and south stretched the ocean. Landsmen, perhaps, would soon have tired of that kind of life, perched on a small island off the coast of South America for eighteen weeks, until one's turn for leave ashore came around. But we liked it there, my two fellow-tenders and myself – so much so that, for twenty-two months on end with the exception of shore leaves, I was greatly satisfied with the life on Three Skeleton Key.

I had just returned from my leave at the end of June, that is to say mid-winter in that latitude, and had settled down to the routine with my two fellow-keepers, a Breton by the name of Le Gleo and the head-keeper Itchoua, a Basque some dozen years or so older than either of us.

Eight days went by as usual, then on the ninth night after my return, Itchoua, who was on night duty, called Le Gleo and me, sleeping in our rooms in the middle of the tower at two in the morning. We rose immediately and, climbing the thirty or so steps that led to the gallery, stood beside our chief.

Itchoua pointed, and following his finger, we saw a big three-master, with all sail set, heading straight for the light. A queer course, for the vessel must have seen us, our light hit her with the glare of day each time it passed over her.

Now, ships were a rare sight in our waters for our light was a warning of treacherous reefs, barely hidden under the surface and running far out to sea. Consequently we were always given a wide berth, especially by sailing vessels, which cannot manoeuvre as readily as steamers.

No wonder that we were surprised at seeing this three-master heading dead for us in the gloom of early morning. I had immediately recognized her lines, for she stood out plainly, even at the distance of a mile, when our light shone on her.

She was a beautiful ship of some four thousand tons, a fast sailer that had carried cargoes to every part of the world, ploughing the seas unceasingly. By her lines she was identified as Dutch-built, which was understandable as Paramaribo and Dutch Guiana are very close to Cayenne.

Watching her sailing dead for us, a white wave boiling under her bows, Le Gleo cried out:

'What's wrong with her crew? Are they all drunk or insane? Can't they see us?'

Itchoua nodded soberly, looked at us sharply as he remarked: 'See us? No doubt – if there *is* a crew aboard!'

'What do you mean, chief?' Le Gleo had started, turned to the Basque, 'Are you saying that she's the "Flying Dutchman"?'

His sudden fright had been so evident that the older man laughed:

'No, old man, that's not what I meant. If I say that no one's aboard, I mean she's a derelict.'

Then we understood her behaviour. Itchoua was right. For some reason, believing her doomed, her crew had abandoned her. Then she had righted herself and sailed on, wandering with the wind.

The three of us grew tense as the ship seemed about to crash on one of our numerous reefs, but she suddenly lurched with some change of the wind, the yards swung around and the derelict came clumsily about and sailed dead away from us.

In the light of our lantern she seemed so sound, so strong, that Itchoua exclaimed impatiently:

'But why the devil was she abandoned? Nothing is smashed, no sign of fire – and she doesn't sail as if she were taking water.'

Le Gleo waved to the departing ship:

'*Bon voyage!*' he smiled at Itchoua and went on. 'She's leaving us, chief, and now we'll never know what – '

'No she's not!' cried the Basque. 'Look! She's turning!'

As if obeying his words, the derelict three-master stopped, came about and headed for us once more. And for the next four hours the vessel played around us – zig-zagging, coming about, stopping, then suddenly lurching forward. No doubt some freak of current and wind, of which our island was the centre, kept her near us.

Then suddenly, the tropic dawn broke, the sun rose and it was day, and the ship was plainly visible as she sailed past us. Our light extinguished, we returned to the gallery with our glasses and inspected her.

The three of us focused our glasses on her poop, saw standing out sharply, black letters on the white background of a life-ring, the stencilled name:

'*Cornelius-de-Witt, Rotterdam.*'

We had read her lines correctly, she was Dutch. Just then the wind rose and the *Cornelius de Witt* changed course, leaned to port and headed straight for us once more. But this time she was so close that we knew she would not turn in time.

'Thunder!' cried Le Gleo, his Breton soul aching to see a fine ship doomed to smash upon a reef, 'she's going to pile up! She's gone!'

I shook my head:

'Yes, and a shame to see that beautiful ship wreck herself. And we're helpless.'

There was nothing we could do but watch. A ship sailing with all sail spread, creaming the sea with her forefoot as she runs before the wind, is one of the most beautiful sights in the world – but this time I could feel the tears stinging my eyes as I saw this fine ship headed for her doom.

All this time our glasses were riveted on her and we suddenly cried out together:

'The rats!'

Now we knew why this ship, in perfect condition, was sailing without her crew aboard. They had been driven out by the rats. Not those poor specimens of rats you see ashore, barely reaching the length of one foot from their trembling noses to the tip of their skinny tails, wretched creatures that dodge and hide at the mere sound of a footfall.

No, these were ships' rats, huge, wise creatures, born on the sea, sailing all over the world on ships, transfering to other, larger ships as they multiply. There is as much difference between the rats of the land and these maritime rats as between a fishing smack and an armoured cruiser.

The rats of the sea are fierce, bold animals. Large, strong and intelligent, clannish and seawise, able to put the best of mariners to shame with their knowledge of the sea, their uncanny ability to foretell the weather.

And they are brave, the rats, and vengeful. If you so much as harm one, his sharp cry will bring hordes of his fellows to swarm over you, tear you and not cease until your flesh has been stripped from the bones.

The ones on this ship, the rats of Holland, are the worst, superior to other rats of the sea as their brethren are to the land rats. There is a well-known tale about these animals.

A Dutch captain, thinking to protect his cargo, brought aboard his ship – not cats – but two terriers, dogs trained in the hunting, fighting and killing of vicious rats. By the time the ship, sailing from Rotterdam, had passed the Ostend light, the dogs were gone and never seen again. In twenty-four hours they had been overwhelmed, killed, and eaten by the rats.

At times, when the cargo does not suffice, the rats attack the crew, either driving them from the ship or eating them alive. And studying the *Cornelius de Witt*, I turned sick, for her small boats were all in place. She had not been abandoned.

Over her bridge, on her deck, in the rigging, on every visible spot, the ship was a writhing mass – a starving army coming towards us aboard a vessel gone mad!

Our island was a small spot in that immense stretch of sea. The ship could have grazed us, passed to port or starboard with its ravening cargo – but no, she came for us at full speed, as if she were leading the regatta at a race, and impaled herself on a sharp point of rock.

There was a dull shock as her bottom stove in, then a horrible crackling as the three masts went overboard at once, as if cut down with one blow of some gigantic sickle. A sighing groan came as the water rushed into the ship, then she split in two and sank like a stone.

But the rats did not drown. Not these fellows! As much at home in the sea as any fish, they formed ranks in the water, heads lifted, tails stretched out, paws paddling. And half of them, those from the forepart of the ship, sprang along the masts and onto the rocks in the instant before she sank. Before we had time even to move, nothing remained of the three-master save some pieces of wreckage floating on the surface and an army of rats covering the rocks left bare by the receding tide.

Thousands of heads rose, felt the wind and we were scented, seen! To them we were fresh meat, after possible weeks of starving. There came a scream, composed of innumerable screams, sharper than the howl of a saw attacking a bar of iron, and in the one motion, every rat leaped to attack the tower!

We barely had time to leap back, close the door leading onto the gallery, descend the stairs and shut every window tightly. Luckily the door at the base of the light, which we never could have reached in time, was of bronze set in granite and was tightly closed.

The horrible band, in no measurable time, had swarmed up and over the tower as if it had been a tree, piled on the embrasures of the windows, scraped at the glass with thousands of claws, covered the lighthouse with a furry mantle and reached the top of the tower, filling the gallery and piling atop the lantern.

Their teeth grated as they pressed against the glass of the lantern-room, where they could plainly see us, though they could not reach us. A few millimetres of glass, luckily very strong, separated our faces from their gleaming, beady eyes, their sharp claws and teeth. Their odour filled the tower, poisoned our lungs and rasped our nostrils with a pestilential, nauseating smell. And there we were, sealed alive in our own light, prisoners of a horde of starving rats.

That first night, the tension was so great that we could not sleep. Every moment, we felt that some opening had been made, some window given away, and that our horrible besiegers were pouring through the breach. The rising tide, chasing those of the rats which had stayed on the bare rocks, increased the numbers clinging to the walls, piled on the balcony – so much so that clusters of rats clinging to one another hung from the lantern and the gallery.

With the coming of darkness we lit the light and the turning beam completely maddened the beasts. As the light turned, it successively blinded thousands of rats crowded against the glass, while the dark side of the lantern-room gleamed with thousands of points of light, burning like the eyes of jungle beasts in the night.

All the while we could hear the enraged scraping of claws against the stone and glass, while the chorus of cries was so loud that we had to shout to hear one another. From time to time, some of the rats fought among themselves and a dark cluster would detach itself, falling into the sea like a ripe fruit from a tree. Then we would see phosphorescent streaks as triangular fins slashed the water – sharks, permanent guardians of our rock, feasting on our jailors.

The next day we were calmer, and amused ourselves teasing the rats, placing our faces against the glass which separated us. They could not fathom the invisible barrier which separated them from us and we laughed as we watched them leaping against the heavy glass.

But the day after that, we realized how serious our position was. The air was foul, even the heavy smell of oil within our stronghold could not dominate the fetid odour of the beasts massed around us. And there was no way of admitting fresh air without also admitting the rats.

The morning of the fourth day, at early dawn, I saw the wooden framework of my window, eaten away from the outside, sagging inwards. I called my comrades and the three of us fastened a sheet of tin in the opening, sealing it tightly. When we had completed the task, Itchoua turned to us and said dully:

'Well – the supply boat came thirteen days ago, and she won't be back for twenty-nine.' He pointed at the white metal plate sealing the opening through the granite – 'If that gives way' – he shrugged – 'they can change the name of this place to Six Skeletons Key.'

The next six days and seven nights, our only distraction was watching the rats whose holds were insecure, fall an hundred and twenty feet into the maws of the sharks – but they were so many that we could not see any diminution in their numbers.

Thinking to calm ourselves and pass the time, we attempted to count them, but we soon gave up. They moved incessantly, never still. Then we tried identifying them, naming them.

One of them, larger than the others, who seemed to lead them in their rushes against the glass separating us, we named 'Nero'; and there were several others whom we had learned to distinguish through various peculiarities.

But the thought of our bones joining those of the convicts was always in the back of our minds. And the gloom of our prison fed these thoughts, for the interior of the light was almost completely dark, as we had to seal every window in the same fashion as mine, and the only space that still admitted daylight was the glassed-in lantern-room at the very top of the tower.

Then Le Gleo became morose and had nightmares in which he would see the three skeletons dancing around him, gleaming coldly, seeking to grasp him. His maniacal, raving descriptions were so vivid that Itchoua and I began seeing them also.

It was a living nightmare, the raging cries of the rats as they swarmed over the light, mad with hunger; the sickening, strangling odour of their bodies –

True, there is a way of signalling from lighthouses. But to reach the mast on which to hang the signal we would have to go out on the gallery where the rats were.

There was only one thing left to do. After debating all of the ninth day, we decided not to light the lantern that night. This is the greatest breach of our service, never committed as long as the tenders of the light are alive; for the light is something sacred, warning ships of danger in the night. Either the light gleams, a quarter-hour after sundown, or no one is left alive to light it.

Well, that night, Three Skeleton Light was dark, and all the men were alive. At the risk of causing ships to crash on our reefs, we left it unlit, for we were worn out – going mad!

At two in the morning, while Itchoua was dozing in his room, the sheet of metal sealing his window gave way. The chief had just time enough to leap to his feet and cry for help, the rats swarming over him.

But Le Gleo and I, who had been watching from the lantern-room, got to him immediately, and the three of us battled with the horde of maddened rats which flowed through the gaping window. They bit, we struck them down with our knives – and retreated.

We locked the door of the room on them, but before we had time to bind our wounds, the door was eaten through, and gave way and we retreated up the stairs, fighting off the rats that leaped on us from the knee-deep swarm.

I do not remember, to this day, how we ever managed to escape. All I can remember is wading through them up the stairs, striking them off as they swarmed over us; and then we found ourselves, bleeding from innumerable bites, our clothes shredded, sprawled across the trapdoor in the floor of the lantern-room – without food or drink. Luckily, the trapdoor was metal set into the granite with iron bolts.

The rats occupied the entire light beneath us, and on the floor of our retreat lay some twenty of their fellows, who had gotten in with us before the trapdoor closed, and whom we had killed with our knives. Below us, in the tower, we could hear the screams of the rats as they devoured everything edible that they found. Those on the outside squealed in reply, and writhed in a horrible curtain as they stared at us through the glass of the lantern-room.

Itchoua sat up, stared silently at his blood trickling from the wounds on his limbs and body, and running in thin streams on the floor around him. Le Gleo, who was in as bad a state (and so was I, for that matter) stared at the chief and me vacantly, started as his gaze swung to the multitude of rats against the glass, then suddenly began laughing horribly:

'Hee! Hee! The Three Skeletons! Hee! Hee! The Three Skeletons are now *six* skeletons! *Six* skeletons!'

He threw his head back and howled, his eyes glazed, a trickle of saliva running from the corners of his mouth and thinning the blood flowing over his chest. I shouted to him to shut up, but he did not hear me, so I did the only thing I could to quiet him – I swung the back of my hand across his face.

The howling stopped suddenly, his eyes swung around the room, then he bowed his head and began weeping softly, like a child.

Our darkened light had been noticed from the mainland, and as dawn was breaking the patrol was there, to investigate the failure of our light. Looking through my binoculars, I could see the horrified expression on the faces of the officers and crew when, the daylight strengthening, they saw the light completely covered by a seething mass of rats. They thought, as I afterwards found out, that we had been eaten alive.

But the rats had also seen the ship, or had scented the crew. As the ship drew nearer, a solid phalanx left the light, plunged into the water and, swimming out, attempted to board her. They would have succeeded, as the ship was hove to, but the engineer connected his steam to hose on the deck and scalded the head of the attacking column, which slowed them up long enough for the ship to get under way and leave the rats behind.

Then the sharks took part. Belly up, mouths gaping, they arrived in swarms and scooped up the rats, sweeping through them like a sickle through wheat. That was one day that sharks really served a useful purpose.

The remaining rats turned tail, swam to the shore and emerged dripping. As they neared the light, their comrades greeted them with shrill cries, with what sounded like a derisive note predominating. They answered angrily and mingled with their fellows. From the several tussles that broke out, they resented being ridiculed for their failure to capture the ship.

But all this did nothing to get us out of our jail. The small ship could not approach, but steamed around the light at a safe distance, and the tower must have seemed fantastic, some weird, many-mouthed beast hurling defiance at them.

Finally, seeing the rats running in and out of the tower through the door and the windows, those on the ship decided that we had perished and were about to leave when Itchoua, regaining his senses, thought of using the light as a signal. He lit it and, using a plank placed and withdrawn before the beam to form the dots and dashes, quickly sent our story to those on the vessel.

Our reply came quickly. When they understood our position, how we could not get rid of the rats, Le Gleo's mind going fast, Itchoua and myself covered with bites; cornered in the lantern-room without food or water, they had a signalman send us their reply.

His arms, swinging like those of a windmill, he quickly spelled out:

'Don't give up, hang on a little longer! We'll get you out of this!'

Then she turned and steamed at top speed for the coast, leaving us little reassured.

She was back at noon, accompanied by the supply ship, two small coastguard boats, and the fire boat – a small squadron. At twelve-thirty the battle was on.

After a short reconnaissance, the fire boat picked her way slowly through the reefs until she was close to us, then turned her powerful jet of water on the rats. The heavy stream tore the rats from their places, hurled them screaming into the water where the sharks gulped them down. But for every ten that were dislodged, seven swam ashore, and the stream could do nothing to the rats within the tower. Furthermore, some of them, instead of returning to the rocks, boarded the fire boat and the men were forced to battle them hand to hand. They were true rats of Holland, fearing no man, fighting for the right to live!

Nightfall came, and it was as if nothing had been done, the rats were still in possession. One of the patrol boats stayed by the island, the rest of the flotilla departed for the coast. We had to spend another night in our prison. Le Gleo was sitting on the floor, babbling about skeletons and as I turned to Itchoua, he fell unconscious from his wounds. I was in no better shape and could feel my blood flaming with fever.

Somehow the night dragged by, and the next afternoon I saw a tug, accompanied by the fire boat, come from the mainland with a huge barge in tow. Through my glasses, I saw that the barge was filled with meat.

Risking the treacherous reefs, the tug dragged the barge as close to the island as possible. To the last rat, our besiegers deserted the rock, swam out and boarded the barge reeking with the scent of freshly cut meat. The tug dragged the barge about a mile from shore, where the fire boat drenched the barge with gasoline. A well-placed incendiary shell from the patrol boat set her on fire. The barge was covered with flames immediately and the rats took to the water in swarms, but the patrol boat bombarded them with shrapnel from a safe distance, and the sharks finished off the survivors.

A whaleboat from the patrol boat took us off the island and left three men to replace us. By nightfall we were in the hospital in Cayenne. What became of my friends?

Well, Le Gleo's mind had cracked and he was raving mad. They sent him back to France and locked him up in an asylum, the poor devil; Itchoua died within a week; a rat's bite is dangerous in that hot, humid climate, and infection sets in rapidly.

As for me – when they fumigated the light and repaired the damage done by the rats, I resumed my service there. Why not? No reason why such an incident should keep me from finishing out my service there, is there?

Besides – I told you I liked the place – to be truthful, I've never had a post as pleasant as that one, and when my time came to leave it forever, I tell you that I almost wept as Three Skeleton Key disappeared below the horizon.

Captain Dingle

SARGASSO

A MAN MAY NOT live his lifetime out on the wide seas and die a coward. If he has the yellow streak in him at the beginning, one of two things must happen: the strong brine of old ocean magically turns the yellow of the coward into the red, red pigment of whole manhood – or he quits.

Men said of Sargasso that he was as yellow as the gulf-weed that gave him his name. From the time when he was picked up adrift in an abandoned ship's boat in the Sargasso Sea, a baby of three, until full manhood, he had spent his lifetime at sea, except for the seven years of enforced residence in Popley Orphanage. And he never quit, which means that he could not be a coward unless an ancient truth lied.

Yet men had seen him turn ashen, greenish-grey, ashiver with fear at the mere sight of a bit of floating weed. Sam Sargasso they had named him when taken ashore, a baby, to be registered a native of Stepney Parish for want of closer data; Sam Sargasso was his name on the articles of a score of ships, his signature on half a hundred discharges. Sargasso Sam they called him as man to man, and as Sargasso Sam every sailor-man sailing the seven seas knew him or had heard of him – as Sargasso Sam the pluckless man.

He held stubbornly to all the beliefs and fears of the sailor. At ten years of age he swarmed down a rain-pipe from his orphanage dormitory, barefoot and naked lest he be identified and haled back to hateful pauperism. At that early age some inner urge forbade him to resign himself calmly to the lot of a poorhouse drudge. Vaguely he feared the sea. Vaguely he had heard hodge-podge stories about his origin, how he had been found in a little boat along with the dead bodies of two sailors and a negro woman dressed as a nurse-girl, floating in the middle of that vast area of golden weed-choked azure sea that fable and superstition have peopled with dead men and filled to congestion with the wrecks and ghosts of dead ships.

Sargasso Sea! He always remembered that name. In later years he remembered how he used to shiver at it, and as a man he shivered even as the boy had shivered.

But his flight from the orphanage was from something yet more fearsome than the Sargasso Sea. He stole over walls and through deserted streets; he stole into a stable and stole a corn sack. And dressed thus simply he fell over a sleeping sailor and woke him up by the effective agency of an elbow and a small bony knee placed firmly and with accidental precision squarely upon a rather rotund stomach.

He was badly scared when the sleeper stumbled up and seized him in one knotted fist, the other knotted member held aloft in angry threat while the wielder gathered his badly disturbed breath. And years afterwards Sargasso remembered that a nearby clock chimed the hour of three o'clock in the morning just as the blow was about to fall, and it did not fall. He remembered, too, through the years, how his captor heard the clock strike, laughed not unpleasantly, and held him off at arm's length while he struck a match. Thirty-five years later he could repeat the precise words in the exact tone used:

'Little shiny fishes! If I ain't caught a little babby marmaid. Wrong ag'in; 'tis a marman; and no ways 'fraid o' ketchin' cold too. Well, well! Sonny, you tromped on yer Uncle Billy's tripes just in time to save him his ship, by all the signs. What you doin' crusin' around in this rig? Ain't you got no home?'

And Sargasso recalled his answer:

'No home, nor any folks, please, sir.'

He recalled, next, being dragged, half-carried, along a lane beside a high brick wall, his captor, guide, self-styled Uncle Billy, staggering a bit, going large and chattering with growing coherence:

'Brig *Pallas*, that's my ship, sonny. Sails on th' early ebb, and 'tis 'most due. If you hadn't trompled on my belly when you did I'd never have heard that church strike six bells. That'd have been eight bells for me sure enough, sonny. Mate's been waitin' to git my berth a long while. . . . So you got no home, hey? Well, well! You want to be a sailor, don't you? Right you be, sonny. Nelson started as a boy, didn't he? Wasn't Paul Jones a gardener's muck spreader? Ain't you as good as them? You come alonga old Bill Gammidge an' he'll make a man o' you!'

He recalled being hustled through a grim gate through which a suspicious face peered before more than a tiny grille was opened;

then up a dizzy ladder and to the decks of a grimy little brig whose shore lines were already slackened off and beside which a small, fussy, belching tug lay impatiently. He remembered the brief but powerful wordy battle between the skipper – his Uncle Billy – and the mate, the chaos of sailing and the mystery of the great river; then there was the haunting memory of the voyage to Demerara, the passage through the Sargasso Sea; his recurrent, inexplicable terror and his desertion of the brig in Berbice.

Boy though he was then and overpowering though his fears were, the sea had called him with an insistence too strong even for his fears. The sea had claimed him for its own. He had shipped as boy in a black-owned sugar coaster; he had eaten sugar-cane and learned to drink rum like water; he had learned seamanship from some of the finest natural seamen in the world; and he had at last gone farther abroad, sailing in better and better ships until he found himself second mate of a tall nitrate clipper trading between Liverpool and Callao.

He was an amazingly good sailorman. In days when steel ships had already replaced ships of wood; when turn-buckle screws did duty for lanyards and dead-eyes; when bowsprits and jib-booms were built of steel all in one piece, fastened down with iron bands instead of chain gammonings; when topgallant masts were rigged to a necklace instead of catharpings and futtock bolts, Sargasso Sam could gammon a bowsprit with chain, rig out a jib-boom and flying jib-boom, take a sheer hulk and fit her for sea from fore-royal stay to spanker lifts in fashion old or new, and never peep inside a book.

But he never mastered his fear of the Sargasso Sea, nor forgot the hoary old tales heard in his youth. Tenaciously he held on to them all, those beliefs and fears of the unlettered sailor. With it all he read assiduously; read books such as few sailors knew the existence of; such as fewer could have read except as a penance, alternative to some horrible punishment. His fear was the more unaccountable. He could never explain it. When an owner, intending to offer him command, quizzed him about his reputation for superstitious terrors, Sam quoted, to the other's astonishment:

'Wouldst thou,' so the helmsman answered,
'Learn the secrets of the sea?
Only those that brave its dangers
Comprehend its mystery!'

'You ought to know it!' the prospective employer had snapped, irritated at being thus dealt with by such a man as Sargasso.

And Sargasso had replied gravely: 'I know its mystery, sir. I don't comprehend it, and I've sailed the world around since I was half a fathom high.'

That command had gone a-glimmering. A skipper who quoted poetry and still hung on to ancient myths and superstitions might be a good sailor, but not good enough for that particular shipowner. So Sargasso remained second mate of the tall Chiliman until the mate left; then he sailed mate and made good. He performed a piece of seamanship during a bitter January gale in the North Atlantic, when he took a boat manned by volunteers and saved forty men and a woman and baby from a derelict four-master, which two nations called heroism, which at least one woman called a miracle.

It brought him his second chance, and this time the offer of command was not laden below Plimsoll with curiosity regarding his beliefs. A steamer had picked up the derelict four-master and towed her to port. The owners sent for Sargasso.

'The *Khedivieh* is sound, Mr Sargasso. She will be put into shape. You may have command for her if you want it. She's going on charter to an American firm, and – '

'Where to, sir?' Sam had asked.

'That I do not know. I understand she is to make at least one voyage out to China, then I believe she will stay a while in the Pacific trade.'

'Sail from here for China, sir?'

'No; you take her to New York with a cargo of coal, then – '

'I'll take her,' said Sargasso Sam, so briskly that his new employer smiled and almost asked him the reason for all his close questioning on seemingly minor matters.

So Sargasso took his big ship under the coal chutes at Barry Docks and went over every new stay and shroud himself after the riggers had finished, while the coal roared into the yawning hatches. Then he walked along the grimy wharf, when the day's work was done for everybody except the coal men, scanning her trim, appraising her shapely line of painted ports; his sailorly eye roved critically over her lofty spars and glistening steel rigging. He had forbidden the mates to bend any sail until the ship was washed of its last coal dust.

'It's the first time I ever heard of a blessed coal wagon trying to get to sea clean, Mr Fisher,' the young second mate grumbled to the mate at supper.

Sargasso had ignored the supper bell. He was still on the dock, inspecting his ship.

'Mr Bunce, ye live and ye learn, if so be ye're able to learn,' the mate had answered with cumbersome wisdom. 'You'll learn that if yer skipper tells ye to get the brooms out and scrub th' coal as it comes down, it's yer duty to do so. Captain Sargasso has th' name of being a sailor-man. Anyhow, he's captain here.'

The second mate finished his meal in abashed silence. The mate had not uttered so many words altogether since they joined the ship a month before. That the notion of cleaning ship before bending sail must surely mean loss of one tide, if not two, was no concern of anybody except skipper and owners, and Sargasso Sam seemed willing to take the responsibility.

Sargasso came down as the mate went to his room for a pipe, and called out full-throatedly:

'Mr Fisher, we finish coaling at ten o'clock tonight. We haul out to the dock head, and you'll see that the hands are turned to washing down at once. Let them start at the mastheads and wash down. There'll be light enough from the pier.'

'The men are ashore, sir,' the mate retorted. 'We shan't get a man of 'em aboard if they hear they've got to wash down at midnight alongside the dock.'

'It is your duty as first mate, Mr Fisher, to see that the hands are turned to at ten o'clock. I could do it if I were mate. No doubt Mr Bunce could do it, too, if he – '

'I can do it!' snapped Mr Fisher sharply. He confided to the snickering second mate, a few minutes later: 'The old story, Mr Bunce! Beggars on horseback; give a man a box of eggs and a bloody big stick and he'll play hell! And ye'll mind, mister, 'tis Sargasso Sam, Sargasso Sam, th' man o' no guts, as is givin' th' orders!'

'Anyhow, he's captain here,' grinned the second mate with relish.

The Skipper could be heard softly whistling in his cabin. Soon they heard him come out to the saloon table and begin to pick bits of food, standing up; and since he could not whistle and eat, he began to utter scraps of verse, some fine, some superfine, some sheer scraps of sailor doggerel.

'Whistlin' sailor!' muttered the mate contemptuously. 'And him chock-a-block full wi' every silly superstition that ever was!'

'Aye, mister, but hear that!' remarked Mr Bunce as the whistle ceased and Sargasso recited with intense fervour:

We are outward bound for the West tonight,
And the yards go up with a cheer;
The bells will ring in the town tonight,
And the men in the inns will hear.

The carts will creak in the lanes tonight,
And the girls will dance to the band;
But we shall be out with the sails to fist,
And the topsail sheets to hand!

'Ugh! Whoever heard o' handin' tops'l sheets, mister?' the mate growled.

'It's poetry,' the second mate retorted. He was interested in his new skipper for all his queerness; perhaps because of it.

'Listen! There! Pure sailor, isn't it?'

Sargasso was walking slowly around the table, a cold mutton chop in one hand, a cup of tepid tea in the other; and between bites and sups he began to sing, as if to himself, a chantey better suited to the roaring of wind and the thundering of sail:

As I walked out one sunny morn to view the fields around,
I spied a pretty primrose lass a-tripping o'er the ground,
Singing:
'Blow the winds in the morning, blow the winds heigh-ho!
Clear away the morning dew and blow, my bully boys, blow!'

He sang through the old song until it reached the point the youthful second mate was eagerly waiting for; then the skipper stopped abruptly with a mild curse of annoyance, as if surprised at finding himself singing such stuff. But the second mate was satisfied.

'There you are, Mr Fisher!' he chuckled.

'The Old man's human and a sailor-man. I like him. D'ye want me to go up-town and find the crowd?'

'Aye, ye might as well. No doubt ye'll be trying now to shape up for my berth.'

The second mate laughed boyishly. He had no yearning to climb by stamping on a shipmate's fingers. He knew where to find the men, and he found them; spent an hour with them, or at least in the same public house, standing them a couple of treats from another bar without intruding: then sent for big Yankee Jack who had been prime leader in song and dance, to say nothing of noisy love-making, and told him all the skipper's fine qualities without saying a word about the washing-down problem.

'Sure, we'll be aboard, mister,' Yankee Jack roared. 'Show me th' scut as renigs. Yer a hot sport yerself, me son, and I like yez. C'm on, have a drink 'longa the boys and I'll bring 'em right aboard. Ship is run right, when mates an' men pulls all together. C'm on! What'll yez have?'

The wisdom or otherwise of Mr Bunce's method was not permitted to develop at once. The men went on board, and Mr Fisher saw to it that the ship was hauled clear of the quay to the haul-off buoys before whispering a word about washing down. Afterwards nothing mattered much, for the men were duly signed-on seamen, the ship was going to sea, and orders were orders. Besides which, only a monkey or a very shore-hungry sailor would think of swarming along the lines to reach the dock.

The big four-masted barque greeted the daylight cleaned of dust. Then the mates bustled the weary, headachy crew into bending topsails and a jib before sending them below to breakfast and a two-hour spell while waiting for the tug. Captain Sargasso had been on deck all the while, criticizing the washing down and the sail bending until the mates were all but frantic and the men mutinous. All Yankee Jack's overnight enthusiasm for mates who pulled with the men, and for a sailor-man skipper, had gone into vapour with the first swish of a broom.

'Hell, he ain't nawthin' but a nigger-drivin' stiff!' was Jack's verdict as he fished in the kids for morsels of meat among the hash. 'Somebuddy'll be puttin' a head on him as big as a binnacle one fine day. Hey, you old son of a cow, thought you didn't have no hell ships in Lime-juice Land!'

The ancient seadog called upon grinned weakly out of a toothless mouth. He was bent and gnarled with years and hard living, and might have been excused had he shrunk from even wordy combat with the formidable Yankee Jack. But he didn't. He reached out bodily, dragged the mess kid over to himself, and cackled while scooping hash into his plate with his sheath knife:

'Nuther there ain't, Yank. You're right. All the hell I've heard here is what you're blowin' off. Guff, I calls it. You ain't used to ships like this yet; or skippers. Wants belayin'-pin soup, you do, then you'd step lively an' stow yer guff. I'm past seventy, I am, and have commanded ships, I have; but you ain't heard me bellerin', hev you?'

Yankee Jack glared fiercely at the withered old man; but the watery old eyes never flinched, and he laughed with growing good humour at the old sailor's pluck.

'You must be Noah, then,' he said; 'an' too darn old to beller.'

'Wrong again, Yank. All wrong. Bill Gammidge is my tally; Bill Gammidge as once was cap'n of the brig *Pallas*, the finest brig as ever swung a stu'ns'l. In the rum and sugar trade she was; that's how come I be here. If I'd stuck to th' sugar now – But that's howsomedever. Main thing is, I give Cap'n Sam Sargasso his fust chance to ship.'

'Aw, yer a liar!' growled Yankee Jack, only seeing the old man's twinkling eyes behind the watery veil; believing he was being made fun of.

'Maybe, Yank, maybe,' the old man shrugged indifferently. 'You're a mighty fine sailor-man, anyhow.'

With the tug came the telegram. Sargasso read it:

'Mr Rouse died yesterday. Postpone sailing until further orders.'

Sargasso read it twice, and again. Mr Rouse was the man who had given him command. He was the senior partner in the firm. All the sparkling enthusiasm of the days before vanished, and Sargasso's face turned sickly grey. He turned to the tug captain.

'Stand by a while, mister,' he said moodily.

'You'll miss the tide,' said the tug skipper.

'Stand by!' To the mate: 'Mr Fisher, rig stages overside and paint a blue stripe around her.' To the second mate: 'Mr Bunce, at eight bells run up the ensign and house flag to half-mast.'

Sargasso paced the poop nervously. The steward's black cat rubbed against his legs. Cursing, he kicked the astonished animal over the rail into the water. In another minute he was down on a line, grabbling with a spitting, fighting cat, dragging it from the water, hurling it to the security of the tug.

'Take it away!' he shouted. 'Take it away!'

All the spring had gone from Sargasso's limbs. He sat in his cabin, entering the various items in his journal, marking places with the telegram folded into a spill. Holding fast to ancient traditions, superstitions, terrors, what-not of the old-time sailorman, it followed inevitably that the sudden change in the even tenor of his first sailing should work havoc with his temper.

'A blue stripe on the first ship I take to sea!' he muttered. His face was ashen. 'And a bloody black cat aboard too! Ugh! Atop of all I lose a tide! Never a breeze but a hurricane! Only wants a nigger woman stowaway now to label the ship for Fiddler's Green.'

While waiting for orders the two mates improved the hour and got more sails bent. They bent jibs and spanker, besides the topsails; they managed to get the three lower topgallants bent, and the foresail was dangling in the gantline when another telegram came on board for Sargasso:

Sail on evening tide. Prepare for lady passenger going to New York, with maid. Letter of instruction borne by passenger.

Sargasso said nothing while the steward was present, but his face went three shades greyer and his firm lip trembled. There was one intense moment when he flung himself down at the desk again, drew paper and pen to him, and got all set to write out his resignation.

'Hell and high water!' he swore, stabbing the pen into the desk pad fiercely. 'They say I'm yellow! Even my officers grin at my beliefs behind my back. The woman's not here yet. Let 'em come! Let 'em all come!' And he bawled for the steward.

'Steward, you'll make up the big state-room for the two women. Lady and maid. Friend of the owners. Get it done right away. And go into town and buy some fancy grub; some live chickens and some fruit. Get a move on!'

Sargasso saw to the necessary details of his own preparation to receive a passenger. The ship still retained her passenger-carrying permit. She was one of the last of the old wool clippers and had been built with passenger accommodations, though now she made other use of it all except that immediately beneath the long poop. There was only the question of setting apart a bath and having the mate fill a water tank over it, then that problem was solved. And noon was not yet come when Sargasso found himself impatiently waiting for his guest.

He went over his ship from forward to aft; then inspected the steward's arrangements.

Lunch would be late, because he had sent the steward away with two sailors to carry his purchases; and that arrangement was good for two hours over and above the necessary time, anyhow. He took a book and tried to read. In five minutes he flung the book across the cabin with an oath.

The book, a collection of short stories and poems, began with a story so obviously written by a landsman that it gagged on a sailor, went on to poems and scraps of sea superstitions, and wound up with a yarn about a Portuguese barque, laden with beef bones and infested with rats, that was caught aback in a squall, dismasted, and doomed to lie in sweltering calms under torrid skies for months, with rats running wild, their eyes glowing at night with phosphorus from their diet of putrid bones. The Portuguese captain put his troubles down to the fact that he had a black cat aboard that was frightened overboard by a black girl who had stowed away and came out one night to steal the cat's food.

'The man's a damned fool!' swore Sargasso as he stamped out to the companion-way. 'If he had hove the black wench over, too, after the cat, he'd got better luck with his weather.'

He stood at the poop rail, watching the crew at work, and felt a bit better because of the clean efficiency of his mates. The sails were all but bent; the ship glistened clean and fresh after the nocturnal washdown. Now that the men had got over their shore heads they worked well and looked like a capable crowd; all but one old man laboriously coiling down a new piece of Manila from which a jib down-haul had been cut. It was full of kinks. The old man handled it in sailorly fashion, in truth, thorough-footing it and dipping the end again, and so getting the kinks out of it; but he was so aged, so far past the meridian that Sargasso mentally put him down for an easy job once they got to sea.

'Just so long as he isn't one of those broken masters sailing 'fore the mast,' he muttered. 'That would put the tin hat on a raft of trouble!'

Along towards evening the passenger arrived. 'I'm Miss Rouse, captain,' she smiled wanly. 'Here is a letter from the firm's solicitor, which I think explains things. Sorry to bother you.'

Miss Rouse was as sweet and fair a bit of girlhood as any sailorman could wish to meet; but Sargasso stared beyond her rudely, with no rude intent, stared hard at a coal-black maid carrying a small suit-case, who looked frightened when she caught his stony glare fixed upon her. The ancient sailor, carrying two more portmanteaus, grinned toothlessly behind the maid, for he thought the skipper was smitten dumb with Miss Rouse's charms.

'Where shall I put 'em, sir?' he asked.

Sargasso snatched himself out of his trance, bawled for the steward, and sent his passenger below. And the old sailor returning from his errand grinned again, tugged at his forelock, and said:

'Pardin, sir. 'Member old Bill Gammidge, don't ye? Him as give ye yer fust berth, sir? Happy t' see ye skipper, sir, Cap'n Sargasso. Good luck, sir, if I might make so free.'

Sargasso stared closely into the old man's withered face, and a scowl darkened his brow. Then the scowl was slowly replaced by a sickly smile, which in turn gave way to a more normal expression as the skipper got a fresh hold on himself.

'Gammidge,' he said, 'you ought to be aft here. But if you must sail in a fo'c'sle, I'm glad it's mine. I want to talk with you some time after we get to sea. Might want some help aft, with passengers.'

'Beggin' y' pardin, Cap'n Sargasso,' the old salt said with a flush of pride, 'orders is orders, as I taught you long ago, sir. If so be you orders me aft, aft I got to come. But I hopes you won't forget as old Bill Gammidge was master of the *Pallas*, as you took your fust v'yage in, and 'taint in natur' for a cap'n to keer a hull lot about bein' second flunkey to a 'Talian stooard, sir.'

There were voices and a girl's fresh yet sad voice among them. Sargasso turned to greet his passengers, striving to work his face into more welcome shape.

Gammidge said hurriedly: 'I 'member, sir, you used to believe a lot o' old fairy tales o' the sea. Don't believe that one about a fallen skipper bein' bad luck. Old Bill Gammidge ain't bad luck to nobody but hisself.'

Then the old man dipped down the poop ladder before he saw the scowl return to Sargasso's face.

Sargasso smiled as soon as he could manage it, for no man might look at Miss Rouse for thirty seconds without wanting to smile. Sargasso wondered what she would look like if she were free from all trouble, so fair and friendly did she appear through the obvious mist of bereavement.

'In case the letter I brought did not tell you everything,' she smiled, 'I am the adopted daughter of Mr Rouse, who was buried today. Apparently I was a castaway, picked up when a baby by one of his ships. I have no claim on his estate and he made no will. But he gave me a good education; so, thank goodness, I am able to shift for myself. I have been told that you, too, were a castaway. Do you hold the same beliefs as I do. Do you believe – '

'The letter you brought told me everything, miss,' Sargasso returned shortly. 'Is there anything lacking in your accommodation? If so, please tell me now. If not, we are ready to sail.'

The lady's big grey eyes opened wider; but she made no more reply than to assure him that her comfort was well looked after, then took up a seat on a skylight locker, produced a well-thumbed, leather-covered album, and began leisurely to arrange some specimens of ferns in it. Sargasso was sending off a message to the tugboat office, jubilant at the prospect of getting to sea at last.

'Oh, captain,' the lady cried, 'can you tell me how to preserve the colour of this weed?' She held up a sprig. 'It was so beautifully golden and now it's turned such a dull grey.'

Sargasso turned to see a piece of faded Sargasso weed. He uttered a curse that shocked Miss Rouse. His face turned ashen. He stamped over to the gangway, overtook his messenger, and strode off himself to get the tug.

A grey dawn. A grey sea. Grey mist and a sluggishly moving ship streaming grey foam from the clean-painted scuppers. The *Khedivieh* was fifteen days at sea. Sargasso sat in his stateroom, reading over his orders for want of something better to do. Head winds, calms, fog, all had fought against him on this his first command. Instead of being three-quarters of the way over to the American side, the big ship wallowed sluggishly in a faint air far to the southward of the shipping tracks. Twice to the northward Sargasso had tacked against the perverse westerly gales. Twice to the south'ard. Now the deep-laden ship had found a breeze, faint and dying, but free, and she moved lazily through a sea that seemed dead.

Far off, it seemed, a shrill-voiced sailor headed a chorus as men braced the yards. Another ill omen. Bracing yards meant that the meagre fair wind was hauling foul, even in dying.

Hay, hay, oh, hay-ay-ay-oh-hay!

'Damnation!' growled Sargasso, and hurled the letter he was reading into a drawer. Then he took it out again and glanced at a paragraph. The paragraph read:

Miss Rouse was picked up adrift in the Atlantic, as we understand you were, Captain Sargasso. She, too, was accompanied by a negro female but whereas your negro was a grown woman, apparently your nurse, Miss Rouse's companion was a child as young as herself. There is in interesting possibility in the coincidence. You and Miss Rouse may fight it out between you. She is determined to make her own living in America as a teacher or governess, though we believe it is not necessary. The maid who sails with her is the same girl who was picked up with her, and is devoted to her. We have heard about your own superstitions, beliefs, fears, whatever you call them. We hope that you will let us know in some future communication how your voyage has turned out in regard to matters other than mere business. Miss Rouse is a merry soul, when not oppressed with grief, and she hinted that she might make you unburden yourself to a greater extent than most people can do. Good luck, captain, etc.

Sargasso went on deck. He glanced around, half hoping to see Miss Rouse, yet glad that she was not there. The mate came to him, having finished bracing the yards.

'Wind hauled, sir,' he said superfluously.

'You're heading too far south,' snapped Sargasso. 'Haven't you learned enough to know that any tack on the polar side is a shorter way home than the equatorial side?'

'Yes, sir; I know that. But this gives a long board, and – '

'Well, Mr Fisher, if you see a bit of yellow weed on the water, tack ship, that's all!'

Miss Rouse came up, wrapped in a fur coat, though it was still summer.

'Ugh!' she shuddered prettily. 'Isn't it lucky you have a chief mate who likes warmth rather than cold? I do hope we see the sunshine soon again. Do you always have this kind of dismal weather in sailing-ships, captain? I have travelled by steamer a lot and never saw such weather. It ought to be warm, too. Shall we see some floating gulf-weed, do you think? I want some for my book.'

Sargasso wanted to be polite more than he had ever wanted anything in life. Miss Rouse affected him like some beneficent ray of warm light; shy naturally, Sargasso worshipped her in silence. Had speech come easily to him he would long since have embarked on an ardent flirtation, if not courtship. Now he tried to fight back a sour contortion of features, turning his back on her.

'Mr Fisher!' he cried. The mate stopped in his pacing. 'Mr Fisher, call the watch. I'll tack ship at once!'

They sailed northerly until wandering icebergs mocked them. On a night when the big ship sailed past a towering moonlit berg that looked like a celestial cathedral, a great four-funnel liner charged from the other side of it, her hoarse siren booming belatedly.

A somnolent look-out, only part of him awake, and that part awed into speechlessness by the apparition of the stately berg, stepped backwards and fell from the *Khedivieh*'s forecastle head at the first sound of that booming siren. A harassed first mate, too intent upon his grouch at a skipper who forced his ship into the ice limits unnecessarily, stared at the oncoming liner, only guessing that a man had gone overboard, and bawled frantic orders.

'Up hellum! Hard up your hellum! Hands to the braces! Jump for your lives!'

With his own hands Mr Fisher let go the spanker sheet and hove with all his might on the wheel. The great liner swerved, her sharp stem missing the sailing-ship by feet; and her colossal bulk side-wiped the other so gently that it scarcely jarred her. But so slight a jar from forty thousand tons, steaming at thirty knots, shook four thousand tons, sailing at eight knots, clear to the keel, and men were flung broadcast. Sails thundered and yards thrashed. Sargasso appeared, white-faced, dragging Miss Rouse by the arm.

'What is it?' he cried. He saw the passing liner. 'Are we cut down? he demanded.

'She only brushed us,' the mate growled. 'Lost a man overboard, though. Knocked him off the forecastle head.'

'Oh, what is the matter?' the girl asked.

She seemed excited rather than frightened. But Sargasso was cursing the liner even as he leaped to the rail, scanning the sea. He caught a glimpse of a waving arm out of the water in the moon path and, with a curt order to the mate to cast him a life-buoy, plunged after the lost look-out, and saved him.

After a long tack to the southward again, the ship approached the limits of the Sargasso Sea, and sunny skies, brisk breezes, and sparkling sprays made each day a tonic. Miss Rouse contrived to delve under the outer skin of Sargasso's reserve; he seemed no longer to care whether the black maid came near or not. Grumbling that had started for'ard stopped as the ship reeled off the knots. But still she was headed by the wind. The north-east trades were unaccountably missing.

'Farther south than usual, that's all,' Mr Fisher stated, discussing the absent winds with Mr Bunce. 'If he'll only stand on south, he'll pick 'em up very soon now.'

'Good thing, too,' quoth Mr Bunce. 'That big Yankee Jack has been shooting off his mouth altogether too much lately. If the chap the skipper saved from drowning hadn't been nigh to take his part, old Bill Gammidge would have got a hiding from Yank for sticking up for the skipper. What I don't see is, why Cap'n Sargasso didn't hold on while he was so far up north and get a good hard slant out of the Westerlies. If we have to beat, might as well have hard winds to beat with.'

'If you ask me, Mr Bunce, I think he's as scared of cold and ice as he is of gulfweed. Shouldn't wonder if that boat rescue he pulled off was more due to somebody in the boat than to himself. Looks yellow to me.'

The youthful second mate stared aghast. Such words coming from a chief mate savoured almost of sacrilege. But the words were scarcely definite enough to warrant a junior reprimanding his senior. They might make a man think; but – well, that's what Mr Bunce did. He thought. And when old Bill Gammidge, at the wheel one night, made bold to repeat almost word for word the mate's language, but as coming from the forecastle, he made up his mind to speak to Sargasso about it at the first opportunity.

The opportunity did not come immediately. Another day found the ship slipping along through a field of golden weed, the wind still heading her. Sargasso remained below until it was time to get his noon observation.

His face paled when he saw the limitless expanse of yellow. He glanced over the stern at the tangled log and turned a shade paler. A shark – a long, lean, wicked-looking shark with a hungry eye – followed close astern.

'Oh, that means that a man is to die, doesn't it?' Miss Rouse rippled. She had come up to watch the taking of the sun, and the skipper's actions intrigued her. 'Surely you don't believe it,' she laughed, accenting the you.

'Let those disbelieve that want to,' he returned curtly, and fell to work with his sextant.

He worked up his sight and plotted his position, his face grim and stern; but he gave no order to tack to the north out of the weed. At four bells in the first dog-watch the cook capsized a copper full of boiling water over himself. The unlucky man died at midnight.

At eight bells in the morning watch, before the watch going below took their breakfast from old Bill Gammidge, the substitute cook, the dead man was buried. Miss Rouse looked on with vivid interest, although her fair face glowed with sorrow.

'Now c'mit this body t' th' deep,' Sargasso gabbled, white to the eyes. 'Until th' sea shall give up – Heave, Mr Fisher! Heave!' he cried nervously, and stepped to the rail.

Miss Rouse was beside him. The grating was lifted at the inboard end; the weighted body slipped from beneath the flag fastened at the upper corners, and plunged almost soundlessly into the yellow weed, leaving for an instant a flash of azure blue, scummed with threads of white foam.

'Oh, are you still looking for that shark?' whispered the girl.

She gazed up into Sargasso's face with a new light in her eyes. He was staring out beyond the place where the body had sunk, too well weighted to give any shark encouragement. The golden weed was suddenly cut by a black fin and Sargasso's eyes glared at it fascinatedly.

'If it goes now, everything is all right, isn't it?' the girl whispered again.

Sargasso stood like a figurehead of oak. The fin darted around in a circle, then started directly ahead of the ship, crossed her bows, and sped aft again. Then it turned its snout towards the rudder, raised its long glistening back clear of weed and water for an instant, and vanished with a flirt of the tail.

'What does that mean?' Miss Rouse asked curiously.

Then she caught the expression on Sargasso's face and stood stock-still in her tracks, while he abruptly turned and left her. She went to Mr Fisher.

'That?' he laughed shortly. 'Old women believe that means the ship will never come to anchor. Old-fashioned sailors believe it, too; those that are weak in the head, miss. I expect we'll tack ship again now.'

'If you mean that Captain Sargasso believes in that, then I think he's too good a seaman to be driven by his beliefs or fears,' she said. 'There must be some reason for such beliefs, anyhow. Didn't the cook die?'

'Hot water, miss, and sharks don't fancy hot water,' the mate laughed unpleasantly.

The ship sailed on, deeper into the weed. Many a tale has been told, many a myth foisted on the gullible, about a vast dead sea of weed, in which tree trunks, islands, floating charnel houses centuries old and derelicts of all ages continue one endless round of eternal monotony, some bearing treasure incalculable, some bearing freight of grinning skeletons, all bearing the unmistakable stamp of ghastly fate. Nothing of the kind obstructed the progress of the big four-masted barque. She encountered weed, thick and long; she had no wind; the Trades were missing; she crept sluggishly where she should have slipped smoothly through the water, but it was only weed and light breezes that hampered her.

Bill Gammidge, monarch of the galley, doctor to all hands, accepted his new job with better grace than most ex-masters would have shown; and as doctor, lord of the grub, he found lots of friends who were not friends or at least doubtful friends before. He soon came to high words with the Italian steward. Blows were only averted by the surprising intervention of Yankee Jack. Then the big sailor stepped inside the galley, grabbed Bill's shirt bosom, and assured him hoarsely:

'You ain't gotta take no guff from him or nobody. See? I like yuh, and the hands like yuh, Bill. You keep on never-mindin', and watch me, see? I'm tellin' yuh!'

Yankee Jack and Mr Fisher had a long talk one evening. Yank was mending a mizzen staysail and was doing a poor job on it. But after so long a chat with the mate seemed very well pleased with the work; so well that when Miss Rouse walked along to say good evening to old Bill Gammidge scrubbing a bucket of clothes in the waist abreast of the galley door, old Bill made room for her beside him on the spare topmast.

'Like a breeze arter a calm, missy, when you come along,' he said.

He laid his old pipe down as a concession to politeness, a reminder of his better days. The girl smiled softly, took up his reeking old cutty and held it to his roughened lips.

'Smoke, Bill,' she said. 'I want you to yarn to me. Isn't this voyage getting rather long?'

'It's so long, miss, that mates is talking to foremast hands like they never ought to. I was master once; master o' the brig *Pallas*, finest brig as ever swung a stu'ns'l. I know. 'Tain't right.'

'Why, what's wrong?' the girl laughed. 'I swear I'm getting fascinated by all this mystery. First, the captain believes in sharks and things; he won't sail into the gulf-weed – '

'He's sailing into it now, ain't he?' broke in Bill hotly. 'I sailed with Sam Sargasso afore you wuz born, missy, meaning no offence. He made his fust v'yage to sea as a boy with me, arter saving me my ship too. So I – '

'Oh, do tell me about it!' cried Miss Rouse, frankly interested at last.

Yankee Jack had rolled up his mizzen staysail and was looking for a hand to help him carry it to the locker. He came towards the galley.

'Got no time now, missy,' said old Bill hurriedly. 'If so be you can spare a minute after supper, I'll spin the yarn. What d'ye want, Yank?'

When the first watch was set and the big ship had settled down to her night arrangements, old Bill Gammidge stood at the foot of the lee poop ladder dressed in a clean dungaree jumper and smoking a new clay pipe. He hated a new pipe. Clean dungarees made him itch; but he waited, whistling through his teeth when he removed his pipe to cool his tongue. And a ghostly, floating, cool white figure came down the ladder to him.

'Have you been waiting long, Bill?' Miss Rouse asked cheerily.

Bill plunged right into his yarn, a bit afraid of the lady, now he had her so near to him under the great low-leaning stars that flooded the sky. He told all about how he had first met Sargasso Sam. How the lad had run away in Berbice. How he had been a thoroughly good lad, promising much as a seaman; but how he was unaccountably obsessed with weird superstitions and crazy fears of Sargasso weed.

'Seems he was only a babby, miss, when picked up in the weed,' Bill finished. 'Got feared, I suppose. But he must have been all I hoped he would be, 'cos he pulled off that life-saving thing as was as good as anything any man ever done. He deserves to command this ship, that he do!'

'I'm so glad,' she said softly. 'I know he is a good man. But don't you think he might do better by sailing south – '

'Beg pardon, missy,' Bill broke in harshly. 'I know there's a lot o' talk. Even the mate is talking, and he never ought to. The men are yapping like dogs. I am an old skipper; skipper o' the brig *Pallas*, finest brig as ever swung a stu'ns'l, and I never see no good come yet of officer nor man blowing off about their cap'n. Cap'n Sargasso, ma'am, knows what he's doing. I'd ha' done the same in his place. Superstitious he may be, but he ain't letting that interfere wi' his duty. No, ma'am! Mark my words! Sargasso Sam ain't no gutless man, such as they tells of. . . . Bid you good night, missy. Beg pardon for my hasty words. I'm maybe an old fool, but Sargasso Sam's all right; yes, ma'am!'

Bill walked away, and astonishingly swiftly Yankee Jack appeared. Miss Rouse ran up the ladder to the poop before he spoke, and he seemed about to come up after her; but Sargasso met her at the ladder head and Yankee Jack melted into the shadows of the waist.

Soon afterwards a small muffled figure crept from the forward cabin door and followed Yankee Jack and Bill Gammidge. As the small figure passed the galley, the faint light from the port shone upon the glistening eyes and shining black face of Miss Rouse's maid. Miss Rouse had found Sargasso alone beside the jigger mast and unexpectedly discovered in him a bright, cheerful strain when she began to ask him about the great stars with which the heavens were alight. She wondered vaguely at his being on watch alone. Knowing a good deal about the sea and its ways, she was afraid at first that he had caught an officer away from his duty, was waiting to catch the delinquent and would prove a sorry companion. But he smiled at her star queries, and she thought a miracle had touched him, so great was the change in his features.

'When Mr Fisher comes aft I'll show you how to take an observation,' he said. 'See that big red star in the west? That's Aldebaran. He's about right for a time sight. Wonder what's keeping the mate.'

'Where is he? Shall I fetch him, captain?'

'Never mind, miss. He went to look at the fore-topgallant mast. Said it was creaking. Good mate, Mr Fisher. Likes to see to those things himself.'

Miss Rouse wanted to say something about mates who talked to the sailors off duty, but the mate appeared and she did not. Then the novelty of being permitted to squint through a sextant and find red Aldebaran blazing at her from the face of a little mirror drove other thoughts from her head.

'Oh, it's fascinating!' she cried.

Then, when Sargasso showed her how to select logarithms, how to compare times and to work out the position of the ship from the sight she had taken, and then to plot it off on the chart, comparing it with his own result and finding it agreed, she thrilled to the sheer human possibilities in him, finding him a very personable man indeed.

'I'm going to have you teach me navigation and go up for my ticket,' she laughed as she left him.

Sargasso remained in the chart room, going over his figures. The mate walked aft to scan the compass.

'Navigators won't be so scarce now, Mr Fisher,' the helmsman grinned impudently.

'Watch your steering!' growled the mate, but gave the man no further reprimand. The man chuckled and spat over his shoulder.

The mellow tones of the poop bell boomed out four bells and the harsher clangour of the forecastle bell answered it. Yankee Jack came aft to relieve the wheel, and Miss Rouse's maid sped behind him, vanishing inside the main-deck door before the relieved helmsman came down the ladder. The relieved look-out approached the poop, calling up to the mate:

'Jager's on th' look-out.' He gave the mate no 'sir', and added in a sidelong undertone, 'Looks like a derelict a bit off th' bow to th' s'uth'ard.'

'Then why in hell didn't you report it?' snapped the mate.

'Aw, take a jump at yerself! I have reported it, ain't I? What's a-bitin' yez?'

'Go for'ard!' stormed the mate. 'I'll talk to you presently!'

'So youse will!' muttered the man.

The mate walked aft, trembling with fury. The man glanced around, saw some dark figures in the waist, abreast of the galley, whistled softly, then darted into the cabin by the main-deck door, peering around for the maid. He stopped short, scared, at the sound of a closing door. Every sound within the ship seemed concentrated in the dim cabin. A small figure emerged from a darkened cabin, stepped to the water bottle in the table rack and filled a tumbler.

The man hissed softly, the maid all but dropped the glass, the next moment she was smothered in the hug of him, laughing boldly up into his face, while two more men appeared in the main-deck entrance.

'Go and bring the mate down here!' whispered the man who held the black maid.

'Not now!' she panted, breathless from his hug.

'Yes, now! You're into it now! You ain't goin' to back out!'

'No, no! But my lady! She's waiting for me! She – '

'We'll take care o' her!' The other two men laughed softly and stepped towards Miss Rouse's stateroom. The maid struggled fiercely.

'Keep out!' she panted. 'Make them keep away, or I'll – '

'Listen!' the man said, speaking into her ear and gripping her hard. 'Fisher's talking as if he's weakened. Get him right away and I'll look after your lady. If you don't – '

'Make them keep out!' the girl insisted, and raised her voice so that the three men cursed her.

'You going?' her captor demanded savagely.

One of the other men laid a hand on Miss Rouse's door handle. The little black maid screamed. The man thrust a hand over her mouth; then he collapsed from her in a sobbing heap, his blood following her knife in a torrent.

The men at Miss Rouse's door stood frozen with panic for an instant. There was a yell and a shot on deck; the sound of an iron door being slammed shut reverberated along the waist. The doors of the skipper and second mate were flung open; the maid darted towards the two men at her lady's door. Then she was caught tight by both of them; the big cabin suddenly filled with men, and big Yankee Jack's roaring voice bellowed orders as he led the attack upon Sargasso.

Sargasso leaped back inside his room, seeking for a weapon. Youthful Mr Bunce, confronted with his first real raw bit of life drama, only knew his duty and with his bare fists he hurled himself forward to do it. On the heels of the last of the mutineers staggered a wheezing, bleeding, tottering figure, the face partly shot away, powder-grimed and horrible.

'Look out, cap'n, look out!' it screamed, then fell. It fell across the body of the man the maid had knifed; and slowly it rose again, gripping in tensed fingers the reddened knife.

Like unseeing fate it lurched straight towards the skipper's door, fell against the crouching back of Yankee Jack, and thrust the steel to the haft in the ring-leader's averted throat.

'Sargasso, I'm a fool! I'm paying!' moaned Mr Fisher, and fell at the skipper's feet, covering with his dead body the pistol dropped by Yankee Jack.

Mr Bunce went down before a rush of foes. Miss Rouse stood in her doorway, horror-stricken at the swift transition from a night of tranquillity to this thing of terror. Somewhere along the starlit deck a lusty voice bellowed threats unless somebody let the owner out of somewhere. Then Sargasso went down, streaming blood from a jagged wound in his forehead as a man hurled a water-bottle at him; and Miss Rouse was rushed back through her door, the key was turned and comparative stillness reigned after the uproar.

Sargasso's head throbbed agonizingly. Cool moisture trickled over his face. His head lay on something soft. His eyes were tightly closed, swollen shockingly. Small hot fingers tried to pry his eyes open; a strange hushed voice crooned to him. The motion under him seemed strange too. With the crooning of the voice another sound was merged and it made him shudder. He tried to speak; his battered head and bruised face forbade it. But he listened intently for that other sound.

'Cat!' he managed to utter, rustily, horribly.

It was all he could say, and there was no music in the tone; but the soft crooning stopped and a small laugh answered him. The crooning went on again, and the cool trickling at his face was sweet. One tight pair of eyelids opened the merest crack under the persevering fingers; a newly risen moon shone full through the crack and he wrenched his head aside in acute pain.

Dimly through his muddled brain the remembrance filtered that moonrise was due around two o'clock am. He had the impression, from the angle at which the moon rays struck his eye, that it was newly risen. He could have told the time more nearly could he have seen the stars. He tried again to speak and could not; but the small hot fingers at his brow quivered when he seized them, and a low, shaken voice told him:

'Keep still. They thought you were dead. I thought so too. You wouldn't have been left here with me if they hadn't been sure you were dead. They left us together to punish me for my part in the – '

A scurry and a squeaking near by; something ran across Sargasso's legs, and the speaker uttered a shuddering cry. There was a soft thud, a louder squeak, a crunch, then the purring snarl of a cat with a kill. Sargasso tried to rise, groping with his hands for support.

'Where – where – where are we?' he gasped, horror giving him halting speech at last.

Small hot hands helped him, guiding his grasp to something familiar yet not of recent familiarity. It was a wooden stanchion in wooden bulwarks he felt, roughened and paintless. He pulled himself up until he stood, facing the moon, sensing it by the lesser darkness that assailed his blinded eyes. Near by his hands found a splintered breech, a broken lanyard of rotten rope, a cracked deadeye.

'Keep hold, just for a minute, sir,' his unseen companion told him, and he heard her soft-shod feet hurrying away.

In a few minutes she returned and put a wooden bowl brimming with tepid, unfresh water to his thirsty lips. And while he gulped greedily, he felt fresh sopping compresses of linen on forehead and eyes. He began to feel stronger. He wanted to move, but the girl made him sit down on what he knew instinctively were quarter bits. Starting to protest, protest was killed by a terrific scurrying and squeaking that seemed to fill the still air. He sat down with a curse, resigning himself to the tireless attentions of his companion in ill luck.

'Soon you can see, now,' she said with a jerky little laugh. 'We might be worse off. You must have been born lucky!'

For an hour she bathed his eyes, silent now from weariness. He thought over her remark. That had been the last thing she said to him: 'You must have been born lucky!' He uttered a laugh that frightened her. But she kept on bathing his throbbing forehead.

'They called me a man of no bowels because I believed in things beyond their vision!' he croaked harshly. 'Said I was a superstitious fool because I knew there was ill luck in the blue stripe; that a shark knew when a ship was doomed; that no good ever came of having a black cat or a black wench aboard. What do they say now?'

The fingers at his brow trembled; the small figure against his body tensed and quivered. But the bathing went on. It went on until, amazingly suddenly it seemed, light burst through his tortured lids. His impatient fingers pried his eyes open and he gazed full at the moon, almost at meridian. Then something soft brushed against his leg. He turned from the moonlight, looked down, saw a huge, fat, glossy black cat with arched back and lifted tail; then looked up and into the wide white-rimmed eyes of Miss Rouse's little black maid. For a moment he stared at her, then laughed loud across the yellow weed-strewn sea.

'A black cat, a black wench, a derelict, adrift in the Sargasso Sea!' he yelled.

A fat rat ran across his hand, resting on the shattered bulwarks. He hurled it at the cat and staggered away around the deck, blundering into things, all but pitching headlong through the broken bulwarks into the sea.

'It's only a rat,' the girl whispered, frightened more than she had been during his quiescence. 'The wreck is swarming with rats, sir. But the cat looks after them. See how fat she is!'

Sargasso laughed unpleasantly, slumping down heavily on a hatch. The girl gave him water and produced from some secret place a few bits of mouldy biscuit. He nibbled and drank, and the girl went on bathing his eyes. While they slowly gained in sight, she told him an astonishing tale that seemed to have no clear beginning, and of which the end was not yet.

'The men listened to Yankee Jack,' she said. 'He made them believe it was only your superstitious fears that made the voyage so long. And Mr Fisher said things, too, which encouraged them. Yankee Jack said the mate would surely side with them, for he had called you crazy. Old Bill Gammidge heard a little; but not much, for they didn't trust him, quite. But he knew they were talking about taking the ship, either putting you and the second mate, and anybody who wouldn't join them, in a little boat or on such a wreck as this if they saw one. They were going to sail the ship to Santo Domingo and sell it. They spoke to me about the people down there. Old Bill couldn't find out about their plans, so he told me to try and get them. I did. I laughed and joked with them at night. I flirted with Yankee Jack and the man they called Sam – the man I stabbed – and they said I should be their lady and have my lady for slave.'

Over the side, fair in the moon path, something white and glistening, ghostly, weird, rose from the sea, and a ghastly sound emanated from it:

'Whoo-oo-oo-ooh!'

'Oh, powerful Gawd!' screamed the girl, relapsing in her terror into the vernacular of her childhood.

Sargasso Sam started; but her tale had reached a point where no fears of his own could steal his attention.

'Only a grampus blowing, child,' he said with a shiver. 'Tell me the rest. Quick!'

She shivered, crushing close to him.

'They got a bit afraid of the mate. So they got talking to old Bill and found he told the truth about once being captain. So when the look-out saw this wreck, he didn't report it until he went to see the mate. They saw more doubt in the mate's attitude and started things so swiftly that I was surprised in the saloon before I could get to tell you.'

'And poor Fisher paid!' muttered Sargasso. 'Yes, he paid. So will you, my girl. You will pay for playing with fire. Do you know just what will happen to us here?'

'Mr Sargasso, Missy Alys says you are a true sailor. You will find some way to save me. They left me here with you they thought dead and laughed when they told me we would drift and drift and drift for a hundred years in the weeds, you a grinning dead man and me never allowed to die. I have paid already. I have been frightened so that my heart is a lump of ice. But you will do something when daylight comes.'

Sargasso Sam laughed harshly. He could see better every minute, and in the bright moonlight the derelict lay bare to his scrutiny. She floated high, but green moss grew out of her decks; the one mast standing, the main lowermast, stood gaunt and white, swinging a long main yard like a gibbet. The remains of a hundred dead rats littered the decks. There was a smell of rot, of death, of putrefaction issuing from the battered fabric. Only the great black cat had any appearance of life. It looked like a fat ghoul in a rifled tomb.

'Do something?' he laughed. 'What was Gammidge doing through it all?'

'They locked him in the galley. I heard him shouting and swearing at them through the port. The Italian steward came out with a knife, too, trying to help; they threw him down in the lazaret. But you will find a way. Missy Alys always said you were a true sailor. She called you a hero when she heard about something you did before you were captain of the *Khedivieh*. She said she believed nothing could beat you.'

The cruel laughter died out of Sargasso's face. As the little black maid rattled on, her own hopes rising as she told of her mistress's confidences, something stern and strong crept into his face. Like a flash of light he saw something that did more than all the years had been able to do for him.

He saw the situation he was in, shorn of all pretence. As desperate as any situation could well be, with every factor there that might prove the truth of his lifelong fears: blue stripe, black cat, black wench, lying shark, everything; here was a little black maid teaching him courage, a black cat rubbing sleekly against his leg, the very derelict he was adrift upon feeling secure at least; and here was a tale that told him the woman he had wanted to worship humbly at a distance had said things about him that placed him on her own plane.

Strength came to him as his eyes opened. He gave the girl his jacket and told her to curl up somewhere and rest. Then he left her with the great black cat purring at her breast and examined the derelict more closely.

The odour guided him to a broken hatch, and his eyes verified the evidence of his nose. The ancient ship was laden with grain. It had sprouted, rotted, swollen, fermented into a mass of unspeakable decay in which thousands of plethoric rats lived and fought, loved and died. It was no mystery how the big cat had survived the untellable period of its imprisonment. It had never had to starve or fight for food; never had cause to grow savage and wild. In the partly rolled hatch tarpaulin lay a pool of bad water. Every time a rain fell the cat's water supply was renewed. If drought came, the rats gave blood.

Under the break of a short half poop a cask of water lay, with scuttle open and a dipper beside it. The dipper was rusted to pieces. The maid had found a broken wooden bucket, and that was what she had fed him water from. An inspection of the galley on deck resulted in the discovery of a drawerful of mouldy hard-tack, the weevils long since dead. Aft, in the cabin pantry, a small keg of salt meat rolled with the ship's motion. A few tins of beef, fish and vegetables completed the tally. There seemed to be evidence of haste in deserting the ship; yet the hull seemed to have made no water in the years, if years had passed.

Sargasso searched hurriedly for papers. He found none. The cabin stank with the rottenness under it. He passed on deck again, gave a swift and all-seeing glance at the weather-beaten old wreck that told him the futility of trying to rig and sail her; then he cast about for some other means of deliverance.

A decrepit boat, split and weather-scarred, sat brokenly in its chocks on the gallows. Sargasso tried the tackles. They came apart in his hand, dry dust of ropes. He put his shoulders to the stern; it surged forward, broke down the chocks, and plunged down and through the broken bulwarks into the sea.

Sargasso leaped after it like a cat. He floundered in the tangling weed, then used the very weed to make fast the boat to the ship. He panted heavily as he climbed back to the deck and his face was white. The touch of the weed shook him to the heart. But the boat was filling. He looked around in the waning moonlight almost despairingly. But his eye roved over the small figure of the sleeping maid; he thought what she had done for him; he recalled what she had told him.

'She believed nothing could beat you!'

With the instinct of a sailor he ran to the forecastle head, knowing that small chains should be there. He tore down from the rotten stanchions two lengths of chain and went to secure his boat. Then, in the last of the moonlight before the dawn, he baled his boat dry, hauled his chain tight and left her until daylight was full.

Through a long blazing day they toiled, Sargasso and the small black maid. Rotten wood, rotten canvas, rotton rope mocked them. They opened tins of food. It was blown and poisonous. They broke open the cask of meat. It was salt beef, so salt that sea water seemed fresh beside it. They ate little, for eating made them thirst, and the water was dangerous. But through it all they laboured. When the sun sank into the yellow sea like a yellow eye, bloodshot, glaring at their presumptuous efforts, they had raised the boat to the deck again, upturned it and plastered the bottom and sides with the best of the inner-hatch tarpaulins smeared with pitch from the one-time carpenter's stores.

'We've done well, girl,' Sargasso grinned.

'You see, your luck isn't so bad,' the girl replied.

'No; if only my luck were as good as it looked to be bad or as good as you seem to think it is, maybe we would get out of the mess before we starve to death. Luck hasn't much to do with it, I'm afraid.'

'Luck goes with work, and a brave man works where another lies down and wails at his luck,' the girl retorted with spirit. 'Miss Alys taught me that,' she added, lowering her eyes before his astonished gaze.

'Damned if I don't think you're right!' he said, and patted her on the head.

Before dark he was whistling, with lips too sore for whistling; he started singing softly. Then he picked up the great black cat and stroked it, its purring sounding like the muffled rolling of drums to his singing:

Many thousand miles behind us,
Many thousand miles before,
Ancient ocean heaves to bear us
To yon well-remembered shore.
Cheer up, Jack; bright smiles await you
From the fairest of the fair,
And her loving eyes will greet you
With kind welcomes everywhere.

It was the low, crooning voice of the little black maid that led the chorus of the beautiful old song:

Rolling home, rolling home, rolling home across the sea;
Rolling home to hearts awaiting, rolling home, dear land, to thee.

'Miss Alys taught me that, too,' whispered the maid, the song ended. 'She says the longest journey has an end. She and me was picked up at sea in worser fix than this, Cap'n Sargasso. She knows.'

'You're right! She knows! You will be rolling home, too, this time tomorrow!' cried Sargasso. 'I've got to see your Miss Alys! Got to tell her something!'

Sargasso slept, but he found and lit a battered lantern first, feeding it with rancid grease from the galley copper, whose lid had kept the rats at bay through endless days. Then he lay near the girl so that the great black cat could guard both from the swarming rats. And at dawn he was astir, mounting to the highest part of the wreck, scanning the sea. Nothing broke the yellow of the weed. The sun came up blazing out of the east; the sky held scant promise of wind.

The maid got food, and he told her to select the best of the stores remaining for the boat and to stopper up the water cask carefully. He finished caulking the boat himself; he spliced pieces of wood together, lashing them with long, tough weed. Tarpaulin made a sail, a sail so rotten that it ripped in hoisting. He made another, double, and it held. Oars he found and a rudder, all rotten, but all he had. Then they put in the stores and water.

'You're not scared?' he asked the girl.

'Me?'

She stared at him. He nodded overside. Ten fathoms away from the boat a mass of weed was being thrown broadcast by a swarm of sharks fighting for something entangled in it. The girl's face turned ashen; her big eyes widened, showing the whites. She saw that he smiled, and shook herself sharply together.

'Didn't I tell you we got to go?' she said shrilly. She glanced around. 'We got to take the cat too. The rats would have eaten us if it wasn't for him.'

Sargasso laughed. All the pet superstitions that had ridden him all his life seemed about to die shameful deaths. He glanced again at the sharks. One, leaving the rest, charged at the boat and rocked it with his rush. The girl was giving the cat a last drink from the leavings of the water cask. Sargasso ran forward, rummaged in the forepeak, but found nothing that he wanted. With a queer grin, he dropped into the hold, scooped a double handful of blue mould from the beams and returned to the boat. Leaning over the low gunwales, he rubbed the blue mess on the paintless sides in a streak passing right around the little craft.

'Now you can come aboard, my lass!' he cried. 'We've got everything now. Being scared of all these things only brings bad luck. We'll try the other tack. Give me the cat. Come on, Satan!'

For two blistering days Sargasso rowed. The water stank and gave out. Food turned to brine in dry mouths. The golden weed mocked them; the wind had no strength. The little black maid wilted towards the second evening. The great black cat mewed thirstily at the sea.

Sargasso rowed. His face turned grey; his lips were dry and cracked. He rowed, and as he forced the leaky boat through the weed he sang croakily:

Blow the wintry breezes,
Blow the winds hi-ho!
Clear away the morning dew,
And blow, my bully boys, blow!

He unshipped his oars at dark, resting uneasily. With his cupped hands he scooped up water and bathed the black girl's face. He wetted the cat's dry nose. It spat at him and sprang the length of the boat at the sting of the salt.

'Now, Lady Luck, it's up to you, old girl!' he croaked, lying down along the thwart.

He dozed for an hour. Then rain on his face awoke him. The boat buzzed merrily through the weed before a brisk squall; the rain poured in a torrent.

'Up, lassie!' he cried. 'Here's water to swim in!'

They caught it in their garments. They filled the little cask with it. The boat was put on a rough course by a star, heading west by north. Another sharp squall half-filled the crazy boat at midnight. Sargasso began to doubt Lady Luck for the first time. The weed had become thinner, the seas were getting up. The maid baled tirelessly, her thirst tempered. Sargasso baled, nursed his decrepit rigging and sang stubbornly:

Blow the wintry breezes,
Blow the winds hi-ho!
Clear away the morning dew,
And blow, my bully boys, blow!

A flying fish flew over the boat, thudded into the sail and fell into his lap. The great cat pounced upon it with a low purr, but Sargasso held it from her. He had seen it in the bright starlight.

'Hold on, Satan!' he laughed. 'Look, lassie! It's a Guineaman, a four-winged flyer. It's good luck. Shall we let Satan have it?'

'Let it go, master. You don't feed no luck to that cat!' the girl cried.

He tossed it overboard and fell to baling, still singing defiantly.

The squall passed and the sea fell calm. But the weed was almost gone, and the great moon came up in a fair expanse of sea but sparsely strewn with snaky yellow lines. Sargasso stood on the thwart, gazing intently around the horizon. Low down in the west red Aldebaran flamed. It winked at him. It flamed again and seemed to laugh at his extremity. Suddenly he stepped from the thwart, laughed queerly, and lifted up the maid to arm's length.

'Look there, lassie! Right over there! See? That's a ship! A ship becalmed like we are! D'ye think you can pull an oar?'

Dawn was near when the tall shape of a becalmed sailing-ship loomed up close to. Sargasso stared hard. There were no lights. The great yards swung in slovenly trim, unbraced. The silence of a dead ship hung about her. But he knew her.

'What's happened?' he muttered hoarsely. 'It's my own ship, lassie; but look at her!'

'Looks like they ain't had all the luck, master,' the little maid answered, frightened at the eerie silence.

Evil as a curse within a church, from some dark cranny in the big ship's fore-part howled a voice in a drunken frenzy. A fiercer voice cursed the howler, and silence reigned again. From high up among the jigger rigging came a cautious voice, a frightened voice:

'Hey, boat ahoy! Boat ahoy!'

'That's old Bill Gammidge!' snapped Sargasso, and urged the boat forward.

'Ahoy, Gammidge!' he answered. 'Come down! I'm Sargasso! What's up?'

'Hully sailor! It's the Old Man, missy!' roared Bill, and a dark blur detached itself from the rolled-up gaff-topsail and began to swarm down the rigging.

Out from the forecastle a figure stepped, peered a moment over the side, but failed to see the boat in the ship's shadow; then yelled obscene oaths upwards and fired a revolver shot at Gammidge in the rigging. Bill stopped with a cry, almost fell. Then he lugged something from his pocket, hurled it at the gunman, who dropped heavily, and Bill continued on down.

'Come on, sir!' he roared. 'They be all drunk 'cept him, and he's out!'

Sargasso was at the rail even as the man fell. He went straight to the fallen man, snatched up the pistol as the man began to stagger to his knees; then, as Gammidge joined him, seeking for the belaying pin he had hurled to such good effect from aloft, other unsteady figures appeared from unseen corners, drunken voices demanded what was wrong, and the leader leaped to his feet with a howl.

'It's the dog-blasted skipper come back!' he screamed. 'Chuck him overboard again or you'll all hang!'

'Keep back!' roared Sargasso, presenting the gun. 'Gammidge, lash that man's hands!'

'He's got no shells in the gun!' yelled the leader. 'Come on, get him!'

The man rushed on tottering legs. Old Bill let fly with his iron pin again, and the leader fell to stay. Over the rail climbed the little black maid, on her shoulder the great black cat. Two men, reaching for Sargasso's useless gun, stopped short at the apparition; Sargasso's empty pistol crunched into their gaping faces, one-two, one-two, and they stumbled blindly away. A figure darted out of the cabin companion-way, heading for Sargasso's back. A smaller figure dropped full upon it out of the jigger rigging, hammered right enthusiastically at the bowed head with something hard, and that danger was averted.

'Thanks, Miss Alys!' said Sargasso curtly. 'Give me that belaying pin now. You can go aft with your maid. You won't want to see this.'

'I've seen worse, and I'm going to stay!' the girl cried.

'Give me the pin!'

He signed to Bill Gammidge to follow and plunged into the forecastle through the uncertain mob, now gathered with bleary eyes about the foremast. As he went he ordered the men to stand to one side; and to those who questioned he added the inducement of good hearty belaying-pin soup.

'Aw, let's dump th' bloody dawg!' muttered one bold spirit.

Sargasso turned upon him like a fury, struck full at his mutinous mouth and felled him.

'Anybody else!' he rasped.

The men slunk away, scarcely daring to mutter. The forecastle reeked with the fumes of whisky.

'Broached cargo, they did, sir,' old Bill said. 'Been drunk an' fightin' ever sence they marooned you on thet thar derelict. I tried to take charge, but they druv me up aloft. Lucky Miss Rouse smelled a rat and climbed up along o' me. I thought it wuz funny as we wuzn't shot at more'n we wuz. 'Parently they wuz short o' ammunition. Phew! Thar's a couple o' stiffs!'

Sargasso speedily found out that it was only a pair of very complete drunks. He dragged them on deck. No others remained in the forecastle.

'Rig the head pump, you men!' he ordered.

The dawn was coming up grey and cool. There was a breath of air in the north-east that promised to grow into wind. Men staggered to obey him. Clumsily, painfully, they got the sea water gushing from the pump. At a nod, Gammidge dragged the drunks under the stream, and there they lay until shocked into consciousness by the chill.

'Now hurry up and deliver your ringleaders in this mutiny!' Sargasso said sharply.

The men at the pump shifted sheepishly, nudging each other whispering.

'Arter Yankee Jack wuz killed, and Sam, there wuzn't no wot ye'd call leaders, Cap'n Sargasso,' said old Gammidge. 'That's bin the trouble wi' em. Him wot I dropped wi' the belayin' pin wuz chief noise, and he looks good an' quiet now, damned if he don't.'

The wretched remnant of the big ship's crew stared at Sargasso in the gathering light of dawn as if he were some awesome creature from another world. As the booze died within them they remembered how they had put him, dead, adrift upon a derelict in company with the little negro maid who had played them false. And through the dull haze of memory the recent reappearance of Sargasso out of nowhere, to recapture the ship unarmed, stood out like a piece of wizardry. They recalled the reputation he had for superstitious beliefs; they were ready to believe him more than mortal at that juncture.

'Goin' to put 'em in irons, sir?' asked old Bill eagerly.

'They're not that important!' Sargasso retorted.

He stepped aside again to tell Miss Alys she might safely retire now. She caught his smile and nodded brightly, seizing her maid's arm and leading her aft. The skipper glanced around the sky, glowing now with warmer light, and saw the rippling water to windward.

'Now, you mutinous scum, you've had your fun!' he cried. 'Lee fore brace, there! Get a hump on you! A hand to the wheel! What did you say?'

He stepped in front of a hulking rascal who muttered as he snatched at a brace. The man glanced at his hard-lined face.

'Nawthin', sir!' he said hastily.

'That's your language!' Sargasso snapped, gave a last scrutiny of the gang and went aft to take charge of his ship.

When the yards were trimmed and the big ship sailed fast to the westward before a piping fair wind, Gammidge relieved the deck and Sargasso went below to refresh himself with a good freshwater wash and a shave. As he felt bodily comfort creeping over him he whistled and sang; and Miss Rouse, in her cabin opposite, listened to the tale told by the maid, smiled, and blushed a little as his song reached her:

As I walked out one summer morn to view the meadows round,
I spied a pretty primrose lass a-tripping o'er the ground.
Blow the wintry breezes, blow the winds hi-ho!
Clear away the morning dew, and blow, my bully boys, blow!
I saddled me an Arab steed, and saddled her another,
And off we rode together like sister and like brother.
Blow the wintry breezes, blow the winds hi-ho!
Clear away the morning dew, and blow, my bully boys, blow!

They met at breakfast. The great black cat sat on the arm of Sargasso's chair, purring like the rolling of drums. The strong fair wind poured through the skylight out of the swollen sails. The cabin was musical with the tumbling of seas outside. The telltale compass overhead pointed true for their point of destination.

'My little maid has told me a wonderful story about you, captain,' the girl smiled. 'Do you know, I have always insisted that you would rise superior to your superstitions in the emergency.'

'So I heard, Miss Alys,' Sargasso smiled back. 'The little lassie told me something of the kind. I'm going to put it all to a grand test soon.'

'I'm sure you have done that already! Why, you came back to your ship, defying Fate with a blue-mould stripe on your crazy old boat, deliberately carrying a black cat, forcing all your old fears to a showdown!'

'Aye, Miss Alys,' said the skipper softly, 'and in forcing my fears to a show down, backed by such an opinion as you gave.'

'And that was?'

'That I couldn't fail in anything I really set out to do.'

'Well, I really believed that,' she laughed with a bright colour.

'Then far be it from my wish to shatter any beliefs of yours, little lady. You may as well start right in making your quarters comfortable in a permanent fashion, Alys – '

'Oh, whatever do you mean?' she cried, wide-eyed and rosy.

'You'll permanently take up your quarters there just as soon as I can find a sky pilot. Don't blush like that! You'll embarrass old Bill when I send him down to eat!'

Swift as thought Sargasso leaned over her, swept her into a hug and kissed her with clumsy tenderness. In the pantry doorway the little black maid gasped delightedly. Sargasso took the companionway steps three at a time and sent old Bill Gammidge to his breakfast.

'Skipper seems purty lively, missy, considerin' wot he's just been through,' remarked old Bill over the hash.

'He's a wonderful man, Bill,' said Miss Alys thoughtfully.

Sargasso's voice came down to them and proved it:

Blow the winds in the morning,
Blow the winds hi-ho!
Clear away the morning dew,
And blow, my bully boys, blow!